IN MY HOOD 3

This is a work of fiction. All of the characters, organizations, and events portrayed in this novel are either products of the author's imagination or are used fictitiously.

www.melodramapublishing.com

Library of Congress Control Number: 2009938147
ISBN-13: 978-1-934157-62-6
ISBN-10: 1-934157-62-7
First Edition: December 2009
10 9 8 7 6 5 4 3 2 1

Editors: Brian Sandy and Candace K. Cottrell
Interior Layout and Design by Candace K. Cottrell (candann.com)

A Novel by

ENDY

Acknowledgements

Giving all praises to the higher power! Without Him I am nothing, with him I can do all things!

I want to send big thanks to my readers, who always support me! I really do appreciate it! Thank you for the feedback and well wishes!

Once again I thank my parents for putting up with me. I love you, Mom and Dad! I want to thank my two daughters for their love and support. Bri and Len, you are my world and keep me on my toes. (Teenagers! Ugh!) I love you girls with all my heart. To my brother Daraine (MU) I love you wholeheartedly.

To all my family and friends, thank you for always supporting me and being there for me in times of need! I want to give a shout out to Linden Pop Warner. Shouts to the staff, coaches, and administrators! Most of all, shouts to the children of the organization, who I dedicate my time to!

To my number one fan, Dennis (STL): I've always left you out, but not this time. Thanks for your continuous support!

Linda Brickhouse and Storm, let get this movement on the move! What up, KiKi Swinson? You know you're my dog!

Crystal L. Winslow, Melodrama Publishing! Crystal, you are truly a breath of fresh air. I really do appreciate you continuously taking a chance on me and my writing. I couldn't have been signed to a better publishing company! Luv you!

I continuously give thanks to all the book vendors, stores, and book clubs that always show me love. Words can't explain how that makes me feel. Thank you!

To my fellow authors, it's always a pleasure to chop it up with everyone. This is a rough business, but we must stay focused and keep our heads above water! Much luv to all of you across the board. Too many of you to name. You know who you are.

This acknowledgment is meant to be short, simple, and sweet. But I do have to mention several people who are also important in my life and I failed to mention in the last acknowledgment.

OOSA Book Club, thank you for always having my back! Ken & Johnny Freeman, thanks for always opening your arms to me! Hey Pam. Anita S. Hey girl, here we go again! Lol . . . Mona & Doral, thanks for making sure that my joints circulated in Maryland! I really appreciated that. My other mother Ni-Ni and my sister Shelly! Thank you for allowing me into your family! Norma: Well, what can I say? You've always supported and I thank you for that. You know you're a damn fool, right? LOL

As always stated, if I've left anyone out, charge it to my head because my heart is truly innocent.

Peace and One Luv!

–E

Foreword

I just put down *In My Hood 3* by Endy and I am amazed by this young lady's talent. Yes, I have read all of her work, but sometimes authors miss the mark in sequels. I know because I have six books published: Thugs and the *Women Who Love Them*, *Every Thug Needs a Lady*, *Thug Matrimony*, *Payback is a Mutha*, *Payback with Yah Life*, *Sleeping With the Enemy*, and coming August 10, *Thug Lovin'*. Whew! Where did the time go?

I am the first street lit or hood author to do a sequel and have been deemed the "Queen of Thug Love Fiction." But once again, Endy hit the nail on the head with this epic tale of the hood. I could relate personally to this story since I have been through hell and back. I know what it is like to grow up in the hood and come out bruised, battered, but not broken.

It was just in 2007 that I met Miss Endy. I had just come home from a nine-and-a-half-year bid in federal prison and was still living at the half way house when she paid me a visit in my office in East Orange, NJ and welcomed me with open arms.

I had been working hard day in and day out trying to put touches on my own projects. But when Endy dropped her latest off at my publishing company, I put everything down curled up in the bed and knocked the story out in one night.

You will not be disappointed. With a raw, uncut approach to what really goes down in the hood, the story will have you wide awake even when you are dog tired. Endy doesn't sugar coat anything in her writing with a huge fan base and following. I know this next story will knock the readers right out of their chairs.

I am Wahida Clark CEO of Wahida Clark Presents. Check me out at www.wclarkpublishing.com. I'm telling you to tell a friend and get ready for *IN MY HOOD 3*!!!!

I'm out!

-Wahida

Prologue

Bodies lay in the middle of the street, and it was raining glass as bullets whizzed overhead and slammed into the windows of the parked cars.

Behind one of the cars, seated on the ground with his back resting against a car door, was an injured Nate, blood leaking from a wound caused by a bullet to his back that went straight through.

He held his hand over the small hole as a trickle of dark red blood oozed into his hands. His breathing was short and heavy. He felt like the world was closing in on him. In his other hand, he held a MAC-10 assault weapon. He couldn't lift the gun. It felt like he couldn't feel his hand, and he couldn't feel parts of his body—mostly his legs.

He sat there with his feet sprawled apart as yet more bullets shot through the broken window of the car and were now slamming into the brick wall of a building, breaking the bricks into pieces. He looked to his left to see young Nyeem sitting behind the car parked next to him.

Nyeem had fear in his eyes as he stared back at Nate. The fear wasn't for his life, but for his uncle, who he thought was going to die.

Nate felt his heart sink when he saw the look in the fifteen-year-old boy's eyes. He looked at the guns Nyeem held in his hand and instantly felt bad. Nyeem was going to be sixteen in one week, but Nate didn't think the boy would see that day. Nate was supposed to protect him.

Nyeem was Ishmael's son, and Nate had made a promise to himself not to let anything happen to him. In his mind, he had failed his friend. Nate was in no condition to save Nyeem.

"Get outta here!" Nate managed to yell to Nyeem.

"I'm not leaving you!" Nyeem told him.

"Don't worry about me. Get the fuck outta here!"

Nyeem stood and bucked shot after shot before returning to his sitting position. Seconds after he let off shots, retaliation gunfire blasted the car he was squatting behind. The pinging sound of each bullet piercing the car caused him to crouch lower.

Behind a car on the opposite side of Nate, Click was losing his mind. He yelled as he fired shots with his automatic weapon like he was in the fight scene of an action flick. Click loved the excitement of a gun battle.

The Spanish gang had come to retaliate for the murder of one of their very own by Leroy's crew. The police had yet to be called, so it was chaos in the streets of Newark that night. In fact, murders had been committed all month, leading up to this night.

Nate began to cough up blood, and Nyeem noticed.

"Click! Cover me!" Nyeem yelled.

Click stood to his feet like Rambo and let the bullets rain. "Aaaahhhh!" he yelled.

Nyeem ran over to Nate, ducking bullets as they flew past and around him. He dove to the ground next to Nate.

When he removed Nate's hand to see how bad the wound was, more blood spilled out from the small hole. He pressed Nate's hand back over the hole. He could see the distant look in Nate's eyes. "Unc, stay with me! Hold on, man!" Nyeem said. "Click!"

"Yo!"

"I gotta get Unc outta here. He needs to get to the hospital!"

For the first time Click actually looked over at Nate and saw how bad he was. "Oh shit! Yo, I don't know how we gonna do that shit without getting dumped on!"

"Call in reinforcement then!"

"Nigga, look around you!" Click yelled.

Nyeem looked around. "Everybody's dead."

"You think?" Click asked sarcastically, referring to the men from their crew who lay dead all over the area.

Nyeem didn't know what he was going to do. He looked at Nate and saw that his eyes were closed. "Unc!" He panicked, shaking him.

Nate barely opened his eyes.

"Unc, I'm gonna get you to the hospital. Just hold on!"

Nyeem looked around frantically. He was trying to find an escape route to get Nate out of there.

Meanwhile, Click was reloading clips into his weapons. He stood just in time to meet one of the gunmen making his way into the street. Click unloaded into the man's face, making him unrecognizable as his face tore away piece by piece before he hit the ground. He ducked back behind the car just before bullets tore through its metal.

Several seconds later, the gunfire ceased. Nyeem and Click looked at each other, wondering what had happened.

Click positioned himself to the rear of the parked car in an attempt to peek out. Just as he did, he saw two Spanish men running in a crouched position toward them. He immediately began to let off shots at the two men, hitting one of them in the leg. The man fell to the ground, screaming in agony. Click then shot the other man in the chest several times. He carefully took aim and silenced the screaming man on the ground by hitting him in the face.

Just then another man made his way across the street, but Click couldn't get him.

"Yo, Nyeem, I think he's coming up on your side." Click pointed his weapon in the direction he thought the gunman was going to come from.

Another man started making his way over to them.

Nate had passed out, and Nyeem was ready to shoot the gunman as soon as he peeked his head out from around the car.

One of the men stepped around the car on Nyeem's side. The young boy panicked, and Click shot the man several times in the stomach, and he fell to the ground several feet away from Nyeem.

Suddenly, bullets sounded off, and Click yelled out. It seemed as if everything moved in slow motion. Nyeem turned to see Click on his knees, his body jerking as he was being riddled with bullets. As the force of each bullet pierced his body, small particles of flesh and blood leaped from his body to the ground. He still held his gun and fired straight up into the air before he fell to his death.

One gunman trained his gun on Nyeem and walked toward him.

"*¡Los tenemos!*" one of the gunmen yelled to the others, letting them know that they got them. He looked around for the others that he'd summoned, but no one came. He turned his attention back to Nyeem, looking at him with evil eyes.

Nyeem looked over at Nate and then closed his eyes, accepting his fate. Shots sounded, followed by a chorus of screams and loud grunts. And then there was silence.

Chapter One

Fifteen Years Earlier

Tears flowed from the twelve-year-old Spanish girl's eyes as she looked down at her dead brother in a coffin. A faint whimper escaped her lips.

Standing next to her was her father, Vinny. He wasn't crying, but you could see the hurt in his ocean blue eyes. Only a few family members bore those unique blue eyes, inheriting them from generations many years before their time. His dark, shiny, black hair was combed back and lay flat upon his head. He was a broad man and stood at six feet two inches.

"Why did they do this, Poppa?" Valencia looked up at her father for answers.

Vinny looked into his daughter's eyes, which were the same unique ocean blue color as his, and his heart melted. She was the only one of his children that inherited those eyes from him. Her puffy eyes were red from crying, and her cheeks were flushed. She wanted answers from her father, her hero.

Vinny looked at his son, Carlos, again and then scanned the crowded cathedral. The church was standing room only. Along the walls and the aisle stood security men from his organization, and an equal amount of men were posted up outside the building as well.

"I don't know, *hija*," he said, brushing her beautiful, thick, black, curly hair away from her face.

It was all he could say at the time. He was so full of rage and pain, he couldn't think of anything comforting to say to his precious daughter, his only child left. He had lost two of his three children, and he vowed that he wasn't going to lose her too. He wanted revenge in the worst way. But right now he needed to grieve and bury his son.

Valencia was the baby of the family, and although her name meant *strong*, she was always protected and spoiled by her father, mother, and older siblings. Vinny was in the drug business and ran a huge territory in Brooklyn and Harlem. Valencia was kept away from anything that had to do with the business. Vinny always kept her busy with things that children did. But she had been especially close to her brother, and unbeknownst to Vinny, her brother Carlos had taught her things about the business and showed her how to defend herself.

Valencia continued to stare down into the open coffin at the man she didn't recognize. But she knew it was her brother by the small sword tattooed on the back of his hand, the very same symbol her father and every man in his organization wore. It was their family symbol. She also could tell the man that lay in the coffin was her brother because of his beautiful, black, shiny hair. Members of the Sosa family all had beautiful, healthy hair. But her brother's face no longer looked the same as it did in life.

He lay there in the plush coffin disfigured. He was gunned down, and his face showed it. Her father wanted the coffin to remain open during the service because he wanted everyone to see the cruel and brutal way in which his son was killed. The undertaker did the very best that he could to fill in the holes all over Carlos's body. Unfortunately his efforts weren't good enough to hide the damage to his face.

Two of the Sosa security men finally escorted Valencia and Vinny away from the coffin and over to the front row of the cathedral.

Mrs. Sosa was already seated there in a wheelchair, which was parked in the aisle next to the front row. She sniffled and wiped her eyes with a handkerchief as she prayed in a low whisper in Spanish.

Mrs. Sosa had been confined to a wheelchair for over ten years, as a result of a hip replacement gone wrong. Interestingly enough, the doctor who performed the surgery somehow ended up dead in the Hudson River.

Once seated, Valencia looked up at her father and tapped his arm to get his attention. He looked down at her, and she pulled him near so she could whisper in his ear.

"Quiero a matar al hombre que llevo' a mi hermano lejos de mi," she said, looking deep into her father's eyes.

Vinny still was at a loss for words after hearing his baby say that she wanted to kill the man who killed her brother. Her declaration made him even angrier at the situation.

Vinny was a dangerous and powerful man. The one thing he wanted was to keep Valencia out of the family business. But after seeing the determination in her eyes, he knew she meant every word of what she had said. It was just the way things were in their family.

It was the next day, after the burial, when Valencia walked into the kitchen, where her mother was preparing dinner.

Mrs. Sosa had been crying, and her puffy eyes showed it. She wheeled herself around the kitchen with ease, preparing the meal for her family. Although she wanted to crawl under a rock, she still had to take care of the family she had left.

"Momma, where's Poppa?" Valencia asked.

Mrs. Sosa simply pointed toward the patio doors that led out onto the deck.

She had barely gotten over her daughter's death, which had happened a year or so earlier, and now tragedy had struck again, with her son's death. At times she hated the life she lived, but she always enjoyed the fruits from her husband's illegal activities. Now it no longer mattered to her whether they had money. She'd lost two of her children because of that lifestyle, and no amount of money in the world was going to bring them back.

Valencia walked out onto the deck and saw her father talking on the phone. He had his back to the patio doors, so he never saw her come outside. As he spoke angrily on the phone, she stood back and listened.

Vinny had security men walking the grounds around the home to ensure the safety of his family, something Valencia was used to, but since Carlos's death, it seemed as if security had been beefed up.

Vinny continued to shout foul obscenities in Spanish while Valencia listened to her father tell whomever was on the phone that he wanted the heart of the man that killed her brother in a jar to sit over his fireplace. She badly wanted to be the one to rip out the man's heart.

"That *hijo de puta* must die," Vinny growled into the phone. Then he turned and saw Valencia standing there. He quickly ended the call and smiled at her, hoping she didn't hear too much of his conversation.

Valencia walked over to her father. As she approached him, he marveled at her beauty, which reminded him of her mother when she was a younger woman. She stood in front of him looking at him with a troubled face. She hadn't smiled since the death of his son, and he missed the pretty smile he was used to seeing.

"¿Qué tal estás?" Vinny rubbed the side of her thin face with the back of his hand.

A petite young girl, Valencia was a late bloomer and hadn't quite fully blossomed into a teenager. Her breasts were just starting to grow, and she hadn't yet acquired a backside, though most of her friends already had shapely bodies, and had all started seeing their periods.

"I'm OK, Poppa. When are you going to teach me to shoot a gun?" she asked.

"¡Hija!" Vinny yelled. He was shocked at her forwardness. "Ven aquí y sientate."

Vinny led her over to the patio chairs to sit. He took a deep breath as he studied her face. He could see the fire behind her eyes. Right then, he knew she was very serious.

"¿Hija, por qué habla asi?"

"I speak that way because I mean it, Poppa. I'm mad!"

"Tales cosas—"

"No, Poppa, speak to me in English," she said, interrupting him. "You know I am more comfortable speaking English."

"OK, *hija.*" Vinny shook his head, understanding that although her native language was Spanish, she was used to speaking English with her friends and other family members born in the United States. "Such things should not have come from this beautiful mouth." He pointed to her mouth.

Valencia didn't respond, continuing to keep a stone face.

"I know you hurt for your brother," Vinny continued, "but this is no way for a young *muchacha* to think."

"But, Poppa, I heard you say that you want the killer's heart in a jar. You feel the same way I do. I hurt too, Poppa. My sister and brother are gone, and since you are doing nothing about it, I will."

Vinny sighed and rubbed his hand across his face. He wanted to find a way for his daughter to understand that it wasn't that easy to take a gun and shoot someone for revenge. He wanted her to know that he would never allow her to get involved in the family business. But little did Vinny know, Valencia knew a whole lot more than she let on.

"*Hija*, I will take care of the *bastardos* who did this to my family, but I will not lose you too. You are too young to understand right now, but you will one day. I promised your mother that I would protect you with my life."

"No! No, Poppa, I will find them with or without you!" Valencia said as she stood to leave.

Vinny grabbed her arm gently to stop her.

She turned to face him as her brows furrowed in a frown, her eyes welled with tears.

Vinny stood and pulled his daughter into his arms. "Oh, *hija*, *eres obstinado*." He called her *stubborn*. "How did you get this way?" He kissed the top of her head.

Valencia pulled back and looked up at him. "From you, Poppa."

"You must never tell your mother. She would lay dead where she sits."

"I promise, Poppa." She wiped the tears that had fallen from her eyes.

"Go change your clothes, and we will leave," he said, releasing her.

"OK." She ran off into the house.

Vinny plopped back down onto the chair and buried his head in his hands. He knew it was wrong for him to teach his young daughter to shoot a gun, but what choice did he have? She was stubborn, and he preferred to be the one to teach her rather than have her to go off on her own.

Chapter Two

OUR BOY

In Newark, New Jersey, the news of the death of Ishmael Jenkins hit the streets. Nate, Click, Dice, Little Cash, and several other members of Ishmael's crew stood around in Leroy's pool hall in a discussion. They wanted answers, and it seemed as if no one was telling them anything.

"Yo, what the fuck, man?" Nate said to one of Leroy's several guards that were there at the pool hall to police the wild bunch. "Where the fuck is Big Roy at?" Nate grilled the big man.

"Just calm the fuck down. He'll be out here in a minute."

"Go back there and tell him to come the fuck out here!" Click chimed in, clearly pissed.

"Yeah!" some of the others interjected.

The crew continued to protest Leroy's whereabouts and what happened to Ishmael. The news had come from an informant who'd overheard the police talking about the night they flooded the street of the abandoned building Ishmael's body was being removed from. He'd made the phone call to one of the crew members, who called the rest to let them know. The bystander made it clear that he'd witnessed Leroy talking with the police out in front of the building.

Click was running out of patience. "What the fuck is the problem, man? What's taking Roy so long?"

"Listen, punk, I told y'all little muthafuckas to calm down!" The guard was clearly irritated by the constant interrogation from the crew.

"Man, fuck you!" Click shouted. "Go get Big Roy!" Click wasn't the least bit intimidated by the guard's large size and status with Leroy.

Dak suddenly walked through the door that led to Leroy's office. He closed the door behind him and marched over to the crew. He stood front and center of the guards as they fell in behind him.

Nate stood in front of the crew, as if he was now in charge. "Yo, Dak, where Roy at?"

"Slow your roll, homeboy." Dak calmly held his hand up, trying to keep the situation under control. "Come with me," he beckoned.

"'Bout time!" Click said.

The crew fell in behind Nate as he followed Big Dak towards Leroy's office.

Dak turned around to see them all walking behind him. "Hold up. Just him," he said, pointing to Nate.

Click protested the loudest. "That's bullshit! I'm going too!"

Dak summoned the other guards. "Man, get this nigga!"

They immediately began marching toward Click, who pulled out his nine and pointed it at the guards, stopping them in their tracks.

"Yo, Click, man, what you doing?" Nate said.

"Man, fuck these niggas!"

"What the fuck is going on out here?" Leroy's deep voice filled the room. He had come from his office into the pool hall.

Everyone stopped what they were doing and focused their attention on him. Some of the young boys had never had the privilege of seeing him up close and personal.

Leroy, with his gangster swagger, glided across the linoleum floor to the center of the hall and was now flanked by his men as they stood before Ishmael's crew.

"Big Roy, man, no disrespect to you, but we just want some answers on what happened with Ish," Nate said.

Click had lowered his weapon and held it down by his side. He still had fury in his eyes.

Leroy looked over at him and studied his face carefully. He could see that Click was hurt. Click held his stare with Leroy.

"Who did it, Big Roy?" Nate asked. "We will slump them niggas with the quickness."

"Naw, young'un, my peoples will handle it. Listen up, fellas!" Leroy shouted to get everyone's attention. "I know y'all niggas is feeling some kinda way 'bout losing Ishmael. He was like a son to me, and he died in my arms, so I feel yo' pain. But I'll be damned if y'all muthafuckas gonna come up in my shit attracting all kinds of unwanted company to my establishment. Now my peoples will handle this! Do I make myself clear?" He eyed Ishmael's crew, instilling fear in most of them. All except Nate and Click.

Some of the young boys mumbled their replies; others simply nodded in agreement.

"From this day on, Nate here will step up in Ishmael's place. If y'all niggas still wanna make some bread, then you answer to him. If you got a problem with that, then take a fucking walk!"

No one moved, more out of fear than anything else.

"A'ight, then y'all get on up outta here. Keep your ear to the streets, and if you hear anything, let Nate know, and we will take it from there," Leroy said, dismissing them. "Not y'all." He pointed to Nate and Click.

"Yo, Roy, I don't roll nowhere without him either." Nate pointed at Dice.

Leroy nodded his head, letting Nate know Dice could hang around too.

Once everyone was gone from the pool hall, Leroy had a talk with the three of them. He let it be known that he wanted to handle Ishmael's killer personally, and although they were close to Ishmael, he felt like Ishmael was like a son to him.

He made sure that he kept his eyes on Click. "You hear me, young'un, right?" he said to Click.

"Yup," Click said without conviction.

Leroy had heard a lot about Click from Ishmael, but now that he would be working for him directly, he had to make sure that Click didn't do anything stupid.

After speaking with the trio, he dismissed them from the pool hall, and he and Dak went back to the safety of his office.

"Dak, we gotta do what we gotta do at any cost to keep how Ishmael died in-house."

"I feel you, Roy," Dak said, sitting in one of the chairs in front of his desk.

"I can't believe that cocksucker Vinny sent his son over here to try to do me in." Leroy shook his head.

"You think that hit was meant for you?" Dak asked.

"Oh, fo' sure, that was for me. I can't believe he still holding onto that jealousy shit from twenty years ago."

"So what you gonna do?"

"I'm gonna put that 'spic' in the ground," Leroy said. "But until then, we gotta keep these young boys busy, 'cause if that little one finds out it was my peoples that put that bullet in Ish, I can see he gonna be our main problem," Leroy said, speaking of Click.

"Yeah, I feel you."

"I'd rather have him on my side than the other side."

Chapter Three

I'M READY

Two Years Later

It had been two years since Vinny began Valencia's shooting lessons. Valencia dedicated herself to practicing. She was now fourteen and almost a professional at using guns. She was experienced with several different guns, and surprisingly she was able to handle an assault rifle quite well. Her gun of choice was the Desert Eagle .50 AE. She loved the handle of the gun, even though it was big, and she loved that it discharged big bullets, not to mention the way the chrome felt in her hands.

She was quickly becoming bored with shooting at the cans that Vinny would have his security men set up for her. She wanted to *really* use the gun.

Today, as she was escorted through the woods to the place where she had been practicing for the last two years, she was flanked by two security men—one man walking in front of her, the other behind her. She was also growing tired of being escorted everywhere, like she was the president's child, and they were the Secret Service. She thought that her mother and father were still very paranoid that someone would come after her to get revenge on her father.

She knew that her father had many enemies, and she wasn't afraid to use her gun if she had to. But that would never happen as long as she had Juan and Mike, the bodyguards she hated. It was embarrassing for her to have to have them following her all day. Even when she went to the mall with her friends, they would follow.

Valencia hated the constant supervision, and she made sure she expressed her feelings to her father, who wouldn't give in to her demands.

Once they arrived at the practice location, Valencia walked straight over to her father, who sat in a lawn chair smoking a Cuban cigar. She stood in front of him, one hand on her hip, the other holding the big gun.

"Poppa."

"Yes?"

"I don't want to shoot at cans anymore. I want to practice shooting at moving targets."

"I don't think you're ready."

Valencia blew air through her nose, frustrated with his response. "I don't want them to follow me anymore either." She pointed to Juan and Mike.

"That is something I need to speak with you about as well. *Hija*, please stop running away from the men I have in place for your protection. You will understand one day, but for now you must stay with them."

"Poppa, you stay with them. I don't want them around me. It doesn't matter anyway, because my sister and brother were still killed when your men were with them. So if anyone wants to kill me, Poppa, those two cannot stop them."

The two men stood there looking at her like they wanted to break her neck.

"No, my child, you mustn't think like that. These men are trained and skilled to protect. I pay them *mucho dinero* to protect you—"

"Poppa, please . . . I am more skilled and trained than they are." Valencia's cockiness came from what she had learned from her brother, not to mention, she was an excellent shooter and had began to take archery lessons. She wanted to be involved with any skill that had to do with violence.

"Excúsame por un minuto." Vinny told the guards to excuse themselves while he talked to his daughter in private.

Valencia waited patiently for her father to speak.

"Hija, listen to me. I know you want revenge, but this is not for a little girl to do. Let me handle this."

In fact, Vinny had tried for the last two years to get revenge, but had been unsuccessful. The timing was never right. To make matters worse, he was now being investigated by the DEA, so he had to fall back and try to keep his nose clean until the heat cooled down.

Valencia huffed and turned her back. She didn't want to hear it. Vinny noticed her behavior. He had never raised a hand nor even yelled at his daughter. But at this point speaking gently to her was not working, and he desperately needed to get his point across. Besides, he'd had enough of her spoiled behavior, which had only worsened over the years.

"*¡Hija!*" he yelled with authority.

You would have thought Vinny had struck Valencia across the face by the shocked look she wore.

"I am not gonna tell you again," Vinny said. "You cannot handle this. You are a child, so be a child. I don't want to hear any more about revenge. If you still want to practice with the *arma*"—He pointed to the gun—"then it's OK with me, but that's where it ends." He waved his hand in a chopping motion.

Valencia stood there steaming mad. She breathed in and out of her nostrils like an enraged bull.

"OK, Poppa, but I will not always be a little girl, and when I am a woman, you will not be able to stop me. I will find who killed Carlos!"

Vinny nodded. He already knew who the killer was, and wanted the pleasure of killing him himself. "When you are grown, if I am still alive and we have not found the killers, I will help you."

Valencia stormed off toward the house, determined to get her way eventually.

Chapter Four

LIL' ISH

The Present

Ishmael's son Nyeem and Doc had been friends since infancy. When Nate took in Nyeem to live with him, he let Doc's aunt babysit Nyeem, and the two friends had been inseparable ever since.

As Nyeem and Doc walked to the corner store, Nyeem's tall, lean, muscular body glided along the sidewalk with a swagger much too advanced for his age. At fifteen, he was wise well beyond his years. His pointy nose seemed to lead the way to his destination. He had his father's dark complexion, his mother's green eyes, and he wore his hair in cornrows that extended down his back just the way his father's did, making him look more like Ishmael than Ishmael himself.

Doc was just as tall as Nyeem, if not slightly taller at six feet three, but his build was much thicker than Nyeem's. He had a lighter complexion and a flat, wide nose with bushy, untamed eyebrows and long eyelashes. Doc had already turned sixteen, and Nyeem was not far behind with a birthday coming soon.

They were the stars of their JV basketball team in high school, so their athletic ability brought on a certain amount of "Hollyhood stardom" for the two. The two of them walked down the street like Hollywood superstars, waving at everyone who called their names. As cars rode by, drivers honked their horns at the pair. The boys would simply throw up their hands, displaying a peace sign or a fist in acknowledgment.

Once they reached the corner, they shook hands with all the young teens posted up there. Nyeem went inside the store, while Doc continued to talk shit with the teens, who sold drugs on this corner and were members of a gang.

Doc wasn't a part of their set, but growing up with these kids did hold a certain amount of weight. So although he wasn't in their gang, he was cool with the members.

"So what y'all NBA niggas 'bout to get into?" Tek asked.

"Shit. Just kickin' it 'round the hood," Doc responded.

"Yo, Doc, you joining the summer league they got going on?"

"Naw, Tek, man, me and Nyeem 'bout to go to basketball camp."

"Oh, word?" Tek asked as he eyed a black four-door Nissan Altima.

Doc also noticed the Altima cruising by, the tinted windows concealing the identity of the passengers.

The other gang members stopped what they were doing and watched the car. Two of the boys put their hands on their concealed weapons, and the car suddenly sped up.

"Yo, who that?" Tek asked.

"Dunno," one of the teens said.

The others simply shrugged their shoulders.

"Yo, Tek, why don't you step off from this shit and come play ball with us? You decent with yours," Doc said.

"Naw, man, this is where I'm comfortable," Tek said seriously. "They like my family. I gotta rep my set. They the only ones who got my back." Tek was living from house to house without parents, so he was drawn to a family of any kind, even if that family was a gang.

"I feel you, but if you change your mind, you can always come with us to this camp."

"Good looking out, Doc, but my school days are over . . . although I don't have a problem bodying you on the asphalt around the way." Tek laughed.

"You crazy as hell." Doc laughed too. "Hmm!" he said, looking at the three teen girls coming down the street.

Tek noticed the expression on Doc's face and looked in the direction Doc was looking.

"Damn!" Tek said when he saw the teen girls, who were all sporting short shorts and low-cut tank tops that exposed their developing breasts.

"Word up!" Doc licked his lips.

Nyeem walked out of the store and over to Doc and Tek. He was about to open his bottle of soda when he followed Doc's and Tek's gazes. He squinted his eyes, trying to see if he knew the girls.

The other gang members went on about their routine of selling drugs and clowning each other, never noticing the approaching girls. As the girls got closer, the other teen boys realized they were nearing and started catcalling, but the girls simply ignored their chants.

Doc, Nyeem, and Tek made an opening so the girls could walk through.

"Hey, Nyeem." Alicia smiled up at him.

"What's good?" he asked with devilish eyes.

"Hey, Nyeem. Hey, Tek. Hey, Doc." The other girls said as they passed through, ignoring the immaturity of the other teens because of their disrespectful way of greeting them.

"Ladies," Doc said.

"What's up, y'all?" Tek asked.

One of the teens stood in front of the door to the store, blocking the girls' path.

"Move, boy!" they yelled at him.

"Yo!" Tek yelled, giving his boys the evil eye. Tek was the leader, and they gave him respect because of his position.

The young boy stepped out of the way and let the girls by.

"Thanks, Tek," the girls said to him as they all walked inside.

All eyes were on the girls' asses as they disappeared into the store.

"Yo, man, Alicia is on your shit," Doc told Nyeem.

"I know she is." Nyeem took a gulp of his soda.

"You need to stop playing and hit that," Tek said.

"Word up!" Doc chimed in.

"How you know I ain't already hit that?'

Doc and Tek burst into laughter.

"Yeah, right, you hit that!" Tek said, still laughing.

"Again, how you figure I didn't?" Nyeem asked.

" 'Cause I know you didn't, nigga. You still a virgin."

"Yeah, a'ight, that's what you think. You better tell your boy," Nyeem told Doc.

"That nigga is far from a virgin," Doc said quickly. "You don't know who this nigga is?" He threw his arm around Nyeem's neck. "This nigga is little Ish, man!"

Nyeem removed Doc's arm from around his neck, not feeling the way Doc was displaying him.

Doc knew Nyeem didn't like that. He had expressed his concerns about that on more than one occasion. One time they were at McDonald's, and an older dude walked up on them.

"Hey, little man," the dude said.

Nyeem and Doc looked at each other, confused. What was going through their minds was, Who was the man calling "little man," when they both towered over him?

"You." He pointed at Nyeem. "I'm talking to you."

"Me?"

"Yeah. Ain't you Ishmael's son?"

Nyeem just couldn't figure out why people would think it was OK to walk up on him at any given time and ask about the father he had never known.

"Yeah, man." Nyeem then turned his back on the man and continued to look up at the menu mounted high over the register.

"Get the fuck outta here! I heard they said that Ish had a son, but I ain't never seen you before. Hell, ain't nobody know he had a son. I knew your father back in the day, man. Your pops was a straight-up dude. Man, the hood was fucked up the day your pops got killed, man." The dude lowered his head as he remembered that fateful day.

Nyeem looked at the man and could see he still hurt for his father.

"I didn't know your mother, but I saw her a couple of times with Ish. She was fire, though. Man, it's crazy to see you are real and not just a rumor. Damn! You look like my boy." The man stood there staring at Nyeem in disbelief.

Because the man was talking loudly, Nyeem began to feel uncomfortable and felt all eyes in the restaurant on him.

"Yo, I know you gonna rise above and take up where my man Ish left off. The game definitely needs another Ishmael Jenkins around here to get some order on things. These little niggas don't even play by the rules no more."

"Naw, man, I ain't my father. I ain't tryin'-a fill his shoes nor replace him. I'm good." Nyeem stepped up to the register to order his food.

"A'ight now, little Ish, you hold yo' head up."

"*Nyeem*, man. My name is Nyeem," he told the man with a straight face.

"Oh, my bad, Nyeem," the man said and walked off. Then he turned to get one last look at the legend's son.

"I hate that shit!" Nyeem told Doc.

"Why, man? I wish my father had some status like your pops did. You just don't understand the kind of power you could have right now."

"Man, I don't want that kinda power. I just want people to leave me alone. But what's fucking with me is, if I wasn't born when my father was alive, how the fuck everybody know I'm his son?"

"Your uncle, man. That nigga probably told everybody. You know your uncle got some pull too, and that was his man. He probably the one who told niggas."

"Yeah, you probably right."

"Come on, man. Get off!" Nyeem pushed Doc when he tried to put his arm back around his neck.

"This nigga is the son of a legend," Doc said, continuing to brag.

At times Nyeem thought Doc abused their friendship, using Ishmael's status a lot in the streets to gain some respect for himself. Besides, Nyeem hated being in his father's shadow.

Doc continued to brag on Nyeem's behalf. "When bitches find out he's the son of a legend, they throw the pussy at him. This nigga been fucking since he was nine!"

"Damn!" Tek responded.

It wasn't far from the truth. After Nate had walked in on Nyeem jerking off in his room, he decided to help him lose his virginity. On his tenth birthday, Nate brought a woman over to the house to give Nyeem his first real nut.

As Doc and Tek talked about Nyeem like he wasn't standing there, Alicia and her friends came out of the candy store. She walked right up to him and stood in front of him. Alicia was a little more developed than the other two girls, with a figure she'd inherited from her voluptuous mother. Men and boys were always trying to talk to her, but she only had eyes for Nyeem.

"What's up?" Nyeem looked down at her.

"You. What you doing standing out here on the block with these clowns?"

"Oh, I ain't out here on the block with them. Me and Doc came to the store, and we was just kickin' it with these cats for a hot minute. What you 'bout to get into?" He grabbed her long ponytail and let it slide down through his fingers.

Alicia loved looking into his eyes. They turned her on. In fact, they turned all the girls on. Alicia was infatuated with Nyeem. He was always dressed in the latest, was on the basketball team, and was fine as hell. Overall, he had it going on.

"Hopefully *we* can get into something." She pointed to herself and then to him.

"Oh yeah? Like what?" He lifted one eyebrow like the wrestler The Rock.

The other two girls were talking with Doc and Tek and laughing at them because they were telling jokes and acting silly.

"It's whatever, Nyeem." Alicia rubbed her hand along his abs.

Nyeem reached into his pocket, pulled out his cell phone, and handed it to her. "Put your number in there," he said, licking his full lips.

Alicia did as she was told and handed him back his phone. "When you gonna call me?"

"When you want me to call you?"

"Don't answer my question with a question, boy," she said, her hand on her hip. "Just tell me when you gonna call me."

"I don't know. Just be waiting by the phone, regardless."

"Oh, so you think you got it like that?"

"Yeah, fo' sure."

She playfully hit his arm. "Oh, you ain't that slick."

"Just answer my call when I do call."

"Whatever, boy! Come on, y'all, let's go," she told her friends and started to walk away.

Nyeem gawked at her physique. He was turned on. Her shorts fit perfectly on her ass, like a pair of panties. Her thighs were muscular and smooth, and her waistline was tiny. The tank top she wore had risen up and exposed her smooth stomach and back.

The other two girls said their good-byes, and the trio walked up the street, while the three boys drooled over their bodies.

Tek interrupted their trance. "So now I know you gonna hit that t'night?"

"Man, go 'head." Nyeem waved his hand at him. "Let's be out, Doc." Nyeem gave Tek a pound and walked off.

Doc did the same and caught up to Nyeem, and the two walked back up the street. They weren't even a good several feet away when a car screeched to a stop behind them. Hearing the screeching tires, Doc and Nyeem turned around to see what was going on.

Three males jumped out of the car and headed toward the corner where the gang members were standing. They approached the other young teens, and they began to argue.

Tek was still standing in the spot several feet away from them and observed what was about to go down. He quickly pulled his gun from the small of his back, walked briskly over to the three teens that had jumped out of the car, and immediately shot one of the boys at point-blank range.

The other boys from Tek's crew scattered, pulled out their guns, and started shooting.

Doc and Nyeem ran up the block to get away from any flying bullets.

"Yo, man, you see that shit?" Nyeem asked.

“That nigga Tek is nuts!” Doc laughed.

Nyeem didn’t laugh. He just kept walking. “Yo, man, what I tell you ’bout that shit?” He stopped and looked at Doc.

“What you talking about?”

“You know what the fuck I’m talking ’bout! Stop fucking telling muthafuckas who my father is. Stop flossing off that shit. I told you before, I ain’t feelin’ that shit!” He turned and walked off.

Doc stood there and watched Nyeem walk away. “Damn, nigga! Why you so sensitive?” He took huge steps to catch up to Nyeem. “Come on, man, it ain’t that serious. Everybody in the fuckin’ hood already knows who you are. You act like I let the cat outta the bag or some shit.”

Nyeem didn’t say a word. He just kept stepping.

“Come on, man, stop acting like a little bitch. I’m yo’ man. What the fuck?” Now Doc seemed to be getting irritated.

“Yo, you just don’t understand, man. I had to hear this shit my whole life, niggas talking ’bout little Ish this, and little Ish that. Then my grandfather talking ’bout my father all the time. I mean, he on some ol’ guilt trip, because he didn’t spend time with my father while he was growing up. So I guess he feels like he needs to make it up with me since my pops is dead. Then I got my uncle on my ass day and night ’bout getting into the business. I’m just tired of all that shit, man! All I wanna do is play ball and go into the league.”

Doc looked at his friend and felt bad for the part he played in making matters worse for him. Sure, he had heard Nyeem tell him on several occasions that he didn’t like it, but he’d always thought that Nyeem was making a bigger deal out of it than it was, until now.

“Yo, man, my bad. I ain’t know it was like that.”

“Yeah, it is, man. That’s what I been tryin’-a tell you.”

“A’ight, calm down. I got you. You my man, and I got you.”

They continued to stroll in silence, both thinking about the situation.

"You still wanna go ball?" Doc finally asked.

"Yeah. Why not?"

The two of them headed off to the park to shoot some basketball and blow off some steam.

Chapter Five

GANGBANGING

"I hear young'un running with them gangs now," Leroy said into the mouthpiece of the phone.

"Naw, he ain't running with no gangs," Nate said. "I told you before, he plays basketball."

"So what? You tryin'-a tell me a nigga can't play sports and still be in a gang?"

"No, Roy, I ain't saying that. Where you hear that shit from anyway?"

"Where you think? The streets." Leroy put the lit cigar up to his lips and began to cough before he could drag on it. He coughed deeply and loudly.

"Yo, you a'ight?"

After he finished coughing, he responded, "Yeah, I'm OK."

"I told you about them cigars, man. You need to leave them shits alone. You know you're sick."

"I'm grown. I was smoking before you was even thought about."

Leroy grabbed a glass of cognac, took a deep gulp, and continued to talk on the phone in the comfort of his bedroom. Since becoming ill,

Leroy had spent all of his time in his bedroom. His room was as big as some apartments.

Meanwhile, downstairs in the main foyer of the house, Dak lay dead on his back. A female stood over him dressed in all black from head to toe. The intruder wore a black nylon mask that covered her entire head. She stood over Dak's body and was holding a machete dripping with his blood. The weapon belonged to Leroy, and the intruder had removed it from the wall where it hung over the mantel. She knelt down beside Dak's body and removed the switchblade, which she had thrown at him when she initially snuck up on him, protruding from his neck. She wiped the blood onto his shirt and retracted the blade before tucking it away in its pouch.

Her perfectly proportioned body resembled an hourglass, with her tiny waistline and curvaceous hips. The fitted black cat suit she wore lay on each curve like a second skin as it clung to her long, shapely, muscular legs and traveled down to her ankles. On her feet she sported a pair of soft black Kung Fu shoes. Because her footsteps were soundless, she managed to sneak up on Dak and throw the switchblade into his neck before he could make a sound.

Dak's huge body lay motionless on the immaculate imported marble floor, his head severed from his huge shoulders and lying just a few inches away from his body. His eyes were cold and distant as they stared up at the twenty-thousand-dollar chandelier Leroy'd had flown in from Italy.

The woman placed the machete she used to dismember his head on the floor next to Dak's body and began to tiptoe away, careful not to step in the puddle of blood leaking from his torso and running along the floor.

"So what's up with my grandson?" Leroy asked, oblivious to the murder that had just taken place inside his home.

"He a'ight," Nate said.

"How is he doing playing ball?"

Nate knew Leroy was becoming forgetful, so he entertained him every time.

"Man, Roy, that boy 'bout to take over the courts. He averages sixteen point three points per game and five point eight assists. I think he gonna make it to be six feet seven easy before he gets to his senior year in high school."

"Yeah?"

Over the years Nate and Leroy had several intense conversations after Leroy confirmed that Nyeem was indeed Ishmael's and Desiree's son. When Nyeem turned four, Leroy revealed to Nate that Ishmael was his son, and Nyeem his grandson. Nate was in shock to say the least.

"Are you shitting me?" Nate had asked.

"Naw, kid, no bullshit."

They were sitting in Leroy's office in the back of the pool hall, and little Nyeem was running around the room, playing with a remote control car Nate had bought for him.

"Yo, for real? Ish never told me that shit."

"He didn't know. I-I-well, it's a long story. I mean I couldn't bring myself to tell him, after the way he was conceived."

"So all this time y'all been making money together, and neither one of y'all knew that y'all was related?" Nate couldn't seem to grasp the concept.

"Son, it's a difficult situation, but I did tell him before he died,"

Leroy said, omitting the part about by whose hand Ishmael had died. That too was an ongoing struggle he dealt with day in and day out.

"I don't know, man. I think he would have wanted to know that you was his father while he was growing up."

Leroy didn't respond. He continued to watch Nyeem play by himself on the floor of the office.

Nate stared at Leroy for several seconds before he spoke again. "Yeah, I guess I could see the resemblance, now that I sit here looking at you. But answer this. How could you watch him grow up knowing he was your son and it not bother you?"

"It wasn't easy, Nate. I . . . it's a long story." Leroy finally turned and looked at Nate.

"I got nothing but time." Nate sat back in the leather chair and waited patiently.

Leroy proceeded to tell Nate the half-truth about what happened back in the day. He told him how Willie Jenkins, who was said to be Ishmael's father and was given his last name, had strung his mother out on drugs. He told him that once she finally got away from Willie, she came running to him. They had an affair, and she had gotten pregnant with Ishmael. Leroy did tell Ishmael the truth about his parentage just before he died in Leroy's arms.

"That's some deep shit."

From that day on Nate and Big Roy shared the responsibility of raising Nyeem.

"Is he ready?" Leroy asked now, referring to Nyeem getting into the drug business.

"Roy, man, I don't know. I been talking to him. He said he don't know if he ready for all that. I told him all the stories 'bout Ish. I told him shit 'bout you and . . . I don't know, man. The boy wanna play ball, and I can't knock him for that."

"Well, him playing ball is one thing, but he needs an occupation that he can retire off of. You know how many niggas think they gonna get drafted into the NBA and don't? Then when they don't get drafted, they don't have a backup plan. I just want him to have a plan."

"Yeah. But how long you think this shit is gonna stay around?"

"As long as muthafuckas are alive, this shit is gonna always be around. This shit didn't start when you were born or when I came along. It's been going on since the beginning of time."

Nate rolled his eyes up into his head, fearing Leroy would start with one of his lectures.

"Just send him over here to see me. I'ma rap with 'im. I ain't seen him in a while anyway. I know the past few years I ain't been in his life like I wanted to, but it ain't never too late."

"A'ight, I'ma do that."

Nate had basically taken over Leroy's business since Leroy had become ill. Leroy was too stubborn to go to the doctor to see why he had been feeling ill the last few years or so. It wasn't just old age. He had been suffering with headaches, weakness, tightening of the chest, and now the coughing fits were taking a toll on him as well. Nate still owned his security company, which had been very profitable, but the hustler in him would never die. He loved being in the hood and mixing it up. In fact, he still did jobs on the side every now and then. The thrill of the cold, hard steel in the palm of his hands would never leave his heart. The cries and whimpers of a victim begging for his life, only to lose it, was one of the biggest rushes he got, next to busting a nut.

But times were changing, and the laws of the streets were changing as well. They didn't have too many runners out on the corners like they did back in the day. The cops were now wise to that and had cut down on street trafficking, and the days of crooked cops seemed to be a thing of the past, with most of the crooked cops either in jail or retired from the force.

Leroy mostly dealt in weight and allowed the corner punks to take the high risks. But Nate gave Click the authority to be in charge of all the street runners and corners.

"Yeah, bring him by here this weekend," Leroy said. "What's going on with all my businesses?"

"It's all good, Roy. Don't worry 'bout the businesses. You need to get to a doctor and get well."

"Young'un, don't tell me not to worry about an empire I built from nothing. As long as I'm breathing air, I'm gonna be on top of my shit. I only let you step up temporarily, so don't let your balls get bigger than your head."

The older Leroy got, the more stubborn he was becoming, as well as grumpier.

"A'ight, Roy, chill out."

Leroy looked up to see the intruder standing in the doorway of his bedroom. "Who the fuck are you?"

She stood there in silence, standing very still as if she were a statue.

Nate noticed the surprise in Leroy's voice. "Who you talking to, Roy?"

"Dak!" Leroy yelled, but got no response. "Who the fuck is this bitch in my house?" he shouted, realizing the intruder was a woman, from the shapely body.

Leroy continued to yell at the intruder as he tried to rise to his feet, but he was too weak to stand on his own, and usually Dak helped him. He also needed a cane to assist him when he walked.

Unfortunately, Leroy didn't know that Dak was dead, and the three men patrolling the grounds of his house were also dead, with switchblades sticking out of their necks.

"Dak!" Leroy yelled again.

Nate continued to try to get Leroy's attention over the phone. "Roy!"

Leroy struggled to stand from the chaise lounge where he sat. He grabbed his pearl-handled cane from the side of the chair to aid him in standing.

"Roy!" Nate yelled. "What's going on? Yo, Roy!"

The intruder reached into the strap of her pouch where her weapon was stationed.

"Muthafucka, you must be crazy coming up in my shit. I'ma show you who you fucking with!" Leroy reached down the side of the chair.

"Yo, Leroy! I'm on my way!" Nate shouted when he finally realized something was horribly wrong.

Before Leroy could remove the .357 Magnum, the intruder used her gun, silencer attached, and pumped a bullet into his right kneecap.

"Aww, you bitch!" Leroy screamed from the excruciating pain, spittle flying from his mouth.

The intruder slowly walked closer toward Leroy and tilted her head to the side, studying him.

Leroy held his knee, trying to get relief. Located on the arm of the chair were several buttons. These buttons controlled the TV, the stereo, and the massager, among other things. This was all designed so that Leroy didn't have to leave his chair. He reached with his left hand and pressed a panic alert button on the arm of the chair, to inform the extra security he had on the premises that he needed help.

She raised the gun and pulled the trigger, releasing yet another bullet. This one slammed into Leroy's other knee. She chuckled lightly as she watched him suffer. It seemed as if this was her plan, to make him suffer before finishing him.

Leroy simply grimaced and grunted. He was so numb with pain from the first shot, he couldn't open his mouth to scream from the pain he now was experiencing in his left knee. He immediately grabbed the left knee and doubled over, his vision becoming blurred.

Leroy continued to try to reach into the side of the chair to retrieve his gun for a second time, but he was too weak. He lifted his head and looked up at the intruder, who had moved even closer. He tried to identify his hunter, but the nylon mask concealed her identity perfectly. He wracked his brain trying to figure out who the woman was. He knew he had many enemies, but none of them were women, at least not to his knowledge.

Leroy took short breaths as it became harder for him to breathe. The phone that rested on the floor from when he dropped it after the first shot began an irritating beeping sound from being off the hook for too long.

"Sit up," she finally said.

Leroy raised his shaking torso. His hands still resting on his knees, he shot daggers at the intruder. He noticed that she had a Spanish accent, and his brain began to process that information.

"Who are you?" Leroy struggled to ask.

"You can call me the 'black widow.'"

"What do you want from me?" Leroy's raspy voice whispered. His mouth was dry, and it was difficult for him to gather saliva to speak. "Do I know you?"

"I want you dead. You killed my brother and sister."

"I don't know you, your brother, or your sister." He grunted. "Take off that mask, you bitch!"

"Of course, you don't know me, but you know my father. He wanted me to do this. You were once my father's best friend."

Finally Leroy's extra security arrived on the premises. They barged into the house and made their way through the house, searching for him.

A smirk crossed Leroy's lips when he heard the commotion of his rescuers. "That's your ass now, bitch!" he yelled as saliva ran down his chin. He had lost control of his lips.

The intruder scanned the room for an escape route. She glided over to a window and opened it. She looked out of the second-floor window. She then placed one leg out of the window and straddled the windowsill.

Hearing the footsteps become louder and faster, Leroy shouted with the last bit of strength he had left, "Up here!"

The intruder raised her gun, took aim, and fired one last time, hitting Leroy in the chest.

Just then the bedroom door flew open. The security men noticed Leroy slumped in the chair and immediately saw the intruder sitting in the window. They began to fire, but she leaped from the second-floor window.

Two men raced to the window and continued to fire into the night, hoping to hit the intruder, who limped as fast as she could into the nearby woods, bullets whizzing past her head. The other two security men ran over to check on Leroy.

Just then Nate came bolting through the door into the room, his gun out. "No!" he shouted, noticing Leroy in the chair with bullet wounds in each knee, and the blood seeping from a bullet wound in his upper chest. He ran over to Leroy and pushed one of the men out of the way. "Roy!" Nate screamed.

In the woods the intruder was well hidden because of her all-black attire. She sat on the ground panting, holding her right ankle and rubbing it. She was in pain. She didn't think that she broke it, though, because she was able to make imaginary circles with her toes.

She looked back at the house, making sure no one was coming after her. She removed the nylon mask, and her black, curly hair fell down around her shoulders. She brushed her hair out of her face and looked back toward the house one more time. When she didn't see anyone, she made her way into the wooded area, limping to her escape.

Chapter Six

WHO DID IT?

As Nate waited at the hospital for Leroy to come out of surgery, he thought about his conversation with Leroy in the ambulance when he had briefly regained consciousness. Leroy had told him something that he didn't quite understand, and then he lost consciousness again, never regaining it.

When they arrived at the hospital, reporters and cameramen flooded the area. *This must be big news for the reporters,* Nate thought as they left the ambulance and rushed Leroy inside the hospital.

Cameras flashed, and the police had to hold everybody back. The reporters yelled out question after question, each hoping to get the first scoop on Leroy's injuries.

"Excuse me, sir," one reporter said, "who are you to Leroy Jones?"

"Sir, is Leroy Jones dead?"

"Who killed Leroy Jones?"

Someone else shouted out, "Was it a drug rival that did this to Leroy Jones?"

Nate just put his head down and ran beside the gurney with the paramedics.

Now Nate sat in the hospital hallway with two of Leroy's men, waiting to hear any news on Leroy's condition. He was being operated on as they waited. Nate was tired after having been up all night.

They had been operating on Leroy for hours. So many emotions were going through Nate. He wanted to go out into the streets and just kill anybody he came in contact with, but he was also tired and sleepy, not to mention starving. He hadn't eaten since the morning of the day before.

It was five AM, and still no word. Nate wanted to bust up in the operating room to see what they were doing. He'd almost gotten himself thrown out of the hospital because he wanted to post two men outside the operating room. But the staff wouldn't allow it, and threatened to call the police.

One of Leroy's men had to contain Nate and calm him down. And they settled for sitting in the hall not too far away from the operating room.

Several times a reporter or two managed to sneak past the police downstairs in the lobby and get up to the fifth floor of the hospital, but they were quickly stopped by the security guard the hospital had standing guard by the elevators.

Nate was tired of sitting there waiting. He felt like he had to do something, anything but just sit there. He stood and took a long stretch.

One of Leroy's men had laid his head against the wall and fallen asleep. The other sat there reading the newspaper.

Nate shoved his hands in his pockets and began to pace the hall.

"Where you going?" Leroy's man asked.

"I need to take a walk or something. I'll be back."

"You need me to go with you?"

"Naw, I'm good," Nate said and walked away.

As soon as Nate disappeared around the corner, the elevator doors opened. A man wearing a fitted baseball cap and a polo shirt with jeans stepped off the elevator, only to meet the hospital's security guard. The tall black man reached in his pocket and held up his identification for the guard, who then stepped aside to let the man through.

He made his way down the hall and stopped at the nurses' station, speaking briefly with one of the nurses. Then he proceeded past Leroy's two men and down toward the operating room area on that floor. He disappeared through the first set of doors leading to the area of the operating room.

Ten minutes later, the man emerged from the double doors. He walked past Leroy's men again, never making eye contact with them.

One of Leroy's men looked up at him, but quickly looked back at an article he was reading, not giving the man his full attention.

The man got on the elevator, and the doors closed just as Nate was making his way back to where he had been sitting.

"Any word yet?" Nate asked.

"Nope."

Just then the doors opened, and out came the doctor with the face mask around his neck. He looked drained. He was followed by two other surgeons and a nurse.

Nate tapped the sleeping guard, and they all stood when the doctors approached them.

The head doctor stopped in front of the men, while the others kept moving forward.

"So what's going on?" Nate asked.

"I'm Dr. Clinton," he said to Nate and the men.

"How is he?"

Dr. Clinton proceeded to tell Nate about Leroy's condition, and then he left them standing there.

Twenty minutes later down in front of the hospital, the reporters, cameramen, and bystanders still crowded the front of the hospital, waiting to hear something about the notorious Big Roy. The police still stood on guard, blocking the entrance to the hospital and making sure only people with credentials were allowed inside.

A spokesperson from the hospital staff emerged from the double doors of the hospital. She was there to read a statement from Dr. Clinton.

Everyone zoned in on the woman. Cameras rolled and flashbulbs popped. Every microphone was shoved toward her so that she could be heard clearly.

She was a petite Caucasian woman with straight blond hair that stopped at her shoulders. She looked to be in her twenties and was dressed in scrubs. She cleared her throat, pulled out some papers, and began to read from them.

"Dr. Clinton, the lead surgeon at St. Barnabas Medical Center made a desperate attempt to save the patient Leroy Jones. Unfortunately, due to difficulty with his heart, Leroy Jones died just twenty minutes ago."

The crowd began to murmur, and the bulbs on the cameras continued to flash.

"Dr. Clinton and the staff did the best that they could, and they would like to send their sincere condolences out to the patient's family. Thank you." She put away the paper.

The reporters fired questions at her, but the woman turned on her heels and walked briskly back inside the hospital.

CHAPTER SEVEN

BIG ROY'S GONE?

The news hit the streets and spread like a forest fire. Everyone was talking about it. Old and young all knew Big Roy. Leroy Jones was loved by some and hated by many, especially law enforcement. It was a sad day in the hood for some, but a celebration for all those who'd always stood in his shadow. Talk was already going around town about who was gonna be the next king. The streets were plotting and planning on how to take over his territories before his body was even cold.

Every barbershop, hair salon, Laundromat, and home television was tuned into a news station that blared the details of the home invasion that ended Leroy Jones's life.

"They finally got Roy," an elderly barbershop owner said to no one in particular. His establishment was one of very few shops still open for business. He'd been there since the sixties, and still cut the hair of his most faithful clientele, at least the ones who were still alive or had hair. He hired three young barbers to keep new business flowing in.

"Yeah, they got my man," the old-timer shoe-shiner added. He bent over while shining a pair of shoes the old-fashioned way. "But I will tell all y'all young punks in here one thing." He stood upright, but his shoulders still seemed to be hunched over from years of shining shoes. He turned and faced the crowded establishment. "Y'all weak niggas ain't gonna never have the type of run my man Roy had."

"Preach, brother!" one of the senior gentlemen said from a corner table where he sat and played checkers alone.

The shoe-shiner continued, "Big Roy was one of the baddest muthafuckas of his time! That cat had all the bitches and all riches!"

"That's right, my brother!"

The younger men groaned in irritation, realizing it was gonna be another preaching session from the old fools. The owner's nephew, Devon, sat on his lazy butt and laughed along with the rest of the young men.

"Yo, a'ight, I'll give it to the old man," one young patron said. "He had a good run, but the key word, gentlemen, is *had*. It's past tense. Big Roy is no more. Now it's time to show y'all old fuckas how to hold it down."

The shoe-shiner asked, "How? By getting all shot up at a young age? By going to prison before you even get off the tittie good?"

The older men in the barbershop began to laugh.

"That's exactly how y'all dumb young punks gonna do it! Big Roy was a genius! He ain't NEVER went to jail a day in his life!" The old man yelled, "Do y'all pissy-wet niggas hear me?"

"Yo, chill out, old man, before you have a heart attack," one of the customers said.

Everybody laughed.

The old shoe-shiner shook his head as he looked at the few other old-timers in the shop. They all read his mind and shook their heads as well.

"Y'all young cats just don't get it. Men like Roy were very smart. They knew how to run a business. Roy might be gone, but let me tell you something." He threw the dirty shine cloth over his shoulders and walked over to the owner's chair. He walked behind the owner as he cut hair and grabbed a picture that was stuck in the mirror, among many others. "This nigga right here"—He walked back into the center floor of the shop and held the picture of Leroy high above his head—"This nigga will never be replaced! You can say what you want, but I bet you a dollar to a dime that there ain't gonna never be another muthafucka to take his place. Now bet me!" He was heated.

"Yo, old man," a young customer said as he stood, having just received a fresh cut. He looked in the mirror, ran his hand over his head, and then turned to face the older man. "I wouldn't bet you shit, because you ain't gonna live long enough to pay me my muthafuckin' money!" He threw the barber a twenty and walked out of the establishment, with laughter from the young patrons following behind him.

Sitting in a chair, waiting his turn to get his haircut, was Mike. He wasn't laughing at all. Back in the day, Mike had always been known to have a vicious crew as well. Retired from the game, the menacing look on his face would make one wonder what he was contemplating at that time.

Chapter Eight

NEWS

The television blared loudly with BET videos. In the kitchen of the newly built townhouse, TJ stood over the stove and turned over the chicken legs he was frying. Grease popped onto the back of his hand, causing him to jump. "Shit!"

His cell phone rang. He walked over to the kitchen table and answered it. "Hey, baby," he said as he placed the phone between his ear and shoulder and walked back over to the stove.

"Are you watching the news?" his girlfriend Dasia asked.

"No. Why? What's up?"

"Go look."

TJ turned down the fire on the stove and placed the fork on the counter before walking into the living room. He grabbed the remote and turned to one of the news channels broadcasting the evening news. On the first station he turned to, he didn't see anything of interest.

"I don't see anything, baby. What's going on?"

"Turn to Channel Four. Hurry."

TJ quickly turned to Channel Four, and a news anchorwoman was announcing the events that took place the night before. In the background was Leroy's house with police tape roped around the area. Up in the right-hand corner of the screen was a picture of Leroy.

"Isn't that the man you said was your godfather?" Dasia asked

"No. My godfather's name is Nate."

"But I remember you telling me about this man. You did know him, right?"

TJ didn't respond right away. He was trying to catch up on what actually happened.

TJ and Leroy had never become as close as he and Nate were. They'd had several one-on-one conversations between his sophomore and senior year of high school, but the very first time he had a sit-down with Leroy was right after killing Nettie.

"You wanted to see me, sir?" TJ asked when he walked into Leroy's office located at the pool hall.

"Yeah, sit down, kid," Leroy said as he sat back in his chair.

TJ was nervous. He knew all about Leroy. Hell, who didn't know Big Roy? He'd seen him cruise through the block in one of his many Cadillacs, but he had never gotten this close to him before or had the pleasure of actually talking to him face to face.

"Nate tells me he has taken you under his wing and deemed you his godchild."

TJ nodded.

"He told me how you took care of that problem we had," Leroy said, referring to Nettie. He waited for a response, but got none.

TJ sat and listened intently. He was always taught to listen and think about what to say before saying it, and that if he had nothing constructive to say, then he shouldn't say anything at all.

"He also tells me you were a good moneymaker and you want to walk away from it all."

TJ nodded again.

"What's the problem? You make good money for a kid your age."

"I lost my mother and my best friend because of that business. It ain't what I want to do with my life. I'm gonna finish school and get up outta here."

"You know how many kids say that same thing you just did? Too many to count, and they all know that getting a square job ain't gonna bring in the kinda cash you can make with me."

"But death and prison ain't worth that kinda cash," TJ said, looking Leroy square in the eyes.

Leroy chuckled. "That's if you weak, kid. If you keep your head on straight, play the game and not let it play you, you'll live to be able to enjoy the bread you make. Look at me. I'ma old man, and I ain't never do a day in jail. Hell, I ain't never did an hour in jail, and I'm living off the fruits of all my hard work."

TJ never blinked. He kept his gaze on Leroy as he spoke. He admired and respected the man, but his mind was made up. He wanted to finish school and go to college. He vowed that after he graduated high school, he would only come back to Newark to visit his grandmother. But she had since died, and he'd never gone back.

"Tony?" Dasia called out to him, bringing him out of his memories. "Are you all right?"

"Yeah, baby. I'm OK."

"Do you know him?"

"Yes, I do."

"I'm sorry to hear he was killed."

"Yeah, me too, baby. I'll get back to you in a few, OK?"

"OK, I'll talk to you later."

TJ and Dasia were college sweethearts. After graduating college they became even closer. He was seriously contemplating marrying her. She was a good woman and gave him his space without crowding him. She wasn't the jealous type, and TJ loved that. He had dated some crazy jealous girls, and he almost lost it on a couple of them. So when he met Dasia and found out she was perfect for him, he made sure he held on to her.

TJ continued to stare at the television although it had since gone to a commercial. He wondered why Nate hadn't reached out to him to let him know Leroy was dead.

It had been a couple of years since TJ had last seen Nate, who had stopped through Virginia a time or two on his way to conduct business in another state, and although he spoke to him at least once or twice a month, Nate usually reached out to him to fill him in on the happenings in Newark. But he called mostly to keep him updated on Nyeem.

TJ took a liking to Nyeem because he reminded him so much of himself when he was younger. He made sure that he also kept in contact with Nyeem to ensure that he stayed in school. TJ didn't agree with Nate and Leroy wanting to pull Nyeem into the drug business, and he made sure he stayed in Nyeem's ear about it.

TJ lived in Richmond, Virginia and loved the slower pace of Southern living. He was making his mark in the accounting world, although he was only just starting out. When he'd graduated from high school, he had his mind set on pre-law, but after failing to win a scholarship, he had to change his major. He was able to qualify for a student loan and used some of the money he had saved from working for Nate for extras, like books and housing. Over the summer, before going off to college at Virginia Commonwealth, he decided to get his BS in accounting, since math was his best subject.

He walked back into the kitchen and removed the chicken from the frying pan, placing it on a plate lined with paper towels. He turned the burner off and picked up his cell phone. Sitting at the table, he began to dial. He sat and listened to the ringing phone go to voicemail.

"Nate, this TJ. Hit me up when you get this message. One!" He ended the call and sat at the kitchen table, thinking about Leroy's death. He suddenly realized just how big Leroy was. Leroy's death was on a news station in another state.

Chapter Nine

WHY BIG ROY?

Ten A.M. the Next Day

Nate sat bedside in a hospital room, where Leroy lay in the bed heavily sedated, tubes down his nose and throat to assist him in breathing, and the heart monitor hooked up to him beeping lightly. He had just recently come out of surgery to have the bullets removed from his body, and all color seemed to have left his face, giving him an ashy look.

Nate sat back in the chair and stared at the sickly man. He hadn't slept since the incident. The television mounted from the ceiling was turned on, but he couldn't hear any sound. He was deep in thought as to what his next move was going to be to get revenge.

The elderly nurse that had been in and out of the room was helpful and made him feel at ease.

Suddenly the news broadcast broke him out of his stupor.

"Hi, I'm Nancy Lipose from the news alert desk bringing you the local news alerts. Late last night, about eleven thirty P.M.*, the known drug lord, Leroy 'Big Roy' Jones, was shot several times in his home. He was rushed to St. Barnabas Medical Center, where he underwent surgery. Later Leroy Jones was pronounced dead due to heart complications. A*

spokeswoman from the hospital delivered the news this morning."

The TV showed a clip of the spokeswoman who read from the paper just hours ago in front of the camera.

"Police responded to a nine-one-one call to this address here in Livingston, New Jersey," the anchorwoman continued. "Leroy Jones was suspected of running an entire cocaine and heroin drug ring for more than two decades. The DEA, FBI, and other local law enforcement have tried for years to bring Leroy Jones in on what would have been the biggest bust of the century. But Jones managed to slip just under the radar of the law on countless occasions. Big Roy has now been stopped. Reporting to you live from the news alert desk, I am Nancy Lipose."

With a frown on his face, Nate continued to stare at the television. He was stunned that the news was reporting Leroy dead. He couldn't figure out from where they got their information. He looked over at Leroy. He looked dead and may have been near death, but he was indeed still alive.

Nate sat back in the chair and thought about how the false news of Leroy's death might play out to his advantage. He pulled out his cell phone and powered it on. The phone came to life, and his voicemail alert sounded off. He ignored it and searched through the contact list for a number. He placed the call and waited for someone to answer.

"Yo, what the fuck happened?" Click yelled into the phone. "I just got back into town, and the first thing I hear is, Big Roy is dead!"

"Click, calm the fuck down," Nate whispered as loudly as he could. He wasn't supposed to use his cell phone in the hospital, but he had to call a meeting with all the workers.

Click was driving back to his place after just leaving the Newark Airport. He had stopped at one of the local liquor stores to purchase something to drink and some lottery tickets when he heard several patrons talking about Leroy's death in the store. He ran back to the car and was just about to call Nate when his cell phone rang.

Click tried to take it down a notch, but was having a difficult time maintaining. "Yo, Nate, what happened?"

"I'll tell you when I see you. I need you to get everybody together and meet me at my crib in like two hours," Nate said, sounding exhausted.

Click didn't respond. He was fuming, and the whites of his eyes had turned red. The veins on the side of his face were bulging. The only thing he wanted to do at that moment was put a lot of bullets in somebody.

"What? How you sound? You gonna tell me what the fuck happened now!" Click yelled.

Nate rubbed his face, becoming irritated. "Listen, Roy ain't dead, but you can't say shit to nobody. As far as we're concerned, he's dead."

Click was more confused now. "What?"

"Just do what the fuck I tell you!" Nate said a little too loudly.

One of his guards stuck his head inside the door, and Nate threw up his hand to let him know everything was all right.

Click and Leroy had grown to be close. Click was just as loyal to Leroy as he was to Nate, and the news of Leroy's death slammed into his heart like a wrecking ball hitting a building.

"Click," Nate said to him.

Click still didn't respond. Nate knew he was still on the phone because he could hear him breathing like a dragon.

"Click, get your head right. We definitely gonna take care of it."

Nate felt he had to reassure him. He knew all too well the type of cat Click was. Click was that hothead, ready-to-buck-off-for-any-reason type of cat, so he needed to keep him grounded before he got the others amped up.

Nate made another attempt to get Click's attention. "Yo!"

"What's up?" Click asked in a calm, almost scary voice.

"Don't fuck this up, man. Just do like I asked, and trust we 'bout to put shit in motion."

"Yeah, a'ight," Click said, unconvinced.

"I'll hit you back later," Nate said and disconnected the call.

Nate looked up to see Nyeem walking into the hospital room. He had completely forgotten to call the young boy and let him know what had happened.

One of Nate's employees had picked up Nyeem from the crib and brought him to the hospital. He looked over at Leroy. "How he doing?"

"He just came out of surgery. He ain't wake up yet. The doctor said he got a weak heart. His blood pressure is up, and Roy got lung cancer. It don't look that good for him."

"Damn!" Nyeem said in a low whisper as he hung his head.

"He just asked me on the phone before this happened last night to bring you to come see him."

"He did?"

"Yeah. Nyeem, c'mere, man. Have a seat." Nate pointed to the chair that sat next to the window.

Nyeem walked past the bed and stared at Leroy. He grabbed the chair and dragged it over next to Nate's chair. "It's 'bout time I tell you the truth about Big Roy."

"What do you mean?"

"He's your grandfather."

"I know."

"No. He's your real grandfather."

"You mean, like blood?"

Nyeem was confused. He had always called Leroy *Grandpop*, but he thought that was out of respect because Leroy had been in his life since he was very young. No one had ever told him that Leroy was his real grandfather. He knew Nate wasn't his real uncle. Nate had worked for his father. And Nyeem knew his father had gotten his product from Leroy, who, according to Nate, Ishmael had looked up to like a father. Since both his parents were dead, Nyeem always thought that Nate and Leroy just took care of him because of their respect for his parents.

Over the years he'd heard different stories in the streets, and so he figured out for himself that neither Leroy nor Nate were his real relatives. In fact, he often wondered who his real relatives were. He wanted to meet somebody, anybody that was a blood relative. But this was something that he'd never asked Nate about. He thought that it would hurt Nate if he asked him about his real family, considering Nate had raised him all his life.

"Yeah, Nyeem, like blood." Nate continued to stare at Nyeem, to see his reaction. When Nyeem didn't respond, he asked him, "What are you thinking about?"

"Why has no one told me about this?"

"I wanted to tell you, but Leroy wanted to be the one to tell you himself. Truth be told, man, I never knew, and neither did your father, because Leroy is your father's father. Leroy didn't tell me the truth until you were about four years old. He didn't want to tell you then because he thought you were still too young to understand. I really believe he was gonna tell you when I brought you by the house, but I never got a chance to do that."

"So why are you telling me now, if he wanted to tell me?" Nyeem was starting to feel a little betrayed. He felt that if Leroy and Nate were like family to him, they should have told him something right away.

Nate looked over at Leroy. "Because, man, I don't think Roy's gonna make it."

"So what you shoulda done was never told me, because I think that's fucked up that y'all would keep something like that from me all this time. You have no clue how I thought I didn't have any real family, how I would be around my friend's family and wish I could feel what they was feeling. And all this time I at least had one blood relative that I knew living right under my nose!"

"Come on, Nyeem, calm down, man. We are your real family, man. We are as real as it gets. If I wouldn't have taken you and raised you myself, you would have ended up in somebody's foster home or something, and there is no telling where you would be right now. Once I found out you was Ish's son, there was no way in hell I was gonna let the system get you. I know my man Ish would not have let that happen to any of my seeds." Nate was seriously hurt by Nyeem's accusations. "Yo, let me tell you something. I am like a real relative to you, because Ish was like my brother. You don't have a fucking clue how tight we were, and as far as I'm concerned, I am your uncle!"

Nate rubbed the back of his neck as tension began to build. He had so many thoughts going through his mind, he felt like he was going to explode. He had to keep a level head, seeing that he was the one in charge, and the last thing he wanted to do was take his frustrations out on Nyeem.

Nyeem sat there still fuming about finally learning he had a blood grandfather only when the man was lying on his deathbed. He thought about how he would never get the chance to really spend time with Leroy.

"Listen, man, I know how it feels not to have anybody in your corner," Nate said. "I was the same way when I was growing up. I mean, I got a moms and a pops, but my mother stayed in and out of jail so much, it was like she was never there. My father was in and out of my life, but then one day he just disappeared. After he left, all I did was jump from house to house with so-called family members. Man, they wasn't my peoples, because they treated me like shit. I didn't eat every day. I wore hand-me-down clothes, and sometimes I couldn't even get in the house because, if it was late, nobody would open the door for me, and I had to sleep on the porch in the dead of winter. Most times when I did get in the house, I slept on the cold kitchen floor because there were so many damn people in the house." Nate stood and began to pace as he remembered those hard times growing up.

Nyeem simply sat there watching him, not saying a word.

"Man, I swear I wanted to set off a bomb in the house and blow everybody the fuck up! They treated me foul as shit! I was bitter as hell, man. I started taking what I wanted. I was tired of being that dirty, skinny kid on the block. I started busting muthafuckas over they heads to get mine. I had no remorse for nobody. I didn't care 'bout shit! But when I met your father, man, on everything that I love, your father showed me nothing but love. Ish was my real peoples, man. There wasn't nothing I wouldn't do for that nigga. Ish was a straight-up nigga, and when I found out you was his seed, I knew I wasn't gonna let you be put into the same situation I had to grow up in. I owe your father my life, man, and by raising you, I am showin' him my gratitude. Now if you still feel the way that you do, ain't nothing I can do about it, but I love you like you was my own. You feel me?"

Nyeem stood, shocked by Nate's story. He felt stupid for the things he'd said. He had always looked up to his uncle, but now knowing Nate's story, he respected him even more.

"Yeah, I feel you, Unc. My bad. I just got caught up."

"It's all good, man." Nate grabbed Nyeem by the back of his neck and pulled him in for a hug.

The two of them stood there embracing for a moment.

"Yo, man, I'm gonna find out who did this," Nyeem said, breaking the embrace.

"Naw, son, you just go to school, play ball, and let the big dogs handle this one. I got this one on lock."

"Yeah, I know you do, but you don't know the type of pull I got on the streets. I know I can find out something."

Nate chuckled. "What do mean, you got pull on the streets? What kinda pull you got? You won't even get in the game, so how you figure you got pull?"

"Yo, a nigga ain't gotta be in the game to hold weight on the streets, Unc. Don't forget who my father is. Niggas be coming up to me all the time talking about my pops. You would think I was some kinda NBA baller or something, the way they treat me out there. It's like I'm in Hollyhood. So I know I can find out something."

"I feel you, but this shit ain't no game. I can't send you out there in the jungle like that with no weapons. Man, once niggas peep yo' game, they gonna come at you spittin' bullets. Naw, you chill out and let me handle this."

Nyeem didn't respond. He just looked over at Leroy and then back at Nate.

"Yo, Nyeem, you heard me, right?" Nate looked at him sternly.

"A'ight, I heard you."

"Don't fuck around, man. I'm telling you, I will know 'cause, just like your father's name is out there, my name is too, and I got eyes on them streets. Don't let me hear no shit 'bout you." He pointed a finger at Nyeem.

"A'ight, man. Damn!"

"Oh, yeah, nobody is to know that Roy is your real grandfather. Keep that shit right here, and it goes no further than this room."

Nyeem nodded, acknowledging that he understood.

"And another thing . . . don't tell anybody Roy is alive."

"Huh?" Nyeem was confused.

"You heard me. Since everybody thinks he's dead, then he will be dead."

"But don't the hospital people know who he is?"

"Shit! I don't even know why they saying he dead, but if that's what's out there on the streets, then we gonna roll with it. That way nobody won't be tryin'-a come up here and finish him off."

"Uncle Nate, they gonna figure it out, man."

"Well, if they do, then they better come hard or go home because, if anybody come for Roy again, we gonna be waiting."

Chapter Ten

BEHIND AN ABANDONED BUILDING

"Hit that bitch again!" the voice yelled.

One man held down the victim, and the other raised the butt of his gun and came down with force across the bridge of the victim's nose, instantly drawing blood.

The victim released a bloodcurdling scream.

"Don't scream now, you little bitch! Hit that nigga again!"

The man barking the orders was none other than a cat named Blaze. He had baby-smooth skin and jet-black wavy hair that was cut low, and was as black as the night. With his physically fit, athletic body and neatly trimmed goatee, he fit the definition of tall, dark, and handsome.

Raised by killers to be a killer, Blaze had earned his nickname from the ruthless way he "blazed" his victims. During his childhood, his parents ran from state to state, fleeing the law and becoming wanted in ten states by the time he was thirteen. His father met his untimely demise in a bank robbery gone wrong. His mother, who was sitting in the getaway car during the robbery, managed to escape.

With his father deceased, Blaze's mother had no other source of income. Since all she knew to do to survive was rob, she thought her best option was to train her only son to take his father's place.

So Blaze learned to use an arsenal, drive a car, and pull off a robbery all before he turned fifteen. When he and his mother were caught trying to rob an armored truck, she was sent to prison to serve three life sentences with no possibility of parole for three previously known murders she'd committed. Blaze was sent off to a boy's facility, where he did fifteen months for robbery.

Once he was released from detention, he was then placed into a foster home, which only lasted for six months before he was returned to a boys' home. Blaze had learned how to master and hone his craft while being locked down in the boys' detention, reading and researching bank robberies and floor plans. He'd escaped from the foster home when he was seventeen and had been on the run from the authorities ever since.

After robbing a local candy store with just a stick in his pocket to imitate a gun, Blaze managed to get enough money to cop a real gun out on the streets. Then he ran into an old friend from the neighborhood, and the two became inseparable. His friend, Triggs, let him stay with him at his aunt's house. Blaze continued to do small-time robberies at night, while Triggs ventured into the drug world.

When Blaze turned eighteen, he was no longer wanted by the boys' home. He was considered an adult and was free to roam the streets without having to look over his shoulder. Triggs, who was also eighteen, had built a little status for himself dealing drugs. Not surprisingly, neither boy finished school.

Although Triggs and Blaze were friends, their illegal endeavors never coincided, until one day when Triggs was having a problem with another street bully known as Black Cat.

Black Cat walked up on Triggs, pulled a gun on him, and took all of his money and drugs. Pissed beyond belief, Triggs came home to borrow Blaze's gun. He wanted to kill Black Cat because he was humiliated and felt punked. When Blaze asked him why he wanted the gun, Triggs blacked out and went into a rant about Black Cat.

"That punk-ass nigga Black Cat took all my shit right out in front of everybody!" Triggs said, tears lining his face.

Blaze was sitting back, eating Chinese food with the money he'd robbed from a small-time dealer. He was trying to put a face with the name. "Who?"

"That muthafucka, Black Cat! Yo, man, just give me your shit! I'm gonna lift that nigga's skull!" Triggs paced in a circle, breathing heavily.

"Hold up, yo. Naw, man, I ain't gonna let you do that. Let me handle this nigga. Show me where he at," Blaze said. Without hesitation, he led the way out of the apartment.

The two searched for Black Cat and finally found him through a source who told them he was in the local bar. They walked up in the bar, and Triggs pointed Black Cat out to Blaze.

With no concern for the patrons in the establishment, Blaze walked over to Black Cat and hit him in the back of the head with his gun, and Black Cat fell from the barstool and crashed to the floor, hitting his head.

Dazed, Black Cat looked up at Blaze and found himself looking down the barrel of a .45.

The patrons sitting at the bar all scrambled away from them. Triggs placed his hand down the front of his jogging suit pants, pretending he was packing too, to keep any wannabe heroes at bay.

"The cat that you robbed tonight is my brother," Blazed growled in the baritone voice he'd developed in his early teens. "You fucked with the wrong muthafucka!"

"Yo, muthafucka, who is you?" Black Cat asked, not recognizing

Blaze.

In fact, hardly anyone knew Blaze, because he didn't hang in the streets. He didn't sell drugs, so he didn't hang out on the corners. He did his robbing and then would dip back into the house.

"I'm your worst fucking nightmare!" Blaze then proceeded to stomp Black Cat in the face, his steel-toe Timberland boots connecting with Black Cat's face several times, sending blood flying. Blaze was a thin, tall teen, standing at six feet three inches, whereas Black Cat was a grown man with a large stomach, so pound for pound, Blaze was the underdog.

"Where the fucking money and product at?"

Black Cat yelled like a bitch, "In my pocket, man!"

Some of the male customers in the bar snickered. They'd been victims of Black Cat's bullying and were happy to see him get what he deserved.

Blaze put the gun to Black Cat's forehead.

"Come on, man, the shit is in my pockets!"

Blaze went into his pocket and pulled out the stack of bills. He handed the money to Triggs, who happily took it. Blaze then reached into the other pocket and retrieved the drugs from a Ziploc sandwich bag. He tossed it to Triggs.

"I should kill your ass right here!" Blaze said, chambering a bullet.

"No!" Black Cat screamed, holding his hand out in defense. Blood filled the inside of his mouth, making all his teeth look red.

When the owner of the bar made his way through the crowd, Blaze turned the gun on him, not knowing what his intentions were.

"Hold up, young man." The elderly gray-haired man held up his hands. "I don't want no problems in my bar. You need to take this shit outside."

"This nigga robbed the wrong muthafucka," Blaze said.

"I understand he got what he got coming to him," the owner told him, "but not in my bar, son."

Blaze kicked Black Cat in the mouth one more time for good measure, and then he and Triggs walked out of the bar.

And that was the start of the two-man team with Triggs as the moneymaker and Blaze acting as the muscle.

The cat that Blaze was now having two of his men handle was a nickel-and-dime wannabe hustler. The twenty-two-year-old had been warned several times by Triggs about dealing in his territory, but the young man was hardheaded. He thought he held some weight because he ran with a couple of dudes whose family had history on the streets. When Triggs came to Blaze with the information, Blaze jumped into action.

The man could barely breathe while the two men put the beating of the century on him.

"So what's up now, nigga? I don't hear you talking." Blaze put his hand up to his ear as if trying to hear the man say something.

With the stomping the man received, all he could do was try to catch his breath when the two men stopped beating him.

"I hope you get the message," Blaze said. "And next time you wanna fuck somebody, do your homework first to find out who you fucking with. Break this nigga off," Blaze said to his men. Then he walked out of the backyard of the abandoned house where they had taken the man for privacy.

The enforcers picked up the two aluminum bats resting on the ground near them and proceeded to swing the bat against the man's kneecaps several times until they heard them crack. The man's screams could be heard from blocks away.

Satisfied with their work, the two men walked out of the backyard and got into the all-black Dodge minivan that they called "the hearse." Whenever they put in work and the target was killed, they used the van to transport the dead body to a dumping place.

Blaze had made a name for himself as the enforcer of the crew that Triggs ran. Blaze, however, was still his own man, and he was partnered in Triggs's business, although he didn't like dealing with drugs. He could never see himself standing out on the corners grinding. If he was out on the block, it was only to talk shit with the fellas, and then he would dip off and go get him a chick to chill with.

Triggs was in the raggedy two-family house where he had his operation set up, walking around in a semi-circle, talking on his cell phone. He had grown into a handsome young man at the age of twenty-five. Always dressed to impress, Triggs was a pretty boy with his golden brown complexion and sandy brown wavy hair. He stood at six feet even and had high cheekbones that sat under a pair of gorgeous brown eyes.

When Blaze walked in, Triggs acknowledged him by throwing his head up.

Blaze went into the kitchen and spoke to the men bagging up the product for sale.

Triggs walked into the kitchen to join the others when he was done with his phone call. "What's up?" Triggs asked as he shook Blaze's hand.

"What's good? Let me holla at you for a minute." Blaze left the kitchen.

Triggs followed behind him and took a seat in one of the chairs in the room at the front of the house.

"Yo, you hear what happened to Big Roy?" Blaze asked.

"Naw, man, I ain't hear nothing. What happened?"

"That nigga is on ice right now as we speak."

"Word?" Triggs asked with a raised brow.

That was the best news Triggs had heard in a long time. He'd wanted Leroy's status for a long time, but with Leroy controlling most of the city, there was no way he could have stepped to him.

If it was left up to Blaze, he would have stepped to Leroy and his crew a long time ago, but Triggs knew they didn't have the muscle to go up against Leroy. He'd known since he was a kid that Leroy had the city on lock, and no one could successfully challenge his position.

"Word up. That nigga is finished, so now we can get that nigga's customers and get this paper up," Blaze said nonchalantly.

Triggs knew his longtime friend was happy about the news. "Yeah, man, no doubt. A'ight, I'm with that. Let's run with this shit."

"I told you that nigga bleeds just like everybody else. But what's fucking with me is, I wished I coulda been the muthafucka that put that nigga to bed," Blaze said, almost disappointed.

Chapter Eleven

KEEP YOUR TRAP SHUT

Later that day at Nate's Place

Everyone gathered at Nate's townhouse. Marijuana smoke filled the living room with a fog, since everyone was "hazing," trying to get their minds off Leroy's death while they waited for Nate to finish a phone call. He was talking to the supervisor of his security company, making sure the supervisor understood what to do in his absence. Nate planned to take time away from the company to find out who tried to take Leroy out.

Nate closed his cell phone and went over to the window. He pushed it up to let in some much-needed air. "A'ight, listen up!" he said. "I need all eyes on me."

Click definitely had his eyes on Nate. He was pissed because Nate wouldn't allow him to do what he did best, which was wreak havoc. He had spoken to Nate just before they all came over to the house, and wanted to tear up the streets when he got the details about Leroy.

Nate ignored Click's gaze and focused on the matter at hand.

"I ain't gonna pull no punches with y'all niggas. Somebody tried to do Big Roy, and that shit ain't cool. I want all hands on deck. I want every muthafucka we got on the streets and in-house to fuckin' rip these streets apart until we find the muthafuckas responsible for this shit!"

"Word up!" Click said, amped.

"I want the muthafucka that did this," one of the men said.

"No doubt," another one said.

"When y'all find that muthafucka, bring his ass to me!" Nate yelled.

"So you don't want us to do him?" Ezel asked.

"Fuck no! I want that muthafucka!"

"You know we ain't gonna find that nigga. He know Big Roy's peoples gonna be looking for his ass," one of the crew members said.

"Well, then flush that muthafucka out!" Nate said, pure evil on his face. "And I want y'all niggas to find the muthafucka that put the hit out too."

"So you think somebody put a hit out on Big Roy?" one of the young runners asked.

Nate just looked at him, his face screwed up.

"What the fuck you think?" Click asked the young runner. "Y'all muthafuckas kill me. Just shut the fuck up and listen! That was a professional hit, and ain't no average muthafucka gonna be able to get past security, kill Dak, and get next to Big Roy. Man, just shut the fuck up!" Click wasn't irritated so much by the young boy's question as he was about being put on a leash. He wanted to be let loose on the streets, and every little thing would bother him until he could do what he did best.

The young teen felt embarrassed because he was getting evil looks from his coworkers for asking the question.

"I'm about to drop something on y'all," Nate said slowly, trying to find the right words to say it.

There were only about twelve members in attendance. Click picked his most loyal men to attend, and Nate had his most loyal men that worked for him at the security company. Then there was Leroy's staff. These were the members that Nate, Click, and Leroy trusted the most. The rest of the organization would never know the truth about Leroy still being alive.

"I want this kept in-house. No one is to know that Leroy is still alive. He's barely alive, but he is still alive." Nate looked into all the shocked and confused faces. "I'm not about to get into how or why. All you need to know is that he is, but he's in a coma. We need to find the jokers responsible for this as soon as possible because, if they find out that he is still alive, they'll come for him again. If I find out that anyone of y'all niggas ran yo' mouths, then do yourself a favor and put a bullet in your own head because if I catch you, you're gonna wish you did!"

Nate was confused to why the news would announce that Leroy was dead, if he knew he was still alive. The hospital knew he was still alive, and Nate hadn't told anyone that he was dead. Although he thought it was better protection for Leroy if everyone thought he was dead, he was still concerned. He remembered the conversation he had with the doctor.

While he sat by Leroy's bed, Dr. Clinton walked into the room to check on Leroy.

"Doc, can you tell me why the media would think my father is dead?"

Dr. Clinton looked over the top of the clipboard. "I think considering the way your father almost lost his life, in the event someone wants to come back to finish the job. I was advised by a very close friend that it would be wise to announce Mr. Jones' death. I apologize for not consulting with you first and hope you will agree with me on those terms."

"I don't want none of y'all to try and go see him. I know niggas is watching us."

No one said a word, and everyone understood. They didn't want any part of Nate or Click.

"So what about the blocks?" another man asked hesitantly, afraid it was a stupid question. "You don't want us to bang while we look for this nigga?" He needed to know, since Nate didn't make it fully clear about that aspect of the job.

"I ain't got shit to do with y'all banging. That's on him." Nate pointed to Click. "My people, y'all still keep doing what you do. Business still gotta run."

Click added, "Yeah, y'all bangers keep banging. Let the niggas that's packing handle all the dirty work."

"Yo, I don't want y'all niggas to start getting sloppy. Don't start fucking up by getting locked up or fucking up the work," Nate said. " 'Cause if any of y'all do, then y'all niggas gonna sit your ass in the joint until I find the muthafuckas that got at Roy. I ain't got time or the bread to be wasting on your dumb asses 'cause, frankly, if it was left up to me, y'all wouldn't even be on the blocks. I would have y'all doing something else, like deliveries and shit. But, like I said, that's Click's thing, and y'all run for him."

Everybody looked around at each other, not saying a word.

"Y'all niggas feel me?" Nate looked at each man closely, and they all seemed to agree. "A'ight, hit the bricks and beat the blocks," he said, dismissing them.

They all rose to their feet, talking and discussing the news from the meeting as they walked out of the townhouse.

Click made himself more comfortable by scooting down on the sofa, now that he had more room.

The four security men remained in the house. Nate had something different for them to do. He wanted to post the men up inside to watch Leroy's house. He already had two men sitting in concealed cars parked on the street watching the house. The police wouldn't allow anyone to go inside the house until they searched the grounds for clues. Nate didn't want any of the sticky-finger cops to walk out of Leroy's house with anything, so the men were put there for that reason.

Nate knew that the police really weren't going to investigate the crime. They hated Leroy. He figured they were probably up in Leroy's crib going through all his shit, trying to find anything to take for themselves. Leroy had one gun that he kept down the side of the recliner. But Nate made sure he took that before the paramedics and police arrived that night. All the men Leroy had patrolling his grounds had registered weapons, so there was no need for him to keep additional weapons on the premises.

Nate wanted to go back to the house to find anything that he could that might give him an inkling of who tried to kill Leroy. His plan was to leave the four men there at the house to patrol the inside and the outside of the house. He wanted to stay at the house for a few days himself, but he needed to be in the streets hunting for Leroy's hitter.

"Yo, man, what's with you telling them young boys that you didn't want them to bang?" Click asked.

"For real, for real? I wouldn't have them out on the blocks, if it was me. Shit ain't like it used to be, and that makes them a high risk. Plus, you know niggas gunning for the spots we got, and them young boys is like targets at target practice, 'cause they ain't holding no armor."

"What the fuck, man! You gave me the authority to get my own crew together to bring in some loot. You told me I was in charge of my crew."

"Yeah, I know I did," Nate said, "but I also told you to use yo' head and work smart, not hard. You're constantly bailing your little niggas outta jail on drug charges, which is costing us money. So the smart thing to do is pull them off the corners and put them on delivering weight."

"Yo, you do what you do, and let me do what I do," Click said, irritated.

"Yo, you still be running into them two Spanish chicks that was down with Nettie?" Nate asked, changing the subject. His head was hurting, and he had no patience to go at it with Click.

"Yeah, I see Jazz around. I ain't seen her cousin in a minute, though. Jazz said Maria was scared straight after that night at the warehouse. Why? What's up?"

"I was riding in the ambulance with Roy when they was tryin-a revive him. He came to, and I tried to get him to tell me who did this to him. He told me he didn't know, but it was a Spanish bitch who tried to do him. Then he just started coughing up blood, and that's when he blacked out again, and they couldn't bring him back out of it. I was thinking, you should see if they know anything, since they Spanish and was into that ass-shaking business. You know how muthafuckas talk, and maybe they might have heard something."

"Hold up. You tryin'-a tell me that Roy said a bitch did him?"

"I'm serious as hell."

"So why you got them niggas out there looking for niggas?"

"Because I'm thinking Roy was delirious or some shit and was talking out his head."

"But what if it's true?" Click asked. "Then we got them cats out there chasing their tails."

"Not really. Because if a bitch did do it, trust a nigga put her up to it."

"A'ight. Next time I see Jazz, I'll kick it with her."

Click put out his roach in the ashtray. He was more confused now than when he first got there. He felt like Nate was holding out on something. He knew Nate got a hard-on from being in charge and calling the shots, and believed he wanted to feed him minimal information, to keep him on the outside. But Click wasn't with the planning and strategy shit and had an agenda of his own. He wanted to just buck on any and everybody, to instill fear in the streets, until somebody talked.

"So what's up?"

"Fuck you mean, what's up?" Nate ice-grilled him.

"I'm sayin', what you 'bout to do?" Click wanted to make sure Nate wasn't just giving orders and not taking any action himself.

"I'm getting ready to hit the streets and try to find out some shit, which you need to be doing too, so get your funky ass up off my couch."

"How Roy doing?"

"Go up there and see him yourself!" Nate shot back.

"Yo, man, I can't go see Roy like that. That shit fucks me up."

Nate was clearly irritated with Click's response. "Whether it fucks you up or not, you need to go pay your respects to Big Roy . . . after all the shit he's done for you."

"Yeah, I know, man, but Leroy is my man and all, and . . . man, just forget it." Click got up and walked to the front door. He didn't want to talk about it anymore. "Where you gonna be at later?"

"I'ma be at Leroy's house checking on things. Hit me on my cell if you need me."

"Yeah, a'ight. I'll be on the streets fucking niggas up." Click half-smiled at Nate as he walked out of the apartment and shut the door behind him.

Nate sat on the chair and buried his head in his hands. He didn't want to go to Leroy's house, but he knew if he didn't do it, no one else would.

CHAPTER TWELVE

BARBERSHOP

The barbershop had closed for the night, but there were still three customers in the shop. The owner had gone home earlier and usually let Devon, his nephew, close up shop for him. Devon didn't cut hair. He mostly ran errands and kept the place clean. He was a two-bit hustler and wasn't kicking up any dust, so most times he stayed in and out of jail. His uncle gave him a job at the shop to try to keep him out of trouble as well as put a few dollars in his pocket, but Devon wanted the big come-up and was just biding his time working in the shop.

The three dudes in the shop had been discussing the death of Leroy. Mike, Tone, and Lex had been living in Newark all their lives. They'd each had their time in the game and had bowed out gracefully and let Leroy have control.

"So what you saying, Mike?" Tone asked.

"I'm sayin', the nigga is dead, and now we can step in," Mike explained while the barber cut his hair.

Tone and Lex looked at each other.

"Yo, man, I ain't with all that. I'm retired from the game. I'm too old for that shit." Tone waved his hand at Mike.

"Too old? Tone, you ain't no older than me, and I'm forty-two," Mike said.

"Yeah, OK, and an old-ass forty-two-year-old nigga ain't got no business calling himself, starting up a drug business. Man, I did that shit when I was younger. Hell . . . you know. You was there. I ain't fucking with these little crazy-ass gangbanging niggas, man. They don't respect the game, nor the code of the streets we used to enforce. Naw, man, you go 'head. I'm good." Tone laughed and gave Lex some dap.

Devon pretended he wasn't listening to the conversation, but he was paying close attention as he swept the floor near them.

"What about you, Lex?" Mike asked.

"Go 'head, Mike. Tone is straight up. We too old to be standing out on the block. It would be one thing for me to have niggas working for me, but, man, you talking about starting from scratch, nigga?"

Lex and Tone fell out laughing.

"Man, fuck y'all niggas! I ain't talking about starting over. I'm talking about just stepping in. Big Roy's shit is already established. We stepping in as the new leaders. We ain't gotta do shit but count dough. The workers are already in place, and all we gotta do is get money," Mike said, painting the picture for them.

The two looked at each other again and burst into laughter.

"Yo, for real, you think them niggas that's loyal to that muthafucka just gonna let us walk up on the set and say we your new leaders? Get the fuck outta here!" Tone said.

They continued to laugh and clown Mike.

"I heard they got every man on their squad out looking for the nigga that did Big Roy. Who's watching the camp?" Mike looked at both of them with raised eyes.

The two men stopped laughing and thought about it.

"Yeah, I see a nigga done got these muthafuckas' attention." Mike reached back, his barber gave him some dap, and they both laughed.

Devon stopped sweeping and sat in one of the barber chairs. He was laughing too as he reached over to Mike and gave him some dap. He definitely wanted in on the deal, because he wasn't really making any money with what he had going on.

"A'ight, man, so what's your plan?" Tone asked.

"Word up! I want in too," Devon said.

The plan was to hit every one of Leroy's corners until the well ran dry. But what these men failed to realize was that the corners didn't belong to Leroy. They were run by Click.

Click pulled his arm back like the string on an archery bow and reeled it forward, making his fist connect with the jaw of the victim. His head flew to the right and almost knocked him to the floor. Spittle flew from his mouth as he grunted from the force of the blow. But he was being held up by two of Click's men, and his body hung loosely in their arms. Blood spots covered the front of his white T-shirt, and sweat covered his face and neck.

Click power-punched him again, but in the stomach this time.

The man hunched forward after receiving the blow. "I ain't do it!" he yelled.

"That's not what I heard." Click gave the man an uppercut.

This punch practically stood the man upright, and he jerked upward. His head then fell forward, and his chin rested on his chest.

"On everything I love, I ain't murk Big Roy," he said, barely able to catch his breath.

Click was on a mission. Despite what Nate told him not to do, he felt like this was something he had to do. Sitting around plotting and planning was not his MO. He was gonna find out who tried to kill Leroy, if it meant he had to kill every nigga in the game.

"Well, if you didn't do it, then you know who did."

"Naw, man, I swear on my mother, I don't know who did Big Roy."

Click pulled his gun from his holster and chambered a bullet.

"Come on, man, my girl is in the room. Please don't do this," he pleaded.

They'd come by the guy's house and waited outside until he came home. Click didn't know if the man had anything to do with Roy's murder, but he knew that dude didn't have no love for Leroy or his crew. So he decided to start with him first.

"Tell me who did it, and I won't do you," Click told him.

"I don't know, and that's the truth," the man said, fear in his eyes.

Click wasn't convinced. "Naw, you know something."

The man's girlfriend, after being awakened by the noise in the living room, came running toward Click to defend her man. She yelled, "What the fuck? What are y'all doing?"

Click gave the woman a stiff arm to the chest, trying to keep her back.

"Danielle, no!" the man yelled, knowing the type of cat Click was. "It's OK, baby. Just go back in the room!"

"Fuck that!" she screamed, arms flailing about, trying to scratch Click in the face.

"Slow your roll, bitch!" Click pointed the gun at her.

She stopped when she saw the gun and began to back up.

"Sit your dumb ass down over there," Click told her, pointing toward the sofa.

"Fuck you!" Danielle gathered saliva in her mouth and spat at Click, hitting him square on the cheek.

Before anybody knew what had happened, Click had pumped two

bullets into the woman's chest, lifting her up off her feet before she hit the floor.

The man hung his head and began to cry for his girlfriend.

Click, saliva running down his cheek, turned to face the man and fired two bullets from his weapon, one of which hit the man in the head and sent blood, brain matter, and bone chips flying into the air, some landing on the two men holding him up.

They jumped back, releasing the man's body to the floor.

"Damn, nigga! Warn a muthafucka next time!" one of the men said. He wiped the blood from the side of his face.

Click stood there breathing fire and ice-grilling the dead man. He didn't say another word. He wiped the saliva from the side of his face with the bottom of his shirt and walked out of the house.

Chapter Thirteen

VIRGINIA

TJ and Dasia cuddled together on the sofa in front of the television. They'd just eaten dessert after the dinner TJ had cooked for them.

"That chicken was good," Dasia said as she lay in his arms.

"Better than KFC," TJ said, brushing off his shoulders.

"Oh, whatever!" She stood and playfully pushed him. "That mac and cheese was the shit, though. Kraft couldn't have cooked it no better." She laughed at her own joke. Actually it was a box of Kraft Macaroni and Cheese that he'd prepared for dinner.

TJ grabbed her and forced her down on the couch. He climbed on top of her and began to tickle her.

"Stop, Tony!" she yelled, unable to control her laughter.

TJ kept tickling her, and Dasia kept right on screaming.

As they played, the news briefly showed the story on Leroy again. TJ stopped tickling her and watched the TV. As he listened to the reporter talk about Leroy's death, he remembered Nate had never returned his call. He reached for his phone to call Nate again.

"What's wrong?" Dasia asked.

"Nothing. My godfather never called me back to confirm that this was true." He pointed to the TV.

The phone rang and went to voicemail again. He ended the call without leaving a message.

"What happened?" Dasia asked, concerned by the look on his face.

"Nothing. He didn't answer. Something is not right. I may have to take a trip up there to see what's up." He looked at Dasia for a response.

She turned her attention back to the TV. "You're gonna go to Jersey?" she asked without looking at him, her voice filled with sadness.

"Yeah, but this man was like family. I mean, he looked out for us, so the respectful thing to do would be to at least go to his funeral."

When Dasia and TJ first began to date, they did everything together. Although TJ wasn't a virgin, Dasia was the first girl he had sex with and felt something. Dasia was different. She wasn't your average teenager. She showed affection, something that TJ never experienced with any girl back in Newark. In his high school years, sex was just a nut, and it seemed as if the boys were all trying to see who could bust off more than the other, having sex with no feelings attached. It was a cat-and-mouse game that TJ played well.

But when he met Dasia and they had their first encounter, she was the one who had the upper hand. TJ remembered clearly. They were in the basement of Dasia's mother's house. Dasia didn't live on campus because she was from Richmond, so she attended school and stayed with her parents.

"Wait a minute," she'd said to TJ, who'd been trying to shove his tongue down her throat, making her gag. "Who taught you how to kiss?"

"What?" He looked at her, confused.

"Who taught you how to kiss? Is this how the girls where you from like it?" she asked, her light country drawl floating in the air.

"Well, yeah, them chicks love it. I mean, they say I'm the best kisser."

"Well, they lied," Dasia said honestly.

TJ's pride was hurt. He released her and sat upright on the sofa.

"Tony, don't get offended." She rubbed his shoulder. "I'm not trying to hurt your feelings."

TJ tried to play it cool. "*Psst*! You ain't hurting my feelings. Trust."

Back in Newark, TJ had an image, one he'd acquired when he sold drugs with his old friend Tyler, who he thought of often. Although he'd stopped slinging, he still was a hit with the ladies, so as far as he was concerned, Dasia didn't recognize a good thing.

"Yes, you are offended, Tony. Listen to me."

"I'm listening," he said, half-pouting, trying to keep a cool exterior.

"I want to show you how to be gentle with a woman. We are fragile and should be treated with tender loving care. You have to be patient with us and explore us." Dasia turned his face to look at her. "Do you understand?"

TJ melted when he looked into her eyes. She had hypnotizing eyes. It was like she could see through to his soul when she looked at him. He nodded in agreement.

"Just take your time and relax," she said, moving in slowly for a kiss.

TJ enjoyed the slow kiss. When the kiss was over, chills ran all through his body, a feeling he'd never gotten when he kissed any other girl. That night TJ's virginity was really taken.

"So you're gonna go?" Dasia asked now.

"Well, yeah, I said that."

"No, you said that you were thinking about going." She got up off the sofa and walked into the kitchen.

TJ walked into the kitchen to find her drinking a glass of iced tea. "What's wrong, baby?" He pulled her into his arms. "Talk to me."

"I'm scared, Tony."

"Why? What are you afraid of?"

"Afraid that something will happen to you."

"Come on, baby, ain't nothing gonna happen to me."

Dasia looked into his eyes. "How can you be so sure?"

TJ couldn't hold her gaze, so he looked away from her.

Once they'd become an official couple, TJ felt comfortable enough to tell Dasia about his past. Over time he had revealed to her everything he had experienced, from the death of his mother, his father disowning him, to his selling drugs when he was younger with his now deceased best friend.

The only thing that TJ never confessed or admitted to Dasia was that he'd committed a murder, and that was because he was afraid his feelings about the murder would be transparent if he ever told her. When TJ had killed Nettie, a sense of calmness like none he had ever felt before washed over him. Although finally getting revenge for his mother was a comfort to him, TJ knew that wasn't the only reason he felt so calm. The act of taking another person's life had actually made his mind relax. These feelings bothered him over years, and he often tried to understand why he felt this way after committing his first murder. But he could never figure it out, so he avoided telling Dasia that one secret.

"Listen, baby, I'm gonna be around family," TJ said, trying to reassure her. "Ain't nothing gonna happen to me. I'm just gonna check on my godfather and my godbrother, pay my respects to Leroy, and then I'm gonna bounce. I will only be gone for four or five days tops."

"Four or five days?" Dasia frowned. "Tony, you just started your job. You can't take off that kinda time."

"Why not?"

"Listen, baby, this job can lead to you making a lot of money. You have been trying to get into this company for a long time and only been there a couple of weeks. Don't blow it by taking time off already."

"Dasia, I hear you, baby, but if someone close to you in your family dies, wouldn't you go?"

"Yes, baby, I would go, but if I started a new job that could turn into a promising career, I wouldn't take the kind of time you want to take off."

TJ wasn't happy with her response, and his face clearly showed his frustration.

Dasia grabbed his hand and held it. "Baby, I'm not trying to discourage you. I just want you to see the logical side of your decision. Yes, by all means, go to the funeral, but go and come back. The normal amount of time that a company gives you off is three days for immediate family, and one for non-immediate family members. Leroy is not your immediate family. Those people are gonna go on to live their lives after this, and if you mess up the opportunity you have now, you will regret it."

TJ sat there silently for a moment. "OK, you're right," he said finally. "I'll really think about it."

Satisfied with his response, Dasia breathed a sigh of relief.

Chapter Fourteen

LEROY'S HOUSE

Later That Night

After taking care of some business, Nate and Nyeem headed over to Leroy's house. They rode in silence before Nate finally decided to speak.

"What's on your mind?" he asked, glancing over at Nyeem, who was looking out the window.

"Nothing. I'm good."

"Naw, you ain't good. I can see it in your face."

Nyeem didn't reply. He simply kept his gaze focused out the window.

"Nyeem, I told you, you didn't have to come if you didn't want to."

"Yeah, I know. I told you I'm good. I'm just thinking about my mother and father. I wish I had the chance to know them." Concern in his eyes, he finally looked over at Nate. "I mean, it ain't like I even had the chance to meet them. I don't even know what they looked like. People keep telling me that I look like my pops with my mother's eyes, but I look at myself in the mirror and I can't figure it out."

"I feel you, Nyeem."

"Do you really, Unc? Do you really feel what I'm feeling?"

"Yeah, I do. My peoples ain't around either. I told you how I grew up. That's why your father and me was so cool. He was like the family I missed."

Nyeem took his gaze off Nate and looked straight ahead. "But at least you got the chance to know your people."

Nate couldn't disagree with that. As fucked-up as his childhood situation was, at least he did have the chance to be with his parents at one time or another.

Nate drove up the street of the quiet, dark neighborhood where Leroy lived. He flashed his high beams twice, and a parked car did the same. Before they could pull the car up to the gate of the driveway, two men got out of the parked car to meet them.

Nate turned off the ignition and got out of the car.

Nyeem stayed in the car and looked at the big, beautiful home his grandfather lived in. It had been a long time since he'd been over to Leroy's house, and he'd forgotten how grand it was.

After Nate finished talking with his men, he removed the police tape that ran across the front of the gate and tossed it to the side. Before making the trip to Leroy's house, he had called the police station to speak with the sergeant in charge, to gain access to Leroy's home. The sergeant told him that it was all clear, that they didn't find anything to lead them to Leroy's murderer.

As Nate got back into his car, another truck with the four security men Nate had assigned to patrol the grounds of Leroy's house pulled up behind his vehicle.

Once Nate pulled his car around the circular driveway to the front door, he looked over at Nyeem before he killed the engine. "You ready?" he asked.

"Yeah." Nyeem grabbed the door handle and opened the door.

After getting out of the car, Nate used his key to open the front door that led to the foyer. The first thing he saw was blood, which reminded him that he had to get in contact with Dak's people, something he'd forgotten to do. An outline of Dak's body was on the floor around the blood.

Nate tried to back out of the house and use one of the other entrances, so Nyeem wouldn't see the mess, but it was too late. Nyeem had already peered over his shoulder and saw the blood.

"Is that Grandpop's blood?" Nyeem asked.

"Naw, that was his man Dak. You remember him, right?"

"Yeah, I remember him." Nyeem kept his focus on the blood as he stepped around it and into the foyer.

"I gotta get somebody to clean up this shit. It stinks in here." Nate pinched his nose to get some relief. He closed the door and then hit the switch to turn on some lights.

Nyeem walked around in amazement. The last time he had been to Leroy's house was when he was seven years old, and he didn't remember much. Since then he had always seen Leroy at the pool hall, Nate's house, or on the streets. His grandfather used to take him places a lot when he was younger. Nyeem used to like to go to the pool hall with Nate, and he loved hanging around the old-timers and watching them play pool, cards, or just talk shit. They would always give him money, because they knew his father very well.

But those days were long gone. Leroy was forced to close the pool hall down because the inspector declared the building unsafe. Although the inside of the pool hall was clean, the foundation was old and worn, so Leroy sold his building to the city, and it was demolished several years ago.

Not long after the pool hall closed, Leroy started to become ill, and the trips they took became shorter and shorter, which meant he saw less of his grandfather. Nate barely had time to take Nyeem to see Leroy between helping Leroy run his business and running his own business, but Nyeem did talk to Leroy on the phone as much as possible.

As Nyeem walked into the living room, he stood in front of a life-sized portrait of Leroy. He studied the picture and could see some of his features in Leroy. He ran his hand along the solid oak fireplace that the picture sat over, and then he looked up at the cathedral high ceilings and marveled at the mural that was painted on them.

"You a'ight?" Nate asked as he joined Nyeem.

"Yeah. Grandpop's joint looks like it's some shit straight outta *MTV Cribs.*"

Nate didn't even bother to correct Nyeem's profanity. "Yeah, this joint is cool," he said as he leaned against the wall.

They both were silent, while Nyeem continued to survey the huge room.

"You hungry?" Nate asked.

"Naw."

"A'ight. Well, let me know if you get hungry. I'm gonna go upstairs to see what I can find."

"A'ight."

Nate walked out of the room and headed upstairs to see if anything was missing, or possibly find a clue as to who had come after Leroy. He walked around and looked into each room, all of which were in total disarray.

"Them muthafuckas!" he yelled.

The rooms didn't look like the police had been looking for any evidence at all. Instead, they looked as if the police was searching for something to take, just like he thought they would do. They had ransacked the rooms, throwing items all about.

Nyeem appeared in the doorway of one of the rooms.

Nate stood in the middle of the room, turning slowly in a circle when he saw Nyeem standing there. "Look at this shit!" he yelled.

"Who did this?"

"Fucking cops!"

Nate had no idea if anything was taken out of the house. Although he had the men set up out front while the police were there, he still didn't know if they managed to slip anything away. The men had told him they didn't see the cops take anything out of the house, but Nate, knowing how sneaky officials could be, was certain they took something, and the security men just didn't notice.

He would have to speak with Leroy to know if anything was missing. But who knew how long it would take for Leroy to come out of the coma?

Nate moved things around with his foot. There was a broken lamp that was shattered into pieces. "Shit!" He kicked the broken pieces out of frustration.

"I'll help you clean it up, Unc." Nyeem walked around the room looking at the things that had been tossed about.

"That's some bullshit. Leroy got a cleaning crew. I was gonna wait till morning and have them come in and do a clean sweep of the place, but they gonna have to come now." Nate looked at his big-face watch and saw it was almost twelve a.m. He pulled out his cell phone and saw he had ten missed calls, including calls from his company, a call from Click, and a couple of calls from his godson, TJ. He rubbed his goatee and sighed.

"What's wrong, Unc?"

"Nothing," Nate said, not wanting Nyeem to be involved in all the shit he had going on.

Nate decided he would call his godson back the next day, because it was late and he knew what he wanted. He also decided to return the other calls in the morning because he knew there was gonna be questions concerning the businesses Leroy owned. His main focus right now was to contact the cleaning crew to straighten out the house and clean up the blood.

Chapter Fifteen

THE BLOCK

Click pulled up to the corner where the young runners from his crew were posted up. He had gotten a phone call from a kid named Seth, who told him to come through the block because he had some information, and that was all he was gonna say over the phone.

Click jumped out of the Benz and made his way over to the corner.

Seth spotted him and walked over to meet him. "I'll be right back!" he yelled over his shoulder to the others.

"What's up?" Click asked, shaking Seth's hand.

"Come on, let's walk."

The two men walked over to Click's car and leaned against it. A nice breeze blew, cooling them off for a moment. It was a hot and sticky night, and kids ran about the streets like it was broad daylight. It was live on the block that night.

"What up?" Click, still pissed about the chick that spat in his face, wanted Seth to get to the point quickly.

Seth wanted to talk to Click about a local cat who was going around bragging about how he was gonna take over Leroy's spot. "That nigga Ace been running his trap," Seth said, folding his lean arms against his chest.

Click knew Ace well. In fact, Ace had always been a shit-talker. He was envious because he desperately wanted to get put on with Leroy and never did. He tried to do a little something on his own, but he wasn't anywhere near as successful as Click and Nate. Click was pushing thirty, and Ace was a few years older, so Click was guessing that Ace was ready to make his move.

"How you know?" Click asked, carefully watching the activity going on around him. Click had to be alert at all times, a trait he acquired because of the things he did, like the double murder he'd committed earlier that night.

"He came through the block popping shit. Everybody heard that nigga. He made sure they heard him. He was tryin'-a play us out in front of everybody."

"What that nigga say?" Click's tone remained calm, although he was pissed inside.

"He was saying some shit 'bout how we better save our money from this last package because, by the time he finish coming off, we ain't gonna be making no more loot. He said he 'bout to take over Big Roy's shit, and he don't want none of us niggas banging for him."

"So what did y'all say?" Click re-adjusted his shoulder holster, securing his gun. Since he was on the books as an employee with Nate's legitimate security company, he was licensed to carry a gun.

"We ain't say shit." Seth was confused. "What the fuck was we s'posed to say?"

"Nothing. Just what you did. What else he say?"

"That nigga was sliming Big Roy, talkin' 'bout how it was good for him that he was on ice. Man, he was talking real slick and confident, so that's why I called. He might be the nigga that did it."

"Naw." Click shook his head. "Ace ain't smart enough to pull that shit off, but that clown might know who did it, and can lead us right to that muthafucka." He got off the car and walked over to the driver's side door.

"So what should we do if he come back around?" Seth asked with his arms spread apart. "Yo," he said as he walked over to the driver's side as Click got ready to get in the car. "Click, that nigga is crazy as shit. We ain't holding out here, and if he comes back wildin', how the fuck we s'pose to protect ourselves?"

Although Ace wasn't big in the drug game, he was nuts. His reckless behavior was one of the reasons Leroy never gave him a chance to run with his crew. A cat like Ace would surely demolish an operation. Ace didn't have a problem creating a scene for the attention, nor did he have a problem pulling his gun out on a joker. Rumor had it that he'd ratted on a few cats, got them locked up, and then stole their stash after the police had taken them away.

"That nigga Ace ain't that damn stupid to fuck with y'all. He know the deal."

Click was confident. In fact, he felt it was a waste of time that he'd rushed down there, even though he thought Seth had some real information.

But Seth wasn't so confident. In his mind he and his boys were out there on the streets wide open for not only Ace, but any other potential hunters who wanted to muscle their way into Leroy's camp.

"Click, man, we out here like sitting ducks. Niggas talking out here, man. They talking real greasy. They ain't fearing us no more," Seth said as a last desperate attempt to get Click to understand the pressure the young boys were under. "Can we at least carry?"

"Yo, Seth, man, shut the fuck up! We still strong in our spot. We still got muscle, man. Hold yo' head. I can't trust that one of y'all niggas ain't gonna just buck at somebody on GP. Naw, I can't take that chance." Click jumped back in his car and started the ignition.

"I can't tell. Y'all got all the muscle out looking for the niggas that murked Big Roy, so how you figure we got protection out here?"

"Seth, get your fucking head right! You killin' me with your bitchin' and cryin' and shit!"

Defeated, Seth backpedaled from the car and watched Click pull away, Jay-Z blasting through the windows.

Seth was nineteen and tall and lanky. He was a good-looking kid with dreads that hung to his earlobes. He was in charge of the block and felt the other guys looked up to him for leadership. But how good of a leader could he be, when he couldn't even get protection for the workers?

"What did he say?" one of the other boys asked as he walked over to Seth, who was still looking down the street at Click's Benz.

"We on our own."

The young boy couldn't believe his ears. "What? How the fuck you figure?"

"Just what the fuck I said! We gotta go for self!" Seth was pissed that Click didn't seem to care about their safety, when they were the ones on the front line. He was the hardest worker, but after what just went down, he felt like all his hard work was in vain.

Sitting two blocks away observing the whole scene was Blaze. The information he was learning could prove useful for his plans.

But little did Blaze know, while he was watching Click, he himself was being watched.

Chapter Sixteen

Wee Hours of the Morning

TJ lay in bed looking up at the ceiling.

Dasia rolled over, opened her eyes, and saw that he was awake. "What's wrong?" she asked, throwing her arm over his chest.

"Nothing."

"So why aren't you sleeping?"

He shrugged. "Just can't sleep."

"Come on, Tony, just tell me what's wrong. Is it because your godfather hasn't called you back?" She made circles on his chest with her finger.

"Something like that."

"So talk to me, Tony."

"Well." He sat up and rested his back on the headboard.

Dasia sat up on her knees and waited patiently for him to talk.

TJ stared at his girlfriend. In his mind he thought he was a lucky man to have her. Dasia had chocolaty-smooth, radiant skin, and her round eyes sat perfectly in her face. She had a little pug nose, and her lips were perfectly proportioned. She stood at only five feet tall and was a full-figured woman, but TJ didn't mind. He enjoyed her thickness. Although she usually stressed about her weight, she wasn't fat in his eyes.

"Baby, it's not like my godfather not to return my call. I mean, he always returns my calls."

"So do you think something happened to him?"

"I don't know."

"Don't you think they would have said that on the news too?"

"No, because the big story was about Big Roy. They not gonna say too much that happened in Jersey. I don't know what to think." TJ rubbed his hand over his head, clearly frustrated.

Dasia sat there picking lint from her T-shirt, deep in thought. She was afraid and was hoping that TJ wouldn't change his mind about going to New Jersey. She had been successful earlier in talking him out of going, or so she thought, but now with him thinking that something may have happened to his godfather, she knew he would change his mind.

"So what are you thinking?"

TJ looked at her. "I'm thinking about going."

"Tony, you said you weren't going."

"No, Dasia, I never said I wasn't going. I said I would think about what you said and take it into consideration."

She sighed and pouted.

"Come on, baby, I can't believe you are asking me not to see about my peoples," TJ said, surprised by her reaction.

"I told you I was scared, Tony. I don't want anything to happen to you if you go up there. You don't seem to understand what happened. Somebody murdered that man, and if you go up there, they could murder you too." Tears filled Dasia's eyes just thinking about it.

Dasia remembered the stories he had told her about his life in Jersey. She wasn't raised in the hood, but she knew about it. When TJ told her about some of the things he'd seen and been through in his life, she was terrified.

But Dasia wasn't just afraid for TJ. She was also afraid for herself, and what him getting murdered could do to her. She knew the goldmine she had in TJ. He was about to be an accounting executive, and she knew the bread that came along with that position. She had plans to lock him down so he would marry her. She had a degree in finance, but she wanted to be a housewife and go shopping all day; live the American dream. If anything ever happened to TJ, then her dreams would be destroyed, and that wasn't something she was going to let happen.

"Baby, you don't know that he was murdered."

"They said it on the news, Tony."

"I don't believe the media. They only tell half-truths, Dasia. I understand how you feel, and I can't explain it to you no better than this. I'm going to go see what happened. I'm sorry, baby, but I would never stop you from going to see your family."

His words cut through her like a knife. She realized she was being selfish. "You're right, and I'm sorry," she said. She leaned over and softly kissed his lips.

"Thank you, baby." He kissed her back.

"Can I come with you?"

TJ looked at her and thought for a moment. He knew there could be danger in Jersey, but there was no way in hell he was ever gonna reveal that to Dasia. He wanted to keep reassuring her that he wouldn't be in any danger. He knew if Leroy really was dead, Nate and the rest of the crew had already started the manhunt for revenge.

"No, baby, you stay here. I'm only gonna go for a couple of days. I will be back before you get the chance to miss me."

"You promise?"

"Yes, I promise." TJ pulled her into his arms.

They embraced, and their minds wandered off in their own

directions.

Dasia was wondering why she couldn't go with TJ if there was no danger. *Maybe he's gonna visit an old girlfriend,* she thought.

TJ knew that if Leroy was dead, he'd feel obligated to do something, and he definitely didn't want Dasia there to witness that. Besides, he wouldn't be able to live with himself if something ever happened to her. He had already lost two very important people in his life—his mother and his best friend Tyler—and he damn sure wasn't going to lose her too. She was too naïve to what went on in the hood, and she'd only get in the way and slow him down. He would go alone to Jersey to handle his business so he could return to his life with her as soon as possible.

Chapter Seventeen

WHO'S YOUR FRIEND?

Jasmine stumbled out of the local bar called Sips. She had been doing tequila shots, courtesy of the horny old men in the bar. She was with an old friend of hers who used to dance at Bodylicious with her. The two women giggled as they staggered along the sidewalk. Jasmine was out partying that night like she hadn't just been told by her landlord that she had to vacate the premises in two weeks. She hadn't paid rent on her studio apartment for the last two months.

"Girl, you shoulda got with that dude," Jasmine said and laughed.

"You outta your fucking mind! That dude had long-ass gray hairs growing out his fucking nose!" her friend Star said. Star was a Spanish chick who once had it going on, but like Jasmine, she had fallen off since Bodylicious closed.

The strip clubs were becoming far and few in between in Newark. The few left open were pretty much dead ends, since the girls who had it on lock were making all the bread, making it hard for any new girls to come in. And the owner was in cahoots with them, refusing to hire any new girls unless they came recommended by one of the dancers who already worked there. So, to make ends meet, Star and Jasmine settled for messing around with the occasional sugar daddy.

Jasmine continued to laugh. "So what, he had hair growing out his nose? I was more interested in the stack he had growing outta his pocket."

"Yeah, you right. He ain't have no problem throwing cash on the bar. That's why I clipped that ass several times." Star laughed.

"Get the fuck outta here! No, you didn't!"

Star reached in her purse, pulled out a bunch of crumpled bills, and showed Jasmine. The two women laughed so hard, they almost peed on themselves. They held on to each other while bent over, cackling like hens.

After they finally caught their breath and managed to straighten up, they burst into laughter again.

A car driving by honked the horn at them, but they kept walking. They were used to honking horns and men howling at them. After all, they were still attractive women. They just didn't have the diva appearance they used to because of lack of money. With no money, it was hard to dress the part.

They continued to stagger along the sidewalk, giggling when the horn honked again.

Jasmine whirled around and yelled at the driver, "What?" But when she saw who it was, a smile spread across her face. "Hey, baby! Where you going?" She staggered toward the car, almost tripping in her stilettos.

Star started laughing again. "If you fall, it's a wrap!" she yelled.

The car pulled over to the curb and stopped just as Jasmine made her way over to it. She practically fell inside the window. "Hey, Click!" She showed all of her teeth when she smiled.

Click smiled back at her. "Damn, Jazz! You fucked up."

"Something like that. I got a little buzz on," Jazz said, holding on to the car for dear life.

"Naw, your ass is twisted." Click laughed.

"Who is that, Jazz?" Star came stumbling over to investigate. She lay on Jasmine's back, trying to see inside of the car.

Jasmine pushed her to the side. "Bitch, you heavy. Get off me!"

"Who is that?" she asked again.

"You don't know him!" Jasmine said over her shoulder. "Where you headed, Click?"

"Click? What kinda fucking name is that?" Star asked while standing behind Jasmine, laughing.

"Don't pay her ass no mind." Jasmine waved her hand. "She is the one that's drunk."

"I'm just making some rounds, checking shit out," Click said. "Where you headed?" Click decided not to ask Jasmine about whether she knew anything about Leroy's murder. He realized she wasn't just drunk, she was one drink away from a coma. Plus, he didn't want to discuss business in front of her friend, who he thought was cute.

"Oh, I'm just walking this chick home because she don't know how to drink and walk, so I have to escort her home." Jasmine's eyes rolled up into her head when she spoke.

"This car is hot!" Star said as she ran her hand along the Benz.

"Oh yeah? You like that?" Click leaned over to get a good look at her.

"Hell yeah! I like shit like this."

"You like anything, with your drunk ass."

"Y'all get in and let me take both y'all home."

"Oh, you ain't gotta tell me twice." Jasmine started to open the front passenger door.

Click called her name to stop her. When Jasmine stuck her head back in the window, Click gestured to her that he wanted Star to sit in the front seat.

Jasmine began to giggle, getting the picture. "You ride up front, Star. I'll get in the back."

Star plopped down in the front, clearly not having full control of her body. "This is nice." She smiled when she got in.

"What's your name?"

"Star." She smiled at him.

"I like that." Click winked at her. "Where you stay at, Jazz?" Click looked through the rearview mirror at her.

"I live on South Sixth Street."

After Click dropped off Jasmine, he looked over at Star.

"So what you 'bout to get into?" she asked him.

"Hopefully you." He gave her a devilish look.

"Well, then in that case, my place or yours?"

"Yours, of course," Click said.

Click didn't do women at his crib. That was his safe haven and the only place he didn't have to look over his shoulders. Only Nate and a few other people knew where he lived, and he planned to keep it that way.

Click didn't have one steady girl. He loved to fuck and was the epitome of the word *dog*. He loved women, and when he wanted one, he would go out and get one. When he didn't want to be bothered, he didn't have to be.

As they walked up the stairs of the apartment building, the stench in the hallway assaulted Click's nose. He followed Star into her apartment and was surprised to see that her apartment was laid. She had a full living room set and a wide-screen television.

Click expected to see a dirty apartment. It wouldn't have been the first time he would've encountered that either. Most of the women he met had it going on in looks and clothing, but he would often find that they kept a nasty house.

Star stumbled as she walked into the living room. Click was on her heels, his eyes glued to her ass. She had a perfectly round ass, and her skinny-legged jeans hugged her body like a second skin. He loved a perfect ass.

Star grabbed Click by the hand and threw him on the couch. She kicked off her shoes and wasted no time climbing on top of him, nestling her vagina onto his semi-erection and shoving her tongue down his throat, kissing him drunkenly while she grinded on his dick, stimulating her clit. They kissed sloppily, groping and feeling each other up.

Click palmed her ass and squeezed it, helping her grind his hard-on.

Star began to pull off her clothing. She sat up, still straddling him, and removed her shirt and bra, all the while grinding and moaning.

Click lay there watching her. Her titties were as big as cantaloupes. He palmed them with both hands. Her head fell back, and she licked her lips, enjoying his touch.

She then began to remove his shirt. He raised himself up and helped her. While he finished taking off his shirt, she went to work on his jeans. Star tried to stand up, so she could take off his jeans, but stumbled to the floor instead. Drunk out of her mind, she began to giggle.

Click removed his jeans while she sat there giggling and trying to get her balance. After getting completely naked, he lay back down, and Star got on her knees and engulfed his hard-on, causing chills to invade his body. He placed his hands behind his head and watched Star go to work on his tool like he was royalty.

She removed his dick from her mouth and licked his shaft from top to bottom. She then twirled her tongue around the head of his dick before sucking on it.

Although he enjoyed the teasing she was giving him by sucking the head of his penis and licking it like a lollipop, Click wanted her to put it all in her mouth. He reached down and grabbed the back of her head, and forced his entire tool in her mouth.

After several minutes of pumping in and out, Click pushed her off him, and she fell back to the floor, her eyes barely focusing. She tried to stand, but kept falling.

Click ignored her clumsiness and reached into his jeans pocket to remove a condom, while Star sat there on the floor lightheaded. The alcohol had taken total control of her body.

Star was thinking she shouldn't have had those two last shots of tequila. Jasmine had enough smarts to know she'd had enough and was ready to go, but Star couldn't leave the shots sitting there, so she downed them just before they'd walked out of the bar. Now she was regretting her decision.

Click got down on the floor with her and ripped off her jeans. Star was so drunk, she didn't have the strength to protest. Click had every intention of taking full advantage of her drunken state. He flipped her over onto her stomach and grabbed her by her tiny waist. Getting up on his knees, he pulled her hips up to him and shoved his thick, rock-hard erection into her anus.

Star felt the sharp pain shoot through her whole body. She tried to scream, but nothing came out of her mouth except grunts. He stroked her vigorously, holding a fistful of her hair and jerking her head every time he slammed into her.

Tears filled her eyes, and she tried to crawl away, but the grip he had on her was too strong. Her weak attempts did nothing but exhaust her more, so she gave up and allowed Click to have his way.

Click fucked Star in the ass so hard, she passed out, her limp body slithering to the floor. But this didn't distract Click from getting that nut. He simply lifted her limp body and kept on pile driving his way to ecstasy.

Once he came, he allowed her body to rest on the floor. He stood and got dressed. He left the condom on his dick until he was out of her apartment, so he could discard it safely. He never left a used condom at any woman's house because he didn't trust them, and he never would.

Click didn't trust women, and for good reason. The way he treated them, they always wanted revenge. Unfortunately for him, Star was no different and was known to be a vindictive woman, just for spite.

Chapter Eighteen

MY PEOPLES

Nate walked back into the house through the back door after letting the cleaning crew out and talking with the men walking the grounds. He wore a T-shirt with his gun holster strapped around his upper body, his gun tucked away in the pouch, black basketball shorts with gray stripes that swung loosely while he walked, white ankle socks, and a pair of Nike sports sandals. He secured the door behind him and made his way through the TV room and into the kitchen. He looked up at the clock mounted on the wall. It read three AM.

He was exhausted. He hadn't had a wink of sleep in over twenty-four hours. His mind was racing, and it wouldn't allow him to sleep, but he knew sleep was necessary for his mind to be sharp. He continued to make his way through the large kitchen, which had an island and six stools around it. As he traveled through another sitting room and into the front foyer, he could see a light coming from the library straight ahead.

Leroy didn't read much, but he had designed the library to look just like one from a favorite old movie. Sometimes he would go into the library to sit and think. He had books upon books of all genres, but he never read them. Just the idea of having a classy library was good enough for him.

Nate reached for the doorknob and slowly turned it. He placed his hand on his gun for safety and opened the door. Once he saw Nyeem sitting in the leather chair, he relaxed.

Nyeem looked up as Nate entered the room.

"Whatchu doin'?" Nate asked as he walked over to him.

"I found this box that had pictures in it. Do you know any of these people?" Nyeem handed him a few pictures he had already viewed.

"I probably won't be able to tell you, since I haven't known Leroy for that long." Nate took the pictures and started viewing them.

"I guess Grandpop did have it going on back in the day. Look at the shit he was rocking." Nyeem marveled at how even back then Leroy was on point when he was a much younger man.

Even though the clothes were out-of-date now, Leroy still rocked tons of jewelry and had expensive cars. In each picture he always had a beautiful lady draped in furs and jewelry on his arm.

"Yeah, he did." Nate kept studying the pictures, shaking his head from side to side. "Naw, I don't know these cats with Leroy."

Both of them looked at the pictures in silence. Some of the pictures were in black and white. Others were so old and worn, the images were fading.

"You think about what you gonna do?"

"Do about what?" Nyeem asked, already knowing what Nate was talking about.

"About coming into the business."

"Come on, Unc, after all that is going on, you honestly think I want to get into this shit? All I want to do is play ball, Unc." Nyeem looked at him with pleading eyes. "Can I just play ball?"

"Yeah, son, you can play ball." Nate felt bad about harassing Nyeem to join the business. He knew now that Nyeem was serious about not wanting to be a part of the business.

It was Nate and Leroy's dream for Nyeem to step into his father's spot. Their plans were to groom him to be better than Ishmael ever was. But times had changed, and Nyeem had a mind of his own. Nate realized then that Nyeem wasn't built for the game, because his mind wasn't in it. It was time to let go of his dream for Nyeem, and allow him to pursue his own dreams.

Nate reached into one of the boxes and pulled out a handful of pictures. He pulled up a chair and sat down to look at them. He was surprised to find a picture he didn't know existed. It was a picture of Ishmael and Desiree the night of their first date at the Copa club. Feelings of sadness and nostalgia overwhelmed him as he looked at his friend standing there hugging the woman he had fallen deeply in love with. The two of them looked so happy.

Nate remembered that night well. As Ishmael left the ballers' club that night to take Desiree someplace else, he and Nate spoke.

"Yo, Nate!" Ishmael called out to him.

Nate made his way through the crowd. "What up?" he asked when he got over to where Ishmael, Desiree, and Derrick were standing.

"I'm 'bout to bounce."

"Word? A'ight."

"I got something else planned for Rae t'night."

"Did you handle that?" Nate asked, referring to the reason Ishmael had originally come to the club.

"Yeah, it's all good. Listen, man, Rick getting ready to bounce too, so do me a favor and keep these clowns straight." Ishmael didn't like that the rest of the crew had been wildin' that night.

"A'ight, I got you. Yo, handle your business."

"It ain't that type of party, man. She's a lady," Ishmael said simply.

Nyeem called out to Nate for the third time, "Unc!"

Nate looked up at him, not realizing Nyeem had called him several times.

"You a'ight?" Nyeem asked.

"Look at this picture." Nate handed him the picture.

Nyeem looked at the picture. "This Grandpop when he was younger?"

"No." Nate paused, a little choked up. The picture brought back memories of Ishmael. "It's your mother and father."

Nyeem looked at Nate to make sure he'd heard him right, and Nate reassured him with a nod. Nyeem looked back at the picture. He couldn't believe his eyes. He was actually looking at the two people who brought him into the world. An emotional rush ran through his veins. He thought his mother was so beautiful. They made a good couple, not to mention they looked so happy.

He ran his finger over the picture, his eyes filled with water, and he was now taking short breaths.

"You a'ight, man?" Nate asked.

Nyeem didn't respond. He continued to stare at the picture, tears racing down his cheeks.

"Nyeem."

Nyeem began to cry.

Nate rubbed Nyeem's shoulder to console him, but that only seemed to make him cry even more.

"Come on, man, it's gonna be all right."

"Why couldn't they be alive?"

Nate didn't know what to say to that.

"Why this had to happen to me?"

"Come on, Nyeem, don't do this, man. I don't know why shit happens, but it does."

Nyeem stood, and the pictures resting on his lap fell to the floor.

Nate also stood. He reached for Nyeem's arm to further console him, but Nyeem pulled away from him and stormed out of the library.

"Nyeeem!" Nate yelled, but Nyeem kept going. Nate walked out into the foyer and watched as Nyeem ran up the steps two at a time and disappeared into one of the bedrooms.

He was about to go after him when one of the security men appeared in the foyer. "Everything a'ight?" the guard asked after hearing Nate yell out.

"Yeah, everything's cool."

Chapter Nineteen

AN ANGEL SENT...

The Next Day

Nate walked into the hospital bright and early that morning with three replacement men on his heels. He was still worried about Nyeem, but after speaking with him this morning, he hoped things would be OK.

Nyeem had locked himself in his bedroom the night before. When Nate went to check on him in the morning, he found the door unlocked, but when he went inside, Nyeem was gone. He called Nyeem's cell phone, and Nyeem told him that he got a ride with one of the security men to go play some ball to blow off steam. Nate understood and ended the call.

Now Nate and the security men got off the elevator leading them to the ICU (Intensive Care Unit). As he walked past the nurses' station, he winked at one of the nurses who sat there, an older nurse with salt-and-pepper hair, who had been very helpful with Leroy when he first came to the unit. She waved at Nate as he walked by.

The two security men Nate had left with Leroy overnight looked exhausted.

They both stood when they saw Nate coming. One of the men

stretched and then bent over to touch his toes, to relieve his stiff back and legs.

"What up?" Nate asked, slapping hands with both men. He walked into the room, and all the men followed him.

The security guard in the room sat in a chair reading a magazine. He also stood and shook hands with Nate.

"Any change?" Nate asked, referring to Leroy's condition.

"He still the same," the man replied.

"A'ight, y'all can go home. Make sure you eat and rest, because I want you back here tonight."

They agreed, and the three men left the hospital room.

"Give me a minute with him," Nate told the three replacements.

After everyone left the room, Nate sat in the chair by the bed. He stared at Leroy for a while. The one good thing about Leroy's situation was that although he was in a coma, he was able to breathe on his own and no longer needed the help of a machine.

"Come on, Big Roy," Nate whispered. "It ain't your time yet."

There was a knock at the door.

Nate stood. "Yeah?"

The door opened, and in walked the older nurse. She smiled. "Good morning," she said as she walked over to the bed.

"Good morning." Nate returned to his seat.

"How are you doing this morning?" she asked, busying herself with Leroy.

"I've had better days."

"Well, don't fret none. Just give it to the Lord. He knows what He's doing."

The older woman was short and chubby with caramel-colored skin. There was an aura about her that Nate couldn't put his finger on. But she seemed to bring a certain calm to him when she was in his presence, and he enjoyed it.

"What's your name, son?" she asked as she changed the urine bag connected to Leroy.

"Nate."

"Really?" She stopped what she was doing to look at him.

"Yes, ma'am."

"My son's name is Nathaniel, but we call him Nate." She disposed of the used bag in a container that had a lock on it. She then walked back over to the bed to check on Leroy's legs and change the dressing on his wounds.

"What's your name?"

"Nurse Justine."

"Nice to meet you, Nurse Justine. How old is your son?"

"Oh, he's in his late forties . . . I think." She stopped and looked up at the ceiling, as if trying to see into her own brain. "Yeah, I think he is." She continued with her duties. "I'm an old woman now. My mind ain't as sharp as it used to be."

Nate didn't respond. He just continued to watch how she did her job so well. It was as if she was programmed and could do it with her eyes closed. She seemed to be so swift but gentle all at the same time.

"You know, my great granddaughter told me I had a birthday coming up." She laughed.

"Yeah?"

"Yes. I had to laugh 'cause I forgot." She continued to chuckle. "Are you an only child?" she asked, never looking over at Nate as she continued to work.

"That I know of."

"Your father is a very strong man."

"Yeah, he is. I just want him to wake up. There is so much I need to talk to him about."

"So tell him. He hears you. He's just in a deep sleep."

Nate looked at her like she was crazy.

"I talk to him all the time. Talking to him can help bring him outta the deep sleep he's in. He needs to hear familiar voices. I talk to him so he can get to know my voice."

Nate listened intently.

Once the nurse was done with her duties, she stood there with her hands on her hips and looked around the room. "OK, I'm done here." She walked over to Leroy. "All right now, suga, I'll be back to talk to you later. Your son is here, and he got some things he wants to talk to you about. Now I want you to listen to him good." She turned to Nate. "Talk to him, son." She pointed at him in a motherly way and walked out of the room.

Nate pulled his chair a little closer to the bed. "Roy, man, I hope you can hear me." He looked up at the door. He didn't feel comfortable talking, but he decided to take Nurse Justine's advice.

"Roy, man, where did you get that picture of Ish and Rae from? Nyeem found all of your pictures, man, and we sat there and looked at them. Then I came across a picture of Ish and Rae. I showed it to Nyeem, and he lost it. I felt like maybe I shouldn't have showed him the picture. I need to talk you, man. I need you to tell me if that was the right thing to do. I need to know if it really was a bitch that tried to kill you."

Nate paused for a moment and stared at Leroy, as if waiting for a response. "Who did you piss off, man? Roy, man, I need you to wake up."

Nate sat back in the chair, frustrated. He felt stupid talking to Leroy. He had a lot of pressure on his shoulders. He had been struggling with making sure that his business was being operated correctly and stressing because he had nothing to go on about who tried to kill Leroy.

And, to add insult to injury, Nyeem was tripping out on the picture of his parents, and he felt he was the cause of that. Last but not least, he was wondering where the media got the idea that Leroy was dead. Though it played in his favor, it was still a mystery to him.

He sat with Leroy for a little while longer, his mind all over the place, but for the moment, he didn't have anybody asking him a thousand questions.

"I'll be back later, Big Roy," he said finally. He looked at him one more time before he walked out of the room.

After Nate gave instructions to the security men, he made his way toward the elevator. As he walked past the nurses' station, he kept his gaze to the floor, deep in thought.

"Just give it to God, baby," Nurse Justine said.

Nate looked over at her and saw the warm smile on her face, and he couldn't help but smile back.

Chapter Twenty

HE'S NOT DEAD

In the upscale neighborhood of Riverhead in Long Island, New York, a cherry red Hyundai Sonata bent the curve at the end of the cul-de-sac. The car slowed down and pulled into the driveway of a beautiful 2700 square-foot colonial home in white with black trim, a three-car garage, and an immaculately landscaped lawn. The house looked peaceful and surreal.

The Sonata pulled up to one of the garage doors and stopped. The engine cut off, and the driver's side door opened. One of the garage doors was open and inside was another car that belonged to her. It was a white Mercedes. Valencia stepped out of the car in a pink-and-white Nike sneakers and a soft terrycloth jogging suit that clung to her body, filling every nook and cranny. She reached back into the car, grabbed her duffel bag, and threw it onto her shoulder. After closing the car door, she then limped toward the front door of the home.

Once inside, two Yorkshire terriers ran up to her feet and sat up on their hind legs, barking.

"Hi, my babies." She smiled and blew kisses at the cute dogs. She then set the duffel bag on the floor and bent down on one knee to pet the dogs. They jumped up and down, trying to jump into her arms. She scooped up both dogs, and they planted wets kisses all over her face. When she stood, she yelped out in pain from her sore ankle.

"Are you OK, madam?" The housekeeper rushed into the foyer of the house.

"I'll be OK," Valencia said. "How's my father?"

"He's not doing so well today, madam. The doctor is up with him now." The housekeeper pointed toward the large flight of steps that rounded along one side of the wall and led to the next level of the house. "Oh, the dogs got loose again, madam, and I'm not going to try to put them back in their gates."

"Don't worry, Shelly, I'll do it."

Valencia put the little dogs down on the floor and proceeded to the back door of the house. She walked out onto the back deck and down the steps onto their land.

The property was bordered by a fence, so the dogs could not escape, but they would harass the neighbors on the other side of their property. Valencia stuck her forefinger and thumb into her mouth and let loose a high-pitched whistle. She whistled two short times, and then the third time she allowed the whistle to last longer.

The bushes and leaves began to rustle, and after a moment, two Rottweilers came bolting toward her. Their huge bodies ran side by side, occasionally bumping into each other, and headed straight for Valencia.

The dogs were several feet away from her when she whistled again, causing them to slow down. Once the dogs reached her, they stopped in front of her, looking up at their master. She petted them on their heads and then turned to walk away. Both dogs were well trained and fell into position, one on each side of her, and escorted her over to their kennel. She opened the large gate and let them in. Neither dog protested. They knew the hand that fed them.

Valencia slammed the gate shut and roped the thick chain around the gate twice, ensuring it was secured.

"The next time you two break out of here, I am going to punish you." She pointed a finger at them, scolding them.

Both dogs seemed to understand what she was saying, because they hung their heads low and walked away into their doghouses then peeked out of the small opening.

"Don't look at me like that. You're bad dogs!" she said before she walked away.

"You need to rest," Dr. Hernandez told Vinny.

"Ah, bullshit!" Vinny waved his hand at Dr. Hernandez, his nephew.

Vinny had a full head of white, curly hair. His naturally tanned skin was graced with wrinkles, showing he had aged. His ocean blue eyes still had a spark. Once a handsome man, the skin on his body hung loosely from his frame due to the large amount of weight he had lost from his illness. He'd been diagnosed with colon cancer and was slowly wasting away.

Vinny sat upright in the chair that was placed next to the hospital bed in the bedroom of his house.

"You are going to have to listen to me, *tío*," the doctor said.

"*Yo no tengo que escuchar de usted!* I feel fine!"

"*¡Sí!* You will listen, and you may feel fine, Poppa, but you are a very sick man," Valencia said as she walked into the bedroom, having heard her father's outburst.

"Ah!" He waved his hand at her, dismissing her too.

"*Primo*," she said to Dr. Hernandez before kissing him on both cheeks.

"Widow," he said, calling her by her nickname.

Valencia's family had given her the nickname "Black Widow" when she turned sixteen. By then she was a sharp shooter, had mastered archery, and was skilled in defense techniques involving the nervous system. Black Widow seemed to be a name that fit her. The black widow spider eats the male after mating, and Valencia had been known to beat up a few of her boyfriends in the past, crippling one by accident by striking a nerve and paralyzing him from the waist down.

The name, given to her by a male cousin as a joke, had since stuck, and everyone except her father called her by that name.

"Your father is a very stubborn man," Dr. Hernandez said. "Can you please talk to him? If he uses less energy trying to move around and takes his medicine, he can live a little longer."

"I gonna live long time!" Vinny said in his heavy Spanish accent.

"Stop that!" Valencia yelled. "Come on, up you go into the bed." She shooed him. "Help please, *primo*?"

Together they placed a frail and protesting Vinny in his bed. He fussed at them in Spanish the whole time, sounding like Ricky Ricardo from the show *I Love Lucy*.

"Quiet, Poppa."

"Just make sure he rests and takes his medicine," Dr. Hernandez said before leaving the room.

"Poppa, why are you so mean to primo? He loves you so much," she said as she sat next to him on the bed.

"Ah!" Vinny dismissed her, pouting like a child.

"I don't know what I am going to do with you. I wish Momma were here. She could make you listen," she said, saddened once again by the loss of her mother years earlier. Most in the family said she never got over the loss of her two children and died from a broken heart.

"Oh, *hija,* I miss your *madre.*" Vinny closed his eyes tightly, thinking of his wife.

Suddenly his demeanor changed. "But I'm angry with you."

"*¿Qué?*"

"Because you missed. I thought I taught you well. You did not kill Leroy Jones."

"Yeah, I did, Poppa. It was on the news."

"No! He is still alive. I know it!"

"Poppa, no, he is not. I know I killed him."

"You must go back and finish him. Please, for me, hija. I want him to die before me. Do it for me, please, *hija.* Kill him for your brother. Kill him for your sister. Kill him for *la gente española.* He spit on our nationality. I want you to kill him and then spit on him!"

Valencia sat there and listened to her sick seventy-two-year-old father cry like a baby for the loss of his family to one man's hand, the man she thought she had gotten rid of. She was sure she'd killed him, but now she would have to return, to make absolutely certain.

Chapter Twenty-One

ACE BOOM

Seth and his boys, Butch, Tae, and Ezel, were standing around talking about a friend of theirs who'd been killed earlier that day.

"Man, all I know is I knew that shit was gonna come back on him," Tae said.

"Word up, but the fucked-up shit was, they killed his grandmoms." Ezel shook his head. "Yo, they ain't have to do that shit to that old lady. She don't bother nobody,"

"That's how that shit be, man. Muthafuckas don't give a fuck no more," Butch said.

"That would be how the game is played today, fellas," Seth said.

As the four of them continued to discuss the incident, they were interrupted.

"What's up, fellas!"

All four looked up into the barrel of two guns.

Ace stood there holding a double-barreled sawed-off shotgun, and his accomplice was wielding a .44 Magnum. The accomplice looked deranged, his face ashy and the whites of his eyes red.

Ace stood there with a stupid grin on his face. "Now how y'all little niggas think y'all gonna work for me when you standing here holding your dicks instead of making my bread?"

Nobody said a word. In fact, Seth was steaming because he had just told Click the other day how he wasn't feeling safe out there without packing. He could have kicked himself in the ass at that moment, because earlier that day he had intentions of going home, getting his gun, and stashing it somewhere in case he needed it, but he never had the chance to go get it.

"Y'all muthafuckas is so easy." Ace laughed.

Seth looked around at the bystanders watching the scene play out like it was a movie. He narrowed his eyes as he ice-grilled Ace.

Ace trained the shotgun on Seth. "You feeling froggish, little nigga? Then go ahead. Leap. I dare you! In fact, I'm begging you. Be a hero and make yo' move."

Seth didn't move. In fact, the only thing that did move on him was the swollen vein on the side of his neck.

"A'ight, fellas," Ace told them, "let's all empty our pockets."

Ace was rocking a trench coat and his partner wore a hoodie with the hood pulled over his head. It was over ninety degrees outside, and it was almost eleven at night. If anybody had some sense, their attire would have been a clear indication that these two were up to no good.

The young boys were all scared, all except Seth, the oldest of the crew and the leader running the corners.

"Move!" The demonic partner finally spoke, scaring the life out the boys.

Even the bystanders made their way to safety.

The boys began to empty their pockets and hand over the money to the partner, who held out a dirty pillowcase.

Ace walked around to each runner to make sure they were emptying everything from their pockets. When it came time for Seth to empty his pockets, he stood there stone-faced.

"Oh, so you still tryin'-a be a hero?" Ace placed the shotgun under Seth's chin.

"Oh my God! Somebody call the cops!" a woman yelled after she emerged from her apartment building and saw the altercation going on across the street.

Ace's partner turned in a split second after the woman yelled out and let off bullets in her direction. She screamed and ducked back into her building as the windows on the door shattered.

Ace started laughing because the three boys hit the ground when the firing began.

Seth still stood there pissed, the shotgun resting under his chin. His crew looked up at him, wondering why he wouldn't just give up the money and the product.

Ace pushed the gun farther into his chin, causing Seth to have to lift his head. His breathing was heavy, not out of fear, but from pure anger.

Having had enough and feeling like they were wasting time, Ace's partner came over and hit Seth on the side of the head with the gun, splitting the skin on his face instantly. Seth fell back hard and hit the ground, banging the back of his head on the cement. The crazy partner ran through Seth's pockets and took all the money he had.

"Where y'all got the product stashed?" Ace asked.

"We ain't got time. Let's go!" The partner tucked away his gun and walked off.

Ace looked at Seth lying there on the ground, and then over at the others, who all lay on their stomachs looking up at him. "Y'all have a nice night." He laughed, tucked the shotgun back into his coat, and briskly walked off to catch up to his friend.

"Oh shit, Seth!" Butch crawled over to him to see if he was still alive.

"Fuck! That nigga is crazy!" Ezel yelled, still shaken up by his near-death experience.

"Yo, man, call the ambulance!" Butch yelled.

As Ezel dialed 9-1-1, Tae pulled out his cell phone and dialed Click.

Chapter Twenty-Two

I-95

TJ was in a rental car traveling on I-95 North. As he drove, he thought about why Nate hadn't returned his call. The more he thought about it, the more he had a funny feeling in the pit of his stomach.

What if something had actually happened to Nate too? It was possible. Would Click reach out to him? What if something had happened to Click too? What would happen to Nyeem?

He pulled out his cell phone and dialed Nate's number again, hoping someone would answer. He put the phone on speaker and laid it on the passenger seat. The phone began to ring.

Nate finally answered the call. "What's up, godson?"

"What the fuck, man?" TJ yelled, pissed now that he realized Nate was all right. "You couldn't hit me up to let me know what the fuck is going on?"

"My bad, man, but you have no fucking idea what's been going on."

"I know I don't, because you ain't call me!"

"Man, calm the fuck down! Let me bring you up to speed on what's going on."

"Please don't tell me you had Big Roy's funeral already."

"Oh naw, man. Yo, listen up. Leroy ain't dead, man. That's some shit the media put out, and I ain't never correct it. I'm playing that shit to our advantage. I'ma call you back later and put you down on everything."

"Too late. I'm on my way up there now."

"Word? You coming up?" Nate was shocked. He had been trying to get TJ to come visit since he went away to college after high school.

"Yeah. I gotta do shit myself because I can't wait for you to reach out to me."

"A'ight, a'ight, I hear you. Well, since you on the way, I'll see you when you get here, and I'll tell you everything then. I need to let you know that shit is about to get hot 'round this bitch, because we 'bout to turn the fucking heat up on blast!"

"I already knew that shit." TJ thought about whether he should continue with the drive or turn back around and go home, since Leroy wasn't dead, but in his heart, he knew he had to see Leroy.

"So you still coming?"

"I'm still driving," TJ said solemnly.

"A'ight, hit me up when you hit the bricks."

"A'ight." TJ pressed end.

Nate then called Nyeem.

"Yeah," Nyeem answered.

"Where you at?"

"I'm chillin'. Why? What's up?"

"I need to know where you at because I got some shit to handle, and I don't know how long it's gonna take. Where you gonna be at?"

"I'ma chill where I'm at."

"You coming back tonight?"

"Yeah."

"A'ight, I'll get back with you later." Nate ended the call.

Nyeem placed the cell phone back in his pocket and leaned over to continue kissing Alicia. They were at one of her girlfriend's houses whose mother worked nights. They sat in the living room on the sofa kissing and feeling each other up. Alicia's friend Tanisha was in her bedroom with Doc.

Suddenly, Nyeem broke the kiss and pulled back from her.

Hot, horny, and ready to give it up, Alicia wondered why he'd stopped. "What's wrong?"

"I just got a lot on my mind." He sat back on the sofa.

"Talk to me. Tell me what's wrong."

Nyeem blew air through his nose, sighing. "It's just so much shit that's going on, and I'm supposed to be going away to camp, and I can't get my mind right. Lately my game has been off because I can't concentrate. I don't want to go to camp and fuck up. They say scouts and pro ballers be there. I don't know . . ." He trailed off, not really feeling like going there with Alicia. He liked her a lot, but wasn't sure if he could trust her with his personal business.

"Well, I'm here if you need to talk to me."

"If I didn't have money and play ball and shit, would you still fuck with me?"

"Yeah, I would. What kinda question is that? I've always liked you, Nyeem. You know that. I mean, you was too busy messing with them other hoes to pay me any attention."

"Naw, it ain't like that. I thought you was stuck-up. That's why I ain't never stepped to you."

"Me stuck-up? Boy, you got me twisted," she said, looking at the commercial playing on TV.

"If I tell you something, would you promise to keep it a secret?"

She looked at him. "Of course I will, Nyeem. I ain't like that."

"Well, my uncle wants me to start banging." He looked at her for a response.

Alicia looked away from him and began to pick at her nails. "Well, I think you should just play basketball. You have a better future finishing school, and a better chance playing ball than selling drugs. But that's just my opinion." She continued to play with her nails.

Nyeem was impressed and relieved at the same time. She just proved to him that she wasn't like the other chickenheads on the block.

Feeling more comfortable, he pulled her into his arms, and they cuddled and watched TV together, while he told her how he felt about seeing the picture of his mother and father for the first time in his life.

Chapter Twenty-Three

POWER-TRIPPING

Click pulled up to the curb and jumped out of the car, followed by two more men in another car. They broke their way through the crowd and saw Seth out cold on the ground, blood running from the side of his head.

"What the fuck happened?" he yelled.

The young boys, afraid of Click, didn't know how he would react to them being robbed, so no one said a word.

He continued to yell. "Y'all muthafuckas don't hear me?"

The security men he had with him began to move the crowd away, while the boys, not knowing what to say, just stood there looking down at their friend Seth as he lay motionless.

Click snatched up Tae. "Tell me!" He growled into the boy's face.

"It-it-it was Ace!" he yelled.

"What did you say?" Click sounded crazed. He heard what the boy said, but he couldn't believe Ace had the balls to actually disrespect him by fucking with his crew.

Butch could see that Tae was shaking in his sneakers. "Ace and some other dude came through here and lifted everything we had."

Click shoved Tae to the ground hard. He pulled his Glock from its holster and aimed it at the crowd of bystanders, and everybody either hit the ground or scampered, knowing Click had issues.

Click's right-hand man, Ameen, turned and said, "Come on, Click, don't do it like this. Let's just go find the nigga."

"Yeah, man, let's go get that nigga and set his ass on fire!" the other man said.

"Click, we called the ambulance for Seth," Ezel said, not wanting to be left out of the loop.

"Naw, fuck that! That's just gonna bring the cops. Get him outta here," he told the two men.

Ameen and the other man scooped up Seth, put him in the back of their car, and pulled off.

Click still stood there with his gun out, his mind racing, his eyes red from anger. *Who the fuck does Ace think he is? Does he know who he's fucking with?*

"What you want us to do, Click?" Butch asked.

"Y'all little niggas go home for now. Don't say nothing to nobody 'bout this shit. These muthafuckas out here gonna say what the fuck they want to anyway. But y'all keep yo' mouths shut. You feel me?" He ice-grilled each one of them.

They all nodded.

"Yo, the cops!" Ezel nodded toward the squad car that was pulling up to the curb behind Click.

"Y'all bounce," he told them.

Before the young boys could walk away, two more squad cars pulled up, and one of the police officers jumped out of the car. "Hold up, fellas! Nobody goes anywhere! Take a curb!"

Click didn't sit on the curb, nor did he turn around. He recognized the cop's voice, and knew the cocky officer was gonna give him a hard time.

The officer's name was Officer Dan Kimble. He'd been transferred from another precinct a couple of years ago. He didn't make a good name for himself out on the streets because, since coming to the precinct, he'd been terrorizing the neighborhoods with his brutality and interrogation techniques. And most officers on the force didn't like him either, because of his arrogant, cocky ways.

It was rumored that Officer Kimble had set Detective Rick Daniels up to take the fall on false criminal charges, forcing him into retirement.

Detective Daniels wasn't the same after the warehouse murder and the loss of the woman he fell in love with, but he continued on with his duties as an officer of the law. He chased Leroy and his crew, trying to be the one who crushed their operation, until Officer Kimble came on board with an agenda of his own.

"Turn around, punk!" Officer Kimble said to Click. "Who the fuck you think you are?"

The other officers proceeded to search the crew seated on the curb, pulling them up by their arms one at a time.

Click slowly turned around, and Officer Kimble immediately spotted the Glock in his hands.

"Hold it! Freeze right there, muthafucka!" he yelled, making sure the rest of the officers heard him.

Click stood there with a smirk on his face, holding the gun down by his side.

"Drop the fucking weapon!" Officer Kimble yelled.

The other officers now had their guns drawn and trained on Click.

Click raised his left arm in the air to show surrender. He slowly bent down and placed the gun he held in his right hand on the ground.

As soon as the gun touched the ground, he was bum-rushed by the officers and forced to the ground. The policemen handled him like he'd just robbed a bank. All the while Click's blood was brewing, as he lay on the ground in his clean clothes, which were being scuffed up as a knee pressed down hard in the middle of his back.

Officer Kimble cuffed Click, while the other two officers held him in place. Once the cuffs were on, Officer Kimble stood and instructed the other two officers to lift Click. He gave orders like he was in charge, although all the officers were of equal rank. They lifted Click and dragged him across the asphalt, plopping him on the curb with the rest of the boys.

"What's up, baby boy?" Officer Kimble asked with a sarcastic grin. "I got your ass now, boy! I been waiting for this day!" He laughed.

The paramedics arrived on the scene and walked over to where the officers had the boys seated on the curb.

"Who needed a paramedic?" one of the EMT workers asked as he held his medical bag in his hand.

"Which one of y'all punks called for an ambulance?" Officer Kimble asked.

No one said a word. Click continued to sit there throwing daggers at the officer.

"Now I know one of y'all called. Somebody called, because we got the same call over the radio," Officer Kimble said.

Still no one opened their mouths to respond.

"OK, I guess it was a false alarm, fellas," he announced. "So in that case, everybody's getting ready to get locked up for prank calling, possession of a firearm, disturbing the peace, and the list can go on, fellas. It's up to you."

With no one confessing, the EMT worker stormed back to the truck, his partner following right behind him. They jumped in the truck, turned off the emergency lights, and left the scene. The other two officers also felt this call was a waste of time, so they got back into their vehicles, knowing what Officer Kimble was capable of.

One female bystander had her phone out, and was videotaping the scene.

Officer Kimble marched toward her. "Get that fucking camera outta here! This is a police investigation scene!"

She quickly backed away to get out of his way. The man she backed into didn't move. He actually had a stone look on his face, daring Officer Kimble to say something to him.

Office Kimble poked out his chest and stopped directly in front of the man. "You ready to go to jail?" he growled at the man.

"For what? I ain't do nothing. You ain't got nothing on me."

"Oh, I can find something if you don't get the fuck off my streets," Officer Kimble assured him with a don't-tempt-me look.

The man slowly began to back away and grabbed the woman's hand.

"Everybody get the fuck outta here!" Officer Kimble yelled to the small crowd.

Slowly everyone began to disperse.

"Get him up!" Officer Kimble told his partner, referring to Click.

The officer snatched Click to his feet. "You dare have a gun on my streets?" He stood inches away from Click's face.

Click grilled him right back. "It's registered."

"Bullshit!" Office Kimble didn't believe him.

A nonchalant Click still held his game face. "If you say so."

"Throw his ass in the car!" He shoved Click toward his partner. "And the rest of you stupid muthafuckas, take your asses home! I better not catch you back out here no more tonight!"

Click sat in the back of the squad car reeking with anger. This wouldn't be the first time he was taken down to a precinct for gun possession. But since he was a partner at Nate's security company, he was authorized to carry one. Each and every time he got hauled into a station, he was released a short time later, until it got to the point where the officers knew him.

But Officer Kimble didn't like Click because of his cockiness, and in Officer Kimble's book, no one was above him. He knew Click was authorized to carry, but was just hoping that Click would slip up one day and he would be the one to nab him.

When the squad car pulled off with Click in the back seat and the crew began to walk away, just a block away Blaze and his right-hand man sat smiling at what they'd just witnessed.

But just two blocks away, somebody in a Chevy Impala sat watching as well.

Chapter Twenty-Four

The Next Morning

This day was even hotter than the day before. The garbage trucks made their rounds, waking up the neighborhood. The gate at a popular corner store owned by Leroy went up with a loud rattle. This store was just one of Leroy's many businesses.

After opening all the gates on the storefront, George, a man in his early sixties, picked up the bundle of newspapers to bring them inside. It was a little after nine am, and he was getting ready for the morning customers that frequented the store before they went to work.

He walked into the store, and not even a minute later, the store's door opened again. He turned to see who had just walked in and saw his buddy Clarence.

"Morning, Clarence," he said.

"Morning, George. It's gonna be a hot one today."

"Yeah. The news said we gonna reach a hundred today," George said as he continued to busy himself with setting up the store and turning on the air conditioner.

Clarence made his way over to the chair George had set up for him. Clarence was retired and came to the store every day to sit with his old friend. George was also officially retired, but he needed the extra money that managing the store brought him. He liked running the store for Leroy because Leroy paid him under the table, and it didn't mess up his pension money.

George turned on the TV mounted from the ceiling, and the two men watched the news.

The door to the store opened, and in walked one of the most beautiful Spanish women that either of them had seen up close and personal, and the two were instantly aroused by her beauty.

Valencia smiled pleasantly at the men as she walked over to the refrigerator.

George craned his neck to get a good look at the woman's ass. She was dressed in a pantsuit. Clarence could see her clearly, and his eyes lit up at the sight.

As Valencia traveled down the aisle, both men looked at each other like they'd hit the jackpot.

George scuffled behind the counter to get a better look at Valencia on the security monitor. Behind the counter there was a monitor that showed four different views of the store. He studied the section of the monitor that showed where Valencia stood. He adjusted the monitor to have a close-up look at the mountain of cleavage that climbed out of the top of her shirt, and was almost drooling.

Valencia abruptly looked up into the camera.

George nearly jumped out of his skin when he realized she knew what he was doing. When he jumped back, he knocked a whole box of Advil painkillers to the floor, creating a loud noise.

Clarence, who had remained seated because his arthritis was acting up, and his knees bothered him, snickered at George, who scurried around, trying to pick up all the rolling bottles.

Valencia made her way over to the counter to purchase the orange juice she'd taken from the refrigerator.

George was so embarrassed, he didn't want to look her in the eyes while she paid for her juice.

Valencia knew he was embarrassed, so she made a point to stare at him while he fiddled around with the keys to open the register.

George had not yet completely finished doing his duties to open the store, so he needed to open the register before ringing her up.

"Gentlemen." She suddenly spoke.

Awestruck, both men looked at her like she was some kind of goddess.

"Do either of you know a Leroy Jones?" She looked back and forth between them.

Clarence looked at George, but George didn't say a thing.

"Excuse me," she said to George.

"Yes, ma'am, I do," George finally responded.

She gave a pleasant smile. "Do you know where I can find him?"

George stuttered, "Umm . . . he . . . Leroy's dead, ma'am." He could feel his body heating up. This woman was turning him on, and she made him nervous.

"Oh, but he is not."

"Yeah, lady, Big Roy is dead. Who are you?" Clarence chimed in, seeing that his friend was having a hard time keeping his drool in his mouth.

"If he's dead"—Valencia began to walk toward Clarence.

Clarence watched her approach, her cleavage jumping with each step. He too began to feel overheated by her sensuality and now understood why his friend couldn't talk.

She stopped and stood directly in front of him. "If you are so sure he's dead, then tell me, have you been to his funeral?" She bent over to give him a full view of her mountains.

“Uh . . . uh . . . no, ma’am,” he stuttered.

“So then he’s not dead. Now tell me where I can find him.”

“I don’t know, ’cause he’s dead,” Clarence said. “Maybe they didn’t want to have a public funeral.”

Valencia turned toward George, giving Clarence a view of her ass. “This is his store, right?”

George nodded.

“You work for him, right?”

“Yes, ma’am.” George was beginning to feel uncomfortable because of the questions, not to mention the fact that, although her mouth held a slight smile, her eyes showed a hint of evil lurking just beneath the surface. “Ma’am, Leroy does not bring me the money. One of his workers pays me. I call them when I need something, and they take care of it. I don’t speak to Leroy directly, and as far as I know, he’s dead.”

George just wanted the woman to leave the store. At this point he realized she was gonna be trouble. A good judge of character, he could always tell when a customer, whether a kid or an adult, was gonna be trouble. This woman that stood in the store smelled like pure evil, and he wanted her out of there.

“Listen, lady,” Clarence said, “the man is dead. If you was looking for Roy for a good time, I’m your man. I can show you a good time.”

Valencia’s blood started to boil. She was trying to be pleasant with the old men, but her patience wasn’t the best. She had a job to do, and wasting valuable time wasn’t on her agenda. Clarence’s last statement was enough to make her throw up in her mouth.

Ignoring Clarence, she asked George, “Who is the worker that pays you?”

“Listen, lady, I don’t know you well enough to tell you my business. I’m sorry, but I can’t tell you that.”

“I have some important business to handle with Leroy. I was

supposed to have met with him this week when I heard the news of him being dead, but I didn't believe it, because someone would have contacted me."

"Well, I don't know what kinda business you got with him, but all I can tell you is that he is dead, as far as I know."

"Well, who is the next person in charge in case of his absence?"

"I don't know," George answered. "I guess that would be Nate. I'm not sure."

"And where can I find this Nate?"

"He owns the security company called Big Tyme Security. Listen, lady, I think you need to leave. I don't know you, and I don't have anything to do with anything other than running this store."

"I can tell you anything you wanna know, lady, but what you gonna do for me?" Clarence asked, chiming in.

Without turning to look at Clarence and entertain his question, Valencia reached inside her suit jacket to the custom belt that circled her waist and snapped in the front, where two switchblades rested, one in each of the two slots on the belt. She removed one blade from its slot while Clarence continued to talk crudely to her.

"Yeah, baby, I will definitely tear that ass up," Clarence said, as if he was better than Leroy, but he had bad knees and was just as old as Leroy. "I don't know what you wanted with old-ass Roy anyway. That nigga can't even walk."

Because of the amount of merchandise that sat on the counter, George couldn't see what Valencia was doing. All he knew was, she was staring at him with piercing eyes, and her back was to Clarence.

Just as George was about to tell Clarence to stop badgering the woman, Valencia retracted the blade from its hiding place and tossed it backward at Clarence, seeing her target from her peripheral vision.

Clarence suddenly became silent, and George was none the wiser as to why until Valencia began to walk toward him, giving him a view of his friend, whose head was resting against the wall, the knife sticking out of his esophagus. George could have shit his pants at the sight.

He backed away from the counter, knocking things to the floor, trying to reach for the panic button to alert the police, but Valencia jumped over the counter with lightning speed, removed the other switchblade, and pressed the button to release it.

The blade shot out, and she placed it firmly under George's chin. He tilted his head back, trying to get relief from the point of the blade.

"You listen to me, you old *puta*! I want you to tell that coward-ass Leroy that I am coming to kill him, and by the time I am finished with him, he will wish he was dead, because I know he's not!" she yelled at George, making him pee his pants out of fear for his life.

Valencia cut George under the chin, not enough to do any real damage, but enough to send a message.

The early-bird runners had emerged to try to get a jump on drug sales. Two fourteen-year-old boys were walking up the street to the store when they spotted a white Benz sitting at the curb in front of the store. It was one of Valencia's luxury cars.

"Yo, look at that shit right there!" One of the boys pointed at the car and began to walk faster, trying to get closer.

"Oh, shit! I bet you that's Big Roy's whip," the other boy said, speeding up his pace too.

"Big Roy dead! How you figure that's his whip? You stupid!" the first boy said.

"I know he dead, but this still could be his shit," the second boy said, realizing he sounded stupid.

They walked along the front of the car, touching the exterior. Then they stepped up onto the sidewalk and ran their hands along the side of the car. They both peered into the front passenger window, so they could see beyond the limousine tint on the windows.

"I'ma get me one of these shits as soon as I get my money right," the first boy said.

"Not before I get mine," the second boy said, marveling at the car's interior.

Both of the teens had their faces pressed up against the window, examining the sound system, when out of the back seat of the car, a Rottweiler jumped into the front passenger seat and started barking wildly, showing his sharp fangs.

The boys jumped back, and the first boy fell to the ground. The dog had scared the life out of them. The dog continued to growl and snap at the air, hoping to get a bite out of the boys.

Back inside the store, George and Valencia could hear the dog going wild. Valencia threw a five-dollar bill on the counter, grabbed her orange juice, and headed for the door.

Once outside, she saw the two frightened boys standing against the brick wall, staring at the dog in the car. She looked back at the dog and then back at the boys. They looked at her and then back at the dog. She simply smiled and walked around to the driver's side of the car.

The dog never stopped barking and clawing at the window.

Valencia got into the car and began to pet the dog. The dog looked at her and then sat down in the passenger seat. As she started the car and pulled out into traffic, the dog was still peering at the boys.

The first teen finally found the nerve to speak. "Yo, that shit was crazy as hell."

"Man, that dog scared the shit outta me."

"You? Man, if I had to shit, it would be in my drawers right now."

"I wonder who that bitch was. She lucky as hell I ain't had my shit on me. I woulda put a bullet in her dog and took her shit," the second teen said, finally finding his courage.

"Nigga, you wouldn'ta done shit, but what you did—scream like a bitch!"

The teen laughed and continued to clown each other.

Chapter Twenty-Five

WHY ME?

Nate had just hung up the phone from speaking with Dak's sister and helping her make arrangements for his funeral. It was decided that there would just be a small service at the funeral parlor for close family and friends. She was having his body cremated, so there would be no burial service. She simply wanted to get it over and done with. Her and Dak weren't that close, but she felt it was the right thing to do.

Nate was especially feeling the stress on this day. He had finally managed to return all the phone calls he'd received over the last couple days. He'd lost some money with his security company because of lack of available manpower for his regular jobs, having taken most of his men and put them on the streets or on watch for him so he could find Leroy's killer.

Bigger than all that, he'd had to go down to the precinct and get Click out of jail. Since Nate was officially Click's supervisor, he needed to provide the proper document showing that Click was licensed to carry a gun. He hadn't gotten any sleep because of all that he had to endure during the night. And the drive to take Click back to his car hadn't helped his stress levels either.

"What the fuck, man? Come on!" Nate said, pissed. "I don't need this shit from you right now! I got too much other shit going on to have to worry about you, Leroy, and Nyeem!"

Click just sat there staring intently at Nate.

"Keep your papers on you, and I wouldn't have to waste time going through this bullshit!"

"Man, fuck you! You don't run me, nigga! I'm a grown-ass fucking man!"

"Then act like it, nigga! This shit is for the birds!"

"Muthafucka, fuck you! I'm out here on these fucking streets, not you! You forgot about the grind in the streets? I'm the muthafucka still mixing it up with these niggas, while you sit back and give orders. You show up on the blocks once a month like some celebrity or some shit, and then you bounce! Fuck that! I ain't about that planning-and-following-the-rules shit! I'ma do what I gotta do out here to get the muthafuckas that I gotta get!" Click yelled, banging his fist on the dashboard.

Nate was seething with rage. His head felt like it was gonna explode. "You know what . . . do you, Click. I know what I gotta do."

Click waved his hand. "Whatever."

"Yeah, what the fuck ever."

It was now ten am, and Nate was running on steam. He needed some stress relief ASAP. His cell phone rang while he was still holding it in his hand. He looked at the caller ID and saw it was TJ.

"What up?"

"Where you at?" TJ asked.

"I'm on my way back to the crib. You here yet?"

"Yeah, I been here."

"Where you at? Why you didn't call me?"

"Because I knew you had a lot going on. I just checked into a hotel and got me some sleep. You gonna be there?"

"Yeah. You coming through?"

"Yeah."

"A'ight, I'll see you when you get here," Nate said, ending the call.

As soon as he ended the call, his cell phone rang again. "Damn!" he yelled out in frustration. "Hello!" he said into the phone, clearly conveying irritation.

It was George. He could barely understand a word the man was saying. George was so flustered, all Nate could make out was that the police were at the store.

"Shit!" Nate made an illegal U-turn to head back across town.

When Nate pulled up to the store, the police had the area blocked. He got out of the car and tried to make his way through the crowd, but was stopped by an officer.

"Step back," the officer said.

"I'm the owner," Nate told him.

The officer let him walk by, and he headed for the store. His cell phone began to ring. It was Nyeem.

"Yeah, Nyeem?"

"Where you at?"

"I'm handling some business right now. What's up?" Nate stopped in front of the store.

"You never gave me the paperwork back to take down to the center to give to Coach Dunkin for basketball camp."

"Damn! My bad, Nyeem. I forgot, man. I'll sign 'em when I get back to the crib. I gotta go. I'll hit you back."

As Nate walked through the store doors, the first person he saw was Officer Kimble. "What the fuck he doing here?" Nate asked under his breath.

Nate avoided eye contact with the officer and walked over to George, who was sitting in a chair with an oxygen mask over his face. A paramedic was taking his blood pressure.

Before Nate could say anything to George, Officer Kimble approached him with his signature sarcastic smirk. "Well, well . . . nice of you to join us. I knew you had something to do with this. You got some questions you need to answer, homeboy."

Nate didn't reply. He simply turned his attention back to George. "You a'ight?" he asked him.

George nodded, not speaking because he was concentrating on taking in all the fresh air that he could.

The paramedic put the blood pressure equipment away. "Your pressure is a little high," he told George, "but nothing to worry about."

"What happened?" Nate asked George.

George removed the mask, looked dead into Officer Kimble's eyes, and put the mask back on.

Nate saw George's eyes move toward Officer Kimble and knew what was up. "Can you excuse us for a minute?" Nate asked, trying his best to be polite.

Just then Nate noticed Clarence's body on the gurney with a white sheet resting over the entire body.

"Take all the time you need. Just as long as you don't leave the store." Officer Kimble walked away.

Nate turned back to George, who had removed the mask and was ready to talk.

George told Nate exactly what happened, including Valencia's threat on Leroy.

"Did you tell these muthafuckas that story?"

Nate didn't need any more pressure on him than he already had. If the police knew someone had threatened Leroy's life, and that Leroy might not be dead, they would definitely start monitoring his actions day and night.

"The only thing I told them sons of bitches was, the Spanish bitch came in here and killed Clarence. I told them she tried to rob the store."

"My man, that's what's up. Good job."

Now Nate believed Leroy had told the truth about a woman trying to do him. But who was this chick? And why was she trying to kill Leroy? Nate desperately needed Leroy to wake up, so he could talk to him and find out the answers.

Nyeem opened the front door to see his godbrother, TJ, standing outside. Nyeem smiled. TJ returned the smile, and the two embraced in a brotherly hug.

"What's up, TJ?" Nyeem broke the embrace and backed into the house, letting TJ come in.

"What's up, baby boy?"

"Nothing, man. Just waiting to go to ball camp."

They both sat down in the living room.

"Yeah? How's it going with playing ball anyway?"

"I'm nice with mine," Nyeem bragged.

"Oh, yeah? Maybe I'll play you a couple of games before I bounce back to VA."

Nyeem laughed. "I don't think you want none of this."

"Please . . . kid, you ain't been having no competition to know what real ball is."

The two laughed and talked for about twenty minutes before TJ realized Nate wasn't there yet.

"Where Nate at?"

"He said he had to take care of some business."

"How you feel about what happened to Leroy?"

Nyeem lowered his head some and then laid it back on the sofa. "I don't know what to think, man."

"It's fucked up, though. Leroy is a good dude. I mean, he was always cool with me."

Nyeem had so many emotions swirling through his body. He was sad at times, and then he would feel angry and want to hurt somebody. But, most of all, he just wanted to be an average teenager and not have to worry about all the drama that had surrounded his life ever since he could remember. "Yeah, I think he's a good dude, but I don't know what he's done to other muthafuckas though, you know? I know a lot of people fear him, and I ain't sure if that's a good thing."

"I feel you, man, but you gotta stay focused. Don't let this shit get to you. Don't get caught up in it. Believe me when I tell you, and I'm telling you some real shit. I been where you are at around the same age as you are now."

Nyeem sat and listened intently. He had nothing but love for TJ, who was always a good influence on him. He did things with Nyeem that Nate didn't have the time to do. Whenever Nate went on road trips, he would always drop off Nyeem at TJ's place until he handled his business, and then he would pick him up on the trip back.

"Yo, man, when I lost my best friend, that shit had me spent. It was like living the nightmare of my mother's death all over again. That shit scared me straight. I'm telling you, Ny, keep your head in them books. Play ball and be the best ballplayer you can be, but make sure your grades are on point because, if balling don't work for you, at least you have an education with a major to help you get a decent job. A high school diploma just don't cut it no more. Feel me?"

Nyeem nodded, letting TJ know he understood.

"If you ever need anything, and I ain't talking 'bout no loot, 'cause y'all got plenty of that shit—I'm talking about advice or a place to crash and get away—you make sure you hit me up. I'm here for you, baby brother. If you need help with your schoolwork, I'm yo' man. I graduated with honors, boy, and I know my shit." TJ smiled.

"Yeah, a'ight." Nyeem grinned.

"So tell me about this shorty you rocking with?"

Nyeem's grin widened. "What?"

"Don't *what* me, Ny. You know what I'm talking 'bout." TJ laughed. "Man, it's all over your face, and it looks like she got you wide open."

"That's bullshit. She don't got nothing open over here."

"See . . . I knew it!"

They laughed and continued to catch up with each other while they waited for Nate to return to the house.

Chapter Twenty-Six

ROBBED

Click was on his way home. He wanted to get in the shower and make something to eat, but the number that showed up on the caller ID of his cell phone led him to believe that things weren't going to be that simple for him. Every time this young teen called his phone, which wasn't often, it was always on some bullshit. He always had some kind of bad news, one way or the other. It was so predictable, Click had started calling the boy *Taboo*.

He took a deep breath and pushed the speaker button. "Yo!" he yelled.

"Click, man, we got jacked last night," Taboo screamed into the phone.

"What the fuck are you talking about?"

"These niggas came through here last night and got us for all our shit. They even took our jewelry!"

"This can't be fucking happening!" Clicked yelled. He slammed his foot on the accelerator, whizzing through the streets. Being robbed twice on the same night from two different crews was a nightmare. Click wanted to taste blood in the worst way.

"Taboo, why you didn't get at me last night when the shit happened?"

"I did try to call you. I called you like ten times, but the phone kept going to voicemail."

Click was about to protest, but he remembered he was locked up last night. His phone, now plugged into the car charger, was turned off when they gave it back to him, since the battery had died overnight.

"Who did the shit?" Click asked, his voice deep and haunting.

"I don't know all them, but I do know one of them. His name is Tone. It was like four of them niggas, and they look like old heads. They broke all of my brother's teeth out the front of his mouth because he wasn't tryin'-a give them his shit. I gotta go back up to the hospital. My mom is up there with him now."

"I know who the nigga is. You go take care of your brother, and I'll hit you later."

"Yo, Click, what about the crew? They wanna know, are you gonna have somebody come through and drop off some more product?"

"Naw, tell them niggas to chill. I'll hit you when I'm ready."

"So what we supposed to do 'bout bread?"

"Listen, I don't need this right now. I got a lot of shit going on. If you ain't stack your grip, and you need some ends that bad, then go work for the next nigga!" Click ended the call and kept speeding, not caring if he ran stop signs.

In his mind it was war. They fucked with his shit, not once, but twice, and he was gonna make sure he handled that situation ASAP.

The white Mercedes pulled up to the front of the Big Tyme Security Company. It was a two-story brick building with immaculate landscaping. The flowers and shrubs were beautifully arranged. The smoke-tinted glass front windows had the words "Big Tyme Security" etched in white letters on them. Valencia looked up at the corners of the building and could see security cameras extending from the roof. She looked at her surroundings, noticing other buildings not far on the fairly quiet street in Millburn, NJ. The other office buildings had minimal movement around them.

She pulled the gear in drive and entered into the driveway leading into a small parking lot on the side of the building where several vehicles were parked. She backed her car into one of the visitors' parking spots before killing the engine.

Valencia leaned over and opened the glove compartment, removed a small automatic weapon, and shoved it down the back of her waistband of her slacks. She then grabbed a much smaller gun and lifted her pants leg, placing the gun in a leg holster.

She removed a switchblade from the compartment and slid it into the empty slot on her belt pouch to replace the blade she'd used to kill Clarence with.

After securing her weapons, she sat there for a few moments thinking about her family. Valencia thought often of her brother and sister. She wondered what their life would be like had they not been killed. She also wondered what their life would have been like had her father not gotten involved in the business. Although, she did understand it was evident to happen back in those days, and she loved living the rich life, not having to want for anything. But she still pondered on if it was all worth the loss of her siblings, and the loss of her mother because of a broken heart. Valencia thought about why she'd become so coldhearted although growing up she was a loving girl. Her brother and sister were her life. She spent most of her time with her brother and sister, until Carlos got into the business with their father. But he's always made sure he made time for her. Carlos would sometimes come into her room when he got home in the wee hours of the morning and would kiss her on the forehead before he went to bed.

She'd always thought if she sought revenge for her family, that all the heartache and pain would go away. This was why she would not give up until the deed was done, not to mention the fact that this was her father's dying wish, and there wasn't anything Valencia wouldn't do for her father.

Valencia walked up to the door and pulled on the handle only to find the door locked. She looked around and noticed an intercom sitting on the left side wall. She pressed the button.

A male's voice came through the speaker. "Yes, may I help you?"

"Yes, my name is Charlene Bloom and I am here to see Nate," she said, using her best professional voice and hiding her Spanish accent.

"Nate isn't here. Was he expecting you?"

"I'm sure he was. He told me to come here and wait and he would be here shortly." She tried to sound convincing.

She was disappointed that Nate wasn't there, but she didn't show it on her face. She knew there had to be a hidden camera where whomever she was talking to could see her. This was why she made sure she adjusted her cleavage to give them a full view of her hilltops.

There was silence.

"Hello?" she said, leaning a little closer to the intercom.

"Yes, I'm here. I was just asking around to see if someone here got any instructions from Nate that you were coming.

"Well, why don't I just come in and wait for him? I'm sure he will be here shortly."

The guard sat in the office and thought about it. He stared at the screen, admiring her beauty.

"Ok," he said and he pressed the buzzer to let her in.

Once inside, she walked over to the double windows in the reception area and waited for someone to come. Those windows were also smoke-tinted.

She looked around the small waiting area. It too was very clean and cozy. Suddenly, the windows to the receptions desk opened, and Valencia turned around to lock eyes with a one of the security men. She produced an award-winning smile, nearly making the guard wet his pants because he was overwhelmed by her beauty.

"Hello," he said, flashing a big smile.

"How are you?" She flirted with her eyes.

"When did you speak with Nate to set up this meeting?" he asked.

"I just spoke with him two days ago and he told me he would meet me here," she responded.

"Can you tell me the nature of this meeting? Maybe there is something I could do to help you."

"Well, yes, maybe you can help me. I came to hire security for my multi-million-dollar company. I wanted to sit down with Nate to go over specific details on the type of security. I am willing to pay top dollar. I also want to hire a personal guard to be with me at all times," she said as she poured on the sexiness.

"I can help you with that; you don't need Nate for that. I'm the manager of the company. Come in," he pointed toward the door that entered into the office. He pressed the buzzer to let her in. Valencia's eyes turned to pure evil when she walked away from the window to enter into the office.

Once inside of the office, the guard extended his hand, allowing her to lead the way.

"Make a right at the second door on your left," he said fully focusing on her round derriere.

As she walked through the office, the other men workers who sat in open desks stared at her with their mouths open. Valencia, used to the attention, proceeded to walk with confidence. She made the left into the office.

"Would you like a cup of coffee or something to drink?" the guard asked.

"Yes, thank you, I would like some water, please."

The guard walked out of the office once Valencia was seated in one of the comfortable chairs in front of the desk. The guard headed toward the office kitchen, followed by several other men all wanting to know who Valencia was. In the meantime Valencia took the opportunity to look around the office. She looked at the pictures that were in a collage on the cork board hanging on the wall. She observed the faces and didn't recognize any of them except Leroy's. And then she came across a picture of Leroy standing next to a handsome man.

"Here's your water," he handed her a bottled water.

"I was admiring the picture display," she said.

"Yeah that was a company barbeque we had a few years ago." He walked over to the board and stood next to her.

She took a sip from the water and continued to stare at the picture while the guard took the liberty to begin naming people in the pictures.

"And in this one this is me, of course. This is Big Roy and Nate," he pointed.

Valencia's suspicions were correct. She had assumed that handsome man next to Leroy was Nate. Now she had a face to go with the name. She took it upon herself and walked over to the chair, ready to get down to business. The guard followed her cue and took a seat behind his desk.

"Excuse me for my rudeness, allow me to introduce myself. My name is Andrew," he extended his hand to her for a shake. Valencia gladly shook his hand.

After twenty minutes of discussing the fake business deal Valencia was pretending to set up, she became restless. She had been slipping questions in on the guard, trying to see if she could get any answers about Nate or Leroy. But Andrew wouldn't budge.

"Is there any way that I could set up a meeting with Leroy and Nate?"

"Um . . . I would have to speak with Nate," Andrew said, now becoming suspicious because of the constant questions concerning Leroy and Nate.

"When did you say you set this meeting up with Nate again?" Andrew inquired.

"It was a few weeks ago," she said looking deep into his eyes.

Something just didn't sit right with Andrew. He thought about how Valencia had told him in the lobby that she spoke with Nate two days ago to set up the meeting, and now she was telling him a few weeks ago. Next she kept asking questions about Nate and Leroy's whereabouts when the primary interest should have been with setting up a contract for security. He sat in thought for a moment before he excused himself from the office.

Once out of the office he walked over to Dave, a co-worker, to speak with him.

"So you came out for a breather, huh?" Dave teased Andrew, implying that he may have been sexing Valencia behind the closed doors of his office.

"Naw ain't nothing poppin' off like that," Andrew said with a serious face as he stood in front of Dave's desk.

"So what's up?" Dave asked, now seeing the concern on Andrew's face.

"Yo, Dave. Man, I don't know," Andrew shook his head from side to side. "I feel like something ain't right with that chick in there."

"What do you mean?" Dave asked, standing up.

"Yo, I just caught her in a lie and she keeps asking 'bout Nate and Big Roy."

"Really?" Dave said more like a statement than a question.

In the meantime Valencia was peeking through the mini-blinds that lined each window watching Andrew speak with Dave in a suspicious way. Her instinct was telling her that her identity may be in question.

"Let me call Nate." Dave picked up the receiver from his desk phone and began to dial Nate's number. Andrew looked back toward his office and thought he saw one of the mini-blinds move.

"Yo, I think she watching us. I think we need to expose this chick and see what's her story," Andrew suggested.

Just as the phone was ringing on the third ring, Dave hung up the phone.

The two men began to walk back toward Andrew's office. When they walked in, Valencia was leaned up against the desk facing the door with both hands behind her back.

"We just spoke with Nate and he said he never spoke to you for any business deals," Andrew lied, trying to see if there was any truth to Valencia's story.

Valencia simply smiled.

"Who are you, lady, and what do you want?" Dave chimed in. He could read Valencia's eyes and knew they were evil.

Dave was trained for this type of situation, and it often came in handy. Dave could see right through a person, from years of interrogation when he once worked for the armed forces.

"I've already introduced myself to Andrew, and I'm sure he told you who I am. I don't see the need for re-introductions. Now are you gentlemen gonna help me with my business venture or not? Because I can take my millions of dollars elsewhere," she simply said.

"I think that would be best if you would just take your money to another company. Like I said, Nate doesn't remember speaking to you. So have a nice day," Dave said sarcastically.

"Wait a minute," Andrew interjected as Valencia stood up right with her hands still behind her back. "We ain't gonna just let her walk outta here without knowing who sent her. Because it's obvious she came here on some bullshit just to get inside," he told Dave. "You better start talking, lady. Who sent you?"

"Yo, what's behind your back? Why you got your hands behind your back?" Dave asked before Valencia could answer Andrew's question.

She didn't move. She stood there and stared at the two men with cold eyes. Dave pulled his gun from his holster, and this caused Andrew to do the same.

"Where is Nate?" Valencia finally spoke with a hoarse voice that no longer held its sexiness.

"Show me what's in your hands!" Dave yelled.

Valencia extended her right hand from behind her back with the quickness, releasing the blade that sailed through the air hitting its mark in Dave's neck. This caused him to drop his gun to the floor and grab his neck as he gasped for air. In the meantime Valencia flipped her left hand out from behind her back and flung the second switchblade that landed in Andrew's right eye, all before he could react to the attack on Dave.

Valencia walked out of the office as if the meeting had gone well. She pranced down the aisle headed for the main door to the lobby as she walked past the horny male employees, who were none the wiser to what had just taken place in Andrew's office.

Pissed, she pulled out of the parking lot of the security company with no more answers than she'd had when she first arrived. But at least now she knew what Nate looked like.

Chapter Twenty-Seven

DUMP 'EM

Nate finally arrived back at his house. After answering all the police officers' questions, he closed up the store and let the ambulance take George back to the hospital for tests. He didn't have anybody else available to run the store in George's absence, which meant Leroy was losing more money.

He'd forgotten TJ was coming over, but was glad to see him. They sat and talked for a while until Nate fell asleep on TJ. He was finally getting some sleep although he was sitting in the chair in his living room.

An hour later, Nate received a phone call on his cell. Inebriated with sleep, he fumbled around, looking for the phone.

"Hello," he said groggily.

"What?" Nate shouted into the phone. "You gotta be fucking kidding me!"

Nate jumped up after disconnecting the call.

TJ walked into the living room after hearing Nate's shouts. "What happened?"

"Two of my employees got murked at my company," Nate

said, rushing around looking for his keys. He staggered from pure exhaustion.

"I'll ride with you," TJ said.

"A'ight. Where the fuck is my keys?" Nate was frustrated.

"On the table right there. Calm down, man," TJ told him, pointing to the keys sitting on the coffee table in front of the chair Nate had been sleeping in.

Nate snatched up the keys and headed for the front door with TJ in tow.

Nate used his keys and bolted through the doors of his security company. About seven employees stood around in the front office. Their facial expressions changed from disbelief and sadness to fear when Nate walked through the doors.

"What the fuck happened?" he shouted and stopped in front of the men.

Some looked down at the floor, while several others looked at each other, trying to see who was gonna actually speak up.

"Nate, we don't really know what happened." The first guard came forward. "All we know is they were in Andy's office with this chick and she came out and they didn't."

"What chick?" Nate continued to shout.

"Some Spanish chick came up in here to do business . . . and . . . I really don't know, man. She had to have been the one to kill them," he trailed off, still hurt of the loss of his co-workers.

Nate rubbed his hand across his face in frustration. He folded both arms across his chest.

"Tell me how one bitch can walk up in my shit and murk two

of my armed employees? Fuck that! Tell me how a bitch can walk up in my security company with an office full of muthafuckas that carry guns?" He shouted at the top of his lungs.

No one said a word, because the truth of the matter is they didn't even know how that could have happened either. All the men were so engrossed in their sexual fantasies with Valencia at the time, no one was in work mode.

"Y'all a bunch of fuck-ups! I pay y'all muthafuckas well enough to protect my shit!" He stormed off down the aisle heading for Andrew's office. TJ followed behind him and then the rest fell in behind TJ.

"Fuck!" Nate shouted when he walked in and saw the two men. He shook his head standing over them, looking down with his hands on his waist.

"Did anybody call the cops?" he said in a demonic voice.

"No, when we found them we called you first," another guard said.

"I can't have them muthafuckas coming up in my shit. I got too much shit going on as is. They gonna be over me like stink to shit!"

No one said a word. TJ stood there looking at the handiwork of Valencia and couldn't believe his eyes. He had seen some shit in his time, but nothing quite like what he was seeing at that moment.

"We gonna have to dump the bodies. I can't bring no more heat on me than there already is."

"Huh?" Some of the men grumbled, while others looked at Nate in disbelief.

"Yo, Nate. You can't be serious?" the first guard asked him.

"I'm serious as shit." Nate's eyebrows formed a frown.

"Yo, man, they got families. What are we supposed to tell them when they come looking for them or report them missing?"

"If the shit is done right, we ain't gotta tell them shit, because they ain't gonna be able to find the bodies. Y'all muthafuckas knew the type of work you were getting into when I hired you. I told you this was a dangerous job and you could lose your life. Don't act like y'all didn't know this shit. And when I hired the ones with families, I told y'all to let your families know." He looked at everyone.

His employees looked defeated. They all stood around with their heads held low, looking at their diseased co-workers.

"Nate, let me holler at you for a minute," TJ said.

Nate turned his gaze to TJ. TJ gestured with a head nod and then walked out of the office. Nate followed him out reluctantly.

TJ was standing by one of the cubicles when Nate approached.

"TJ, man, right now I gotta take care of business. What do you want?" Nate said.

"Slow your roll, Nate. You're not thinking with a clear head right now. I'ma be the voice of reason. You tryin'-a dump the bodies of dudes who worked for you. They got families and you want your co-workers to do the dirty work. Man, I don't think that's a good move." TJ shook his head.

"Yo, man, when I need your advice, I'll ask you for it."

"I ain't givin' you no advice, bruh, I'm being straight up with you. Do you honestly think none of them cats in there ain't gonna roll over on you? You showing them right now that you don't give a fuck about them being your workers. If you do some shit like that to the two dead cats, then you would do the same to them." TJ paused and noticed he had Nate's attention. "I'm saying them cats will roll over on you, Nate, and that's some straight shit."

"Yeah, I feel you, but if I report the murders, they gonna shut my shit down, man."

"But wouldn't you rather them shut your shit down temporarily to investigate the murders of your workers for the bitch that did it, instead of suspecting you for murder when they find the bodies?"

Nate stood there thinking for a moment. "Yeah, a'ight." He walked off back to the office.

"Listen up fellas. I got a lot of shit going on and y'all know that. I wasn't thinking with a clear head. I'm gonna call the cops and one of y'all call their families. When the cops get here, tell them the truth. I'm gonna find out who this bitch is who did this shit one way or the other."

Nate didn't let on to anyone that he was suspecting it was the same woman who came into Leroy's store that morning and killed Clarence. But in his mind, he had to find her by any means necessary.

Chapter Twenty-Eight

REVENGE.

The Next Day

Mike walked his albino pit bull down Seventeenth Street. The dog practically pulled him along, although Mike was five feet eleven and weighed almost 220 pounds. Mike was talking on his phone with Tone about how well the hit on Click's spot had gone the night before, in addition to the hits they'd already carried out.

As he walked and talked, an old, beat-up brown Chrysler followed him. The car drove past him and made a left turn at the end of the block. Mike never looked over at the car, even though the muffler was bad, and it made a roaring noise when the car accelerated.

Mike was feeling really good because they'd actually come off big with the robbery the night before. It just so happened they'd robbed one of Click's most profitable blocks.

The sad part about it was, the head runner, Taboo, had every intention of contacting Click to have him come scoop up the money. Taboo had all of the money on his person, which wasn't a wise thing to do. He definitely broke one of the rules of the game. He'd even brought the money from the previous package with him to the corner.

So Mike, Tone, Lex, and Devon all got a good piece of change once they split the profit. But they wanted the jackpot, and for them to get the pot of gold, they had to crawl before they could walk.

After Mike finished talking on the phone, he placed his cell phone back in his pocket. He turned the corner and walked into Westside Park. He removed the huge collar from around his dog's neck and smacked the dog on the butt, and the dog took off running, chasing birds. Since there was no one in the park at that time of the morning, it was safe for the dog to run free.

Mike found a spot on a cement wall and took a seat.

The brown Chrysler circled the block again, but this time the doors opened, and two males jumped from the car, running low. Then the car pulled off and continued down the street.

Mike played with his cell phone while his dog ran and barked at the birds and squirrels. He looked up to see the dog chasing a squirrel up a tree. The dog sat there looking up at the tree. Mike went back to surfing the web on his phone.

After several moments went by, Mike looked back up, only to find his dog gone. He looked around but didn't see him anywhere. When Mike stood, he saw his dog lying on the ground in the distance. "Duke!" he yelled out for the dog, but the dog didn't move. "Duke!"

Mike started to walk toward his dog. There was still no reaction from Duke. He began to pick up his pace as his heart started to beat a little faster. He realized something was wrong. He began to jog, and the closer he got to Duke, the more he knew something was wrong.

"Duke!" Mike stopped short when he got to Duke, and tears almost filled his eyes. His dog was dead. Duke had two bullet wounds to the head and a deep gash from his chest all the way down to his testicles.

Mike looked around frantically, trying to find out who might have done this to his best friend. He whipped his head around from side to side, turning his body in a complete circle, only to see nothing. He got down on his knees and held his dog's head in his hands and that's when he noticed the needle sticking out of the side of Duke's neck.

Just as he was about to remove the needle from Duke's neck, Mike heard rustling behind him and whipped his head around, only to receive a bullet to the forehead. When the gun discharged, there was no sound. The gun had a silencer, and Mike never knew what hit him. His body fell on top of Duke's.

Click pumped two more bullets into Mike's head as he stood over him. He then nodded toward Ameen, and they ran out of the park to the waiting Chrysler.

Click had discovered that Mike and the rest of his crew had robbed several of his spots, leaving Click with five of his seven blocks shut down, including the one Ace had hit. Click had heard Mike was the brain behind it all, and now he'd pumped some bullets into it.

Chapter Twenty-Nine

GANGS

Nate finally signed the basketball papers for Nyeem, and then TJ agreed to ride with him to go handle all of his and Leroy's business that he'd been ignoring since Leroy got shot. Just as he suspected, the police shut down his security company for investigation on the double murder. He wasn't happy about the situation, but at least the police were on the lookout for the Spanish female who'd done the killing. Nate didn't have time to see Leroy that morning, so he made the necessary phone calls to his security team to do the shift change on their own. After confirming with the guard at the hospital that Leroy's condition hadn't changed, and that Nurse Justine was taking good care of him, he felt better about not having time to go by the hospital.

While Nate and TJ cruised the streets, Nyeem made his way over to Doc's house, so they could walk down to the center together to hand in their camp papers and play a few games of hoops.

As Nyeem turned the corner and started the walk up Doc's block, he spotted Tek and his crew standing outside a house, a few houses away from Doc's house. He decided to make a pit stop to kick it with Tek before going on to Doc's.

"What up, money?" Tek slapped hands with Nyeem.

"What up, Tek?"

"Where you headed, kid?"

"I'm gonna go scoop up Doc, so we can take our camp papers down to the center." Nyeem leaned against the parked car.

"Oh yeah, that's right. Y'all niggas 'bout to go to NBA camp."

"Naw, man, not NBA. It's just gonna be a few retired NBA ballers there to help with the training and shit."

"Oh, a'ight. That still should be a'ight, though."

"Yeah, I'm ready for it. I need to get away from this joint for a few. After my birthday I'm outta here."

"Yeah, when is that?"

"It's next week."

"Oh, that's what's up. Maybe we can celebrate you and Doc going away to camp with a party at my crib, with shorties and all up in there," Tek said, liking his own idea.

"That's what's up. I'm with that, and you know Doc gonna be with that shit too."

"A'ight, so it's on then." Tek looked at Nyeem and smiled. "Yo, man, I'm proud of y'all niggas, man."

"Word?" Nyeem shook Tek's hand, letting him know he was grateful for the comment.

"Yeah, man, 'cause if y'all wasn't doing the ball thing, y'all niggas probably would be out here banging with us."

"Yo, man, you ain't gotta bang. You could be going to camp too."

"Naw, man, I'm sixteen and I left school at twelve, so ain't no going back for me. I'm good, though, but y'all two niggas ain't built for this shit. That's why I'm glad y'all holding yo' head."

It was funny to hear Tek talk like that, because Nate had just spoken to Nyeem about gangs earlier that morning.

"Nyeem!" Nate had called out to him from the kitchen.

Nyeem appeared in the doorway of the kitchen. "What's up?"

"Word is, your boy Doc is running with them gangs."

"Where you hear that shit from?" Nyeem twisted up his face. He looked at the eggs left in the frying pan and turned up his nose. Since recent events, he hadn't had much of an appetite, and eggs definitely weren't his top choice on the menu. He walked over to the refrigerator and peered inside.

"That ain't important." Nate raised an eyebrow. "You fucking around with them niggas?" he asked, leery of Nyeem's nonchalant answer. Someone had seen Nyeem and Doc talking with Tek on several occasions, and everybody knew Tek was in a gang.

Nyeem looked over the refrigerator door at Nate with serious eyes. "Unc, why you tryin'-a play me out?"

"It ain't 'bout tryin'-a play you out. I asked you a question." Nate walked over to the sink and placed his breakfast plate inside.

"No. Hell, no. OK?" Nyeem dipped his head back into the refrigerator.

"Watch your mouth!" Nate pointed a finger at Nyeem. He shook his head as he leaned against the counter. "Leave that gang shit alone, Nyeem, I'm telling you. You think your father's name gonna keep you protected with them niggas, but trust, them Bloods and Crips don't give a fuck 'bout your father. These young gunners don't have any respect for the game no more. That's why I'm tryin'-a set you up right, where you don't have to deal with niggas like that."

Nyeem rolled his eyes upward and closed the refrigerator door after not finding anything appetizing to eat. In fact, he had suddenly lost his appetite completely.

Nate couldn't be any further from the truth. Neither Nyeem nor Doc were in any gang, and Nyeem was tired of people watching him and then running back and telling his uncle lies. But what hurt the most was that Nate would even think he was that stupid to be in a gang.

Nyeem was also tired of hearing the stories of the legendary Ishmael Jenkins, who single-handedly ran the streets, didn't take no shit from no one, and had the illest crew in the city with his partner Derrick.

Living in a man's shadow wasn't what Nyeem wanted. He longed for his mother and father all his life. He had the picture that he'd found of them with him, and he was gonna keep it near and dear to his heart. But he didn't want to continue to live as the resurrected Ishmael Jenkins.

If Nyeem was contemplating joining a gang, it wouldn't be because he was trying to be like his father, it would be because he was trying to escape his father's legendary status.

"Yo, Nyeem!" Doc yelled out of the first-floor window of the two-family home where he lived, his body partially hanging out the window as he leaned forward and looked down the street at Nyeem and Tek.

Nyeem looked up and threw his hands in the air, acknowledging his friend.

"C'mere, kid!" Doc beckoned.

"Hold up, Doc!" Nyeem said, holding one finger in the air. "A'ight, y'all." He gave pounds to the gang members he and Tek had been chopping it up with and stepped off down the street.

"What's good?" Nyeem asked Doc after arriving at his house.

"It's all good, baby. Yo, Ny, you got your papers?"

"Yeah, nigga, I told you that shit on the phone. Hurry up!" Nyeem said, growing impatient.

"Man, shut up!" Doc laughed. "Come on, man, you know me. I gotta get my swag on." he said.

Nyeem cracked up laughing at how silly Doc was acting. He didn't have a shirt on, and he looked funny hunching his shoulders while dancing.

Pop! Pop! Pop!

Suddenly shots rang out, hitting Doc several times in the chest, causing his body to jerk around in the window, and tires screeched, leaving the smell of burning rubber in the air. Then there was silence.

Everyone outside hit the turf. Tek hit the ground, pulled out his gun, and crawled over behind a parked car. He began to fire after the fleeing car.

Nyeem looked at his longtime friend hanging out of the window, bent over at the waist, blood running down his arms and dripping from his fingertips.

Everyone else began to come out of hiding, and the crew came running down the street.

"Yo, Ny, man, you a'ight, kid?" one member of the crew yelled.

But Nyeem didn't say a word. He stood there and watched as his friend's body slowly slid out of the first-floor window and crashed into the bushes right under the window.

"Damn, that's fucked up! Doc!" Tek ran over to his body.

As everyone huddled around to see Doc's bullet-riddled body, one of the gang members said to Tek, "It was them same niggas from the other day, Tek!" reminding him of the boy he'd killed at point-blank range. Apparently the dead boy's crew had returned for revenge.

Still Nyeem said nothing. He stood there stewing. He and Doc were supposed to go to camp together next week and had planned to get drafted into the NBA together. All these thoughts swam through his head, but nothing could bring his friend back.

Chapter Thirty

THE SET

Click rolled up onto the set where Tek and his gang stood around drinking and smoking haze. When he rolled up on them, they were on alert, ready to brandish their weapons, until they realized who he was.

Click and his sidekick, Ameen, jumped out of the car and walked over to the gang members.

Tek stood from the step he was sitting on to go greet Click, and they shook hands.

"What up?" Click said when he approached Tek.

"I'm fucked up right now. My boy is gone," Tek said, referring to Doc's death.

"Yeah, we all are." Click looked at the rest of the young boys, who were getting high as their way of grieving for their friend. "So what y'all little niggas gonna do 'bout that situation?"

"We 'bout to buck on them niggas," Tek said with sleepy-looking eyes, high from the weed he'd smoked.

"Y'all got the game fucked up," Click said.

"Whatchu' talking 'bout?" Tek asked, perplexed.

Ameen stood an easy six-four and had a medium build. His unapproachable look always instilled fear in most. "What he saying is, if that was your boy, y'all little mu'fuckas should be out there like bloodhounds, sniffing them jokers out and putting some lead in they asses."

"I'm saying we gonna get them niggas," Tek defended.

"When?" Click shouted, disappointed.

No one said a word. In fact, they feared Click. Although he wasn't of the gang mentality, everyone knew him, gangbanger or not.

Click shook his head and walked off from the gang members, leaving them standing there with their bottom lip hung open. He and Ameen jumped back into his car and sped off down the street.

After receiving information from some locals on who the rival gang members were, he and Ameen sat patiently in front of the triggerman's house. Click pulled his fitted cap down over his eyes and reclined his seat back a little while he waited patiently for the boy to come home. He and Ameen had switched vehicles in Click's collections of cars. They were sitting in an old burgundy Buick Skylark with tinted windows. The body of the car looked beaten and worn, but under the hood was a brand-new engine that would blow any racecar off the track. Neither man spoke as they listened to Jadakiss spit mind-numbing lyrics into the air.

After another ten minutes went by, there was finally some movement. Click looked at his watch, and it was one-thirty in the morning. Walking down the sidewalk toward the building they were parked across the street from, came the shooter with another gang member. The two of them were engaged in a conversation as they walked with their heads down, looking at the ground.

Ameen eased his door open and slid out of the car. Click had removed the bulbs from the interior, so when the door opened, a person couldn't see who was inside of the car when it was dark. Ameen made his way up the street a little.

Click saw him cross the street like a black cat. That was his cue. He opened the driver's side door and hopped out of the car. He walked over to the boys, approaching the building with both his hands behind his back. With his fitted pulled down over his eyes, he tilted his head back a little, so he could see the boys coming.

"Yo, who dat?" the shooter asked his friend as they approached Click, who was standing in front of the building.

"Shit if I know," the other boy responded.

"What up?" the shooter asked Click as they reached him.

"You holding?" Click asked simply.

"Naw, man, you better go up the block with that shit. Ain't nothing over here," the shooter said, not trusting Click because he'd never seen him in the neighborhood before.

"How 'bout holding this for me then?" Ameen said, standing behinds the boys.

They both turned around startled, and locked on the arsenal Ameen was pointing at them. Then when they heard the sound of bullets being put in chambered, they looked back at Click, who was now pointing twin .40's right at them.

"Yo, man," both boys said at the same time, as if they'd rehearsed.

"You know Doc?" Click stared at the shaking boys.

"No. Who?"

"The nigga you murked today," Ameen responded.

They both looked back at him and then back to Click.

"Yo, man, I ain't mean for him to get hit. We was after that punk,

Tek, man," the boy said.

His friend looked over at him, disappointed in the way he was selling out.

"Too late for that," Click said. "Bleed 'em."

"No!" both boys yelled in unison.

Ameen let a bullet rip to the back of the head of one of the boys.

The shooter tried to run for the front steps of the building, but Click let two bullets go, one from each gun, ripping into the back of his neck and spine. The boy fell face first into the door and slid down onto the steps. Click then walked over to the steps and pumped two more into the back of the boy's head.

Neither shot that left Click's or Ameen's gun could be heard because of the silencers they had attached to the guns.

Ameen began to walk over to the getaway car when Click turned back and pulled out his camera phone and took a picture of the shooter.

"What the fuck was that for?" Ameen inquired once Click got into the car.

"Making it a little bit easier for my boy to deal with," he said as he sent the picture to Nyeem's phone with a message that read: "Doc can get his revenge when he see them niggas up top!"

"Make sure you erase that shit off your phone."

"Already done." Click started the car, pulling off slowly from the curb, but not before he took one last look at the work that he and Ameen had put in.

The hearse, with Blaze driving, rode past and looked at the two dead boys just after Click pulled off. He continued to drive by as the van picked up a little speed, trying to catch up to Click's car.

Then the Chevy Impala pulled around the corner several seconds later, and the mystery man also observed the display of dead bodies.

Chapter Thirty-One

CLICK'S REVENGE

The next day

The sun was high in the sky, and the carwash on South Sixteenth Street was packed with cars. The line to get into the carwash was long, and the chances for the workers to get a break were slim. It seemed every time they would get the line down to about four cars, when they looked up again, the line would be even longer than before. Cars were double parked as the niggas with loot politicked and checked out each other's whips. Music blared from car speakers loudly as if the car owners were in competition with each other, all trying to see whose system was rocking the loudest.

Ace stood out front talking with one of the customers, who was getting his tires glazed by one of the workers.

"Yeah, I see you shining," the dude said, referring to the ice Ace was now rocking.

Not only had Ace managed to rob one of Click's corners, but he had accomplished hitting one of the stash houses as well. Since Click had never responded to Ace's hits, Ace believed he had the shit on lock.

"Yeah. I'm 'bout to take over all this shit. This carwash right here 'bout to be mine too," Ace said.

"Nigga, how you figure? Big Roy owns this." The man twisted his lips up at Ace, not believing him.

"Nigga, Roy is breathing dirt right now!" Ace said, waving his hand at the man.

"Yeah, but he got people to run his shit. My man Nate is next in line, and you know him and that crazy nigga Click ain't 'bout to give you shit!"

"See, son, that's where you're wrong. I'm robbing them niggas blind, and they ain't stepped to me yet. Them niggas is soft as butter. They can't breathe and function without Big Roy." Ace was talking real loud, and the patrons were all tuning in. He knew he had everyone's attention and made sure he played it up. "Yeah, man, muthafuckas think it's a joke. I want muthafuckas to come for me and watch what the fuck I do!" He walked around in a circle, holding up his shirt to reveal his gun.

The man that was talking to him simply shook his head. He stepped away from Ace and bent down to wipe off some water from the lower frame of his car.

Just at that moment, the man heard a grunt and then a whoosh of air. When he looked up, Ace was standing there holding his neck while blood ran down his fingers and neck. The air had rushed out of his body, and he was now gasping, trying to maintain his balance, his eyes stretched wide and his mouth gaped open.

The man he'd been talking to stood there stuck on stupid. He knew what was happening, but he couldn't move.

Next, bullets slammed into Ace's face, one going straight through his eye and coming out the back of his head. The other two hit him in the cheekbone and jaw. Ace stumbled about as everyone realized what was going on.

"Oh shit!" someone yelled.

Several other patrons hit the ground, not wanting to get hit by the flying bullets, but the intended target was dead on his feet, and the shooting had stopped.

Ace finally fell to his death after being struck ten times in different parts of his body.

"Did you see that shit sticking out of his neck?" one patron asked, referring to the flesh that hung from his neck where a bullet had entered his esophagus.

Click and Ameen placed their guns with the silencers on their laps. Parked across the street, they sat back to watch the work that they'd put in.

Ace had unknowingly signed away his life with Click, thinking he was home free because no one came after him.

"Yo, looks like our work is done here, right?" Ameen looked over at Click.

"Oh, no doubt."

"I say we go peel some more niggas' skulls."

"Word, most definitely. But first I wanna run by Nate's crib and check on my nephew."

"Who? Nyeem?"

"Yeah, man."

"A'ight." Ameen started the car and pulled off into traffic.

Chapter Thirty-Two

MY BEST FRIEND

TJ, Nate, Click, and Nyeem sat in the living room of Nate's townhouse. Ameen had dropped Click off. Nyeem sat with his head leaned back on the sofa, his arm covering his eyes.

"I know how you feel, Ny. Man, I know what's going through your head. I been there, remember?" TJ asked.

Nyeem didn't say a word. In fact, he felt worse than he did before he got the picture mail from Click of the dead boy.

"Nyeem, do you hear TJ talking to you?" Nate asked.

Nyeem removed his forearm from his face, exposing red, wet eyes. He looked up at Nate.

"Ny." TJ knew that look in Nyeem's eyes all too well. "Look at me, man."

Nyeem took his gaze off Nate and turned to TJ.

"Don't do it, man. I know what you're thinking. I lost my best friend at about the same age as you. I know it's not fair, but don't try to handle it yourself. It's not your fault, and you can't fix it." TJ was very serious about what he was trying to tell Nyeem.

Click sat there and stared at Nyeem, feeling sorry for him. He liked Doc. Doc was a good kid, and he knew how Nyeem felt. He'd also lost his good friend Dice. They were inseparable like Doc and Nyeem had been. But Click felt differently than TJ. His frame of mind was to get with them little wannabe gangsta niggas and turn them all into Swiss cheese.

"You hear me?" TJ asked again.

Nyeem nodded, then hung his head low, staring at the floor.

"Did you hand them papers in to go to camp?" Nate asked.

"I ain't going," Nyeem said.

"Aw, naw, you going. I know you lost your boy and all, but life goes on, and you love ball. I told you them gangs ain't shit," Nate said.

"I told you before, we ain't in no gang!" Nyeem yelled.

"Bullshit, Nyeem!" Nate jumped to his feet. "That was one gang going after another, and Doc was part of that shit, whether you want to believe it or not! You might not have been jumped into the gang, but you was hanging with them niggas!"

TJ jumped up and stopped Nate, not knowing what his intentions were. "Hold up, Nate, man, the kid is grieving for his boy. Calm down, man. I don't think he was in any gang. I mean, they knew them cats because they went to school with them. A person can't help who they know."

"I understand he's grieving, TJ. He ain't the only one going through some shit here, but that still ain't no excuse to give up."

"I feel you. And he didn't say he was giving up. He just said he didn't want to go to camp," TJ explained, trying to get a grip on the situation.

"Me and Doc was going to camp together!" Nyeem yelled. "It was all his idea to go in the first place. He had the hookup to get us in!"

"So now you not gonna go?" Nate asked. "Your boy would want you to go, Nyeem! If I let you back outta this, then the next thing you know, you gonna drop outta school 'cause you don't want to go without your boy. No, I won't let you give up on something you love! You going to camp, period!"

"Yo, man, why don't you let the kid live?" Click said.

"Fuck you, Click! 'Cause I'm two seconds from fucking you up anyway!" Nate was still pissed at Click for his actions the other night.

"Oh, word?" Click stood, ready for whatever Nate was bringing. He too had a lot of shit to deal with and wasn't up for no games.

"Word, muthafucka!"

TJ was still standing in front of Nate and was now trying to keep him from charging Click. "Hold up, Nate! Y'all niggas need to calm the fuck down!"

"Naw, *T*, man, let that nigga go! He feeling himself right now. I'ma show him who he fucking with!" Click said, placing his hand on his gun.

"Oh, yeah, nigga? What you gonna do? I got a fucking gun too, muthafucka!" Nate began to reach for his gun.

"You know what? Hell, yeah, I'm going to camp, because I need to get the fuck away from y'all muthafuckas!" Nyeem yelled and stormed out of the room. He went into his bedroom and slammed the door.

Everybody stood there and looked at each other. Click was still fuming, but he sat back down in the chair.

Nate made an attempt to go after Nyeem, but TJ grabbed his arm and stopped him. "I got him," TJ said and walked off toward Nyeem's room.

Chapter Thirty-Three

BLACK WIDOW

Jasmine sat in the pizza restaurant with Star, who was telling her all about her encounter with Click. Star was still sore from when he invaded her rectum. He had split her there, and it still bothered her when she sat down.

"I can't believe you would even set me up with a *puta* like that." Star rolled her eyes and then took a sip of her soda.

"Me? Set you up? I don't even remember that night. You are the slut, *mamacita*, so don't go blaming me."

"But he is your friend. You should have told me."

"Like I said, I don't even remember what happened that night in the first place. And he is not my friend. I did a couple of jobs with him back in the day when I was running with that loco Nettie." Jasmine waved her hand at Star and continued to eat her slice of pizza.

Star, playing with the straw in her cup, pouted as she thought about the way she was treated like common street trash. The more she thought about it, the angrier she got. "I was thinking about getting somebody to fuck him up," she said.

"Who? Can't nobody you know fuck with Click. Listen, Star, you don't want to start messing with Click. He ain't the one. He works for Big Roy, and they will kill you and whoever you get."

Jasmine warned her in Spanish, so no one sitting within earshot could understand her. The pizzeria was located next to a bar, and several people stood around outside and inside the restaurant.

"Devon can."

Jasmine couldn't believe her ears. "Devon? The-dude-that-sweeps-the-floors-in-the-barbershop Devon?"

"Yeah."

Jasmine burst into laughter. "You can't be serious. That jerk is a straight-up punk! What makes you think that he got any work for Click?" She still chuckled while she talked.

"Because he's down with Mike and them."

Jasmine suddenly stopped laughing.

Now it was Star's turn to clown her. "Yeah, I see it ain't funny no more, huh?"

"Whatever." Jasmine waved her hand at Star. She did know about Mike, Tone, and Lex from back when she stripped at Bodylicious. They were definitely ruthless then. She knew they had nothing on Leroy's camp. Actually nobody did, but that crew held their own.

"OK, so why would Mike and them want doofy-ass Devon around them?"

Neither woman knew that Mike was dead.

"Because they 'bout to take over Big Roy's shit and come off. He said he gonna take care of me too."

Star and Devon had been screwing around with each other off and on for several years. Star would never get serious with him because he didn't have enough cash to take care of her needs, but Devon was so in love with her, he settled for seeing her whenever she had time for him. Now that Star was at an all-time low, hearing Devon talk about how they were gonna be the new kings of the streets had her dreaming dollar signs.

Sitting two booths away was Valencia. She had stopped inside the pizzeria to get a bite to eat, and to see if she could overhear any conversations about Leroy, knowing that people in the hood talked.

She heard everything the girls were talking about. Hearing Leroy's name piqued her interest. She'd been running into dead ends, trying to find out if he was dead or alive. She'd even checked with all the hospitals and came up with nothing. She was actually contemplating going back home to Long Island when she heard the girls talking.

Star sucked her teeth and rolled her eyes. "You obviously don't know Devon either."

Devon had come by to see her and revealed to her the plan to take over Leroy's territory and come up big. Of course, Star was all in.

"I do know Devon, and like I said, he can't fuck with Click. Trust, if he does get with him, Big Roy's boys are gonna be all over him *a prisa, mamí.*" She snapped her fingers.

"Well, all I know is, Devon is down with Mike and them now, and they gonna be strong."

"Just let it go, Star. Trust me, I know. I been with them, and you know I told you what I went through. Thank God, I'm still alive."

Star sat there pouting. She knew about what happened with Jasmine and her sister Maria, and how her cousin Marisa was killed. But Jasmine wasn't suffering like she was. She wanted revenge on Click in the worst way.

"Anyway, forget about that right now. I need to find a place to live, or I'm gonna be on the streets soon," Jasmine said.

"You? I was just looking at my bills the other day, and I can't even pay my light bill, and I don't have all of my rent for next month."

"So why don't we just stay together and then we can pay the bills?"

"You don't have a job either, Jasmine. All that's gonna do is have both of us on the streets."

The two women ate the rest of their meal in silence. Jasmine thought about what she was gonna do to get money to save herself from being homeless, and Star was contemplating letting Devon know what Click had done to her.

"Excuse me, ladies," Valencia said, standing in front of their table.

Neither of them even noticed that she had walked over to them because they were so absorbed in their own thoughts.

"I don't want to seem like I was being nosy, but I couldn't help but overhear that both of you are having money problems. I have a way that both of you could make two thousand dollars."

Jasmine and Star, their mouths wide open, looked up at this woman.

"Ladies, my name is Black Widow." She extended her hand for a shake.

The two women looked at each other and then back at Valencia.

Later Jasmine and Star discussed the Black Widow's proposition while they walked to Star's apartment.

"I don't know, Star, that chick seemed weird to me."

"Listen, Jazz, she is legit, and no matter how weird she seemed to you, she got dough to throw away."

Jasmine, deep in thought, kept walking with her head down.

"I ain't see you refuse the five hundred down payment she threw in our laps at the pizza parlor," Star said.

"I'm not stupid, Star. I need this money to pay my back rent."

"OK then, and you can get the rest of it when we do what we gotta do." Star was all too willing to get the fifteen-hundred-dollar-apiece balance.

"Yeah, but I don't know if I want to fuck with the people she tryin'-a mess with. I been through this shit before, Star. It feels like a recurring nightmare is about to happen."

"Girl, ain't nothing gonna happen to us. We gonna look out for each other. I got your back, and you got mine." Star threw her arm around Jasmine's neck, hugging her.

"When you mess with people like Leroy Jones, the only thing that's gonna have our backs is a bullet."

Star realized how serious and scared her friend was, and she tried to understand, but in her mind, no matter what, she was gonna make the two thousand dollars with or without Jasmine. And if Jasmine did back out, she would ask Widow if she could get Jasmine's part too.

Chapter Thirty-Four

LONELY

Click left Nate's place, and Nate called Doc's mother, offering to assist her with making arrangements for her only child's funeral. He consoled the grieving mother and offered to pay for the whole funeral.

In the meantime, TJ knocked on Nyeem's door, trying to get the angry boy to open up. "Nyeem, it's me, TJ. Open the door, man."

No response.

"I know how you feel, man. It feels like you're all alone."

Still no response, so TJ leaned against the wall next to the door.

"Listen, Ny, man, my mother was murdered too. You know the story. I don't know who my father is either. So I'm in the same boat as you. Nate took me under his wing and took care of me, and I turned out OK."

Nyeem said nothing, nor did he open the door.

"Sometimes I feel like I'm alone too even now, but I know I'm not. I'm your brother, Nyeem. I've always told you that. I'm here for you, man, no matter what it is." TJ heard the lock click.

Nyeem opened the door slightly and walked away from it, and TJ pushed open the door and walked inside.

"Yo, I heard that one of Leroy's blocks got jacked by Ace," Triggs told Blaze. "If other niggas gunning for Leroy's shit, how we gonna get in?"

Blaze sat on the sofa flipping channels with the remote.

"Just cool out," he told a hyper Triggs. "That's actually a good thing. Let them niggas beef it out over that shit, 'cause they gonna cancel each other out, making it that much easier for us. Just chill, Triggs. I got the shit all planned out."

"Well, if you got shit planned out, when you gonna let me in on what's planned?"

"Because you gonna start tripping like you already doing now." Blaze pointed his finger at Triggs, but he continued to watch the TV.

"Man, fuck that! What's up?"

"You worry 'bout the paper, and let me do what I do best 'cause when I get ready to unleash, the morgue is gonna be standing room only, piled up with dead niggas."

Unbeknownst to Triggs, Blaze had been cruising the streets, checking out the happenings in the neighborhood. Normally he didn't do this unless he got the urge to do a robbery. He had cut down tremendously on robbing, but once in a blue moon, the urge would hit him and he would go out and commit a robbery just to keep up his skills. But for the last few days he'd been watching everything play out for Leroy's camp, and no one was the wiser. He knew where Click's stash houses were.

He'd also realized Nate had been making trips to the hospital every day. He wasn't sure who he was going to see, but he'd spotted him and sometimes some of his boys all going into the hospital.

On one occasion he'd tried to follow them inside, waiting by the lobby elevator to see what floor they would get off on, but other people always got on, preventing him from getting the information he needed.

Regardless, Blaze knew it was just a matter of time before Leroy's whole operation folded, and he was waiting for the right time to step in. His patience came from the planning and scheming he always did before he caught his robbery victims off guard. His mother had trained him to be patient and plan ahead. Sometimes, mothers did know best.

CHAPTER THIRTY-FIVE

BROTHERLY LOVE

"I want you to go to camp," TJ told Nyeem. "Don't let anything interfere with what you love to do. Nate was right about that." He sat on the bed next to Nyeem.

"Man, I can't deal with this shit half the time. It's always something going on, and then Unc be taking that shit out on me."

"Naw, Ny, you can't look at it like that. See, Nate means well. I mean, he may not know how to show it, but he cares a lot about you, man. He loves you like you was his own. He comes from that street mentality, so he doesn't show any emotions that would be considered soft." TJ stood, walked over to the wall, and started looking at some of the posters Nyeem had displayed.

"He feels like he gotta be hard on you in order to make you hard," he continued. "Honestly, I don't think he knows how to be no other way, man, but I wouldn't take it personally. It's his way of showing that he cares. Shit, he probably ain't never cried a day in his life." TJ laughed.

Nyeem chuckled a little as well.

TJ walked past the dresser and saw the picture of Ishmael and Desiree resting there. He picked up the picture and looked at it. "Damn!

I remember them, even though I was younger. They was good peoples, especially your moms." He turned to Nyeem.

"Yeah, that's what y'all keep telling me, but I can't say that my life woulda been any better if they were alive, because they was living this lifestyle too."

"I know what you mean. I told you my moms was an alcoholic. I know she dabbled in getting high, but she loved to drink. And, to me, she might as well have been getting high, because drinking is just as bad. So I was always around drugs when I was younger. But I did love my mother to death, man. No matter what, she made sure we had." TJ stared off into space, thinking about his mother, Beverly.

Nyeem looked up at him and saw the same look of loneliness on TJ's face that he often had on his own face. "You really miss your moms, huh?"

"Do I?" TJ placed the picture back on the dresser. "I miss my mother so much, at times I feel like I want to just crawl up in a corner and cry."

Nyeem looked at him, surprised. "You cry?" He pointed to TJ.

"Come on, man, I'm human." TJ laughed. "Yeah, I do sometimes, not often, and you better not tell anybody." He playfully punched Nyeem.

"I won't, TJ. You're like the brother I don't have. I wish you could live here."

"Listen, baby bruh, I am your brother, and I'm just a phone call and less than six hours away. You can always come stay with me on the weekends, to get away. I told you that."

"Don't you got a girlfriend or something?"

"Yeah. And what that mean? You are my family, my little brother, and to me, that takes precedence any day. Speaking of girlfriends . . . why don't you call yours? Maybe she can help take your mind off things." TJ looked at him sideways, a devilish grin on his face.

Nyeem started laughing. "Go 'head, man."

"Call her, man. It will make you feel better."

Nyeem nodded. "OK, I will."

"Speaking of which, I gotta call my girl. She been blowing up my phone, but I ain't have the time to answer it 'cause y'all niggas been wilding out." TJ laughed.

"That's them fools, not me."

"A'ight, so you straight? You gonna go to camp and stay focused in school, right?"

"Yeah."

"Listen, your man Doc would want you to do this. Do it, and each time you accomplish something, talk to him. I do that all the time with my boy Tyler. It helps."

"Thanks, man," Nyeem said.

"Don't thank me, man. It's all love."

TJ grabbed Nyeem, and they gave each other a brotherly hug.

As TJ walked out of the room, Nyeem picked up the phone to call Alicia.

TJ made his way down the hall and into the living room. "Oh, you still here?" TJ asked when he saw Nate.

Nate looked up at him. He had nodded off. "Yeah. Is everything a'ight?"

"Yeah, he's cool. You and Click need to calm the hell down. I can't believe y'all niggas still beasting, as old as y'all is."

Nate smiled. "I ain't that much older than you."

"You got me by at least twenty years."

"Yeah, but I look good." Nate stood and headed for the door.

TJ followed him.

Nate stopped at the door and turned around to face TJ. "And don't get it twisted, nigga. I don't have you by twenty years. It's just a little over ten years, and that's it." He flung open the front door and stepped out into the humidity.

"Ten, fifteen, twenty, what difference does it make? It's all the same to me. You old as shit." TJ closed the door behind him.

They drove off together, headed to the hospital to check up on Leroy.

During the drive, Nate reached into the middle console and produced a 9 mm handgun. He handed it to TJ.

TJ looked at the gun. "What's this for? We gonna need this shit to go into the hospital?" He looked over at Nate.

"Naw, man. I feel the need to give it to you. You may need it. I mean, you know how we roll, and we got muthafuckas who definitely gonna test us. Remember, they think Leroy's dead, and that means it's open season for these niggas to try to move in on us."

TJ knew the risk he would be taking when he decided to make the trip up north, but he didn't have any intention of participating in the drama. He'd thought about it on the drive, and Dasia was right. Anything could happen to him, and all that he'd worked hard for would go down the drain.

"Listen, man, I'm not saying that I want you to get down with us and use it. I mean, I know how you feel about that. And, if I ain't never tell you before, I'm proud of you. But, like I said, you know how we roll, and you may have to use it to protect yourself."

"No doubt."

TJ studied the gun, moving it from hand to hand. He hadn't held a gun since he was a teen. He felt calmer just holding it. He checked the safety and placed the gun down the front of his jeans.

"Naw, man, we don't roll like that," Nate said. "That gun is registered, and I do have you on the books as an employee, so you are registered to have a weapon with my security company. Look in the back seat and get that side holster."

TJ grabbed the holster, adjusted it, and hooked it to the waist of his jeans. After placing the gun in the holster, he relaxed in his seat.

As TJ and Nate got off the elevator at the hospital and made their way down the hall, Nate saw his two security men sitting in their chairs. When they saw him, they stood.

"What's up?" He shook hands with the men. "This is my godson, TJ."

"What's up?" TJ shook hands with the two men.

"That old lady nurse been asking about you," one of the men said.

"A'ight," Nate responded.

Then he and TJ walked into the room.

When TJ saw Leroy lying up in the bed all ashy-looking and skinny, all the blood drained from his body. Leroy looked bad. The last time he'd seen him, he was built and vibrant. What he was looking at now was a frail, thin, and sickly man who had more gray hair than black. TJ's heart sank right to the bottom of his stomach.

Nate noticed the look on TJ's face. "You a'ight, man?"

TJ couldn't speak. All he could do was stare at Leroy.

"Come on, man, pull up a chair and have a seat," Nate said. "It ain't as bad as it looks."

Before either of them could take a seat, Dr. Clinton walked into the room.

"How you doing?" Nate asked the doctor. He shook his hand. "This is my son," Nate said, introducing TJ. He knew if he didn't tell the doctor that TJ was his son, he would have made TJ leave the room, since only immediate family was allowed in the ICU.

"Hello, son," Dr. Clinton said. He turned his attention back to Nate. "How are you today? I was just about to call you."

"What's wrong?" Nate was alarmed by the serious look on the doctor's face.

"Well, your father has an infection, and gangrene has set in. I'm afraid we're going to have to amputate his legs."

"What?" Nate asked.

TJ continued to listen carefully.

"His legs are badly infected due to poor circulation. The blood is just not circulating properly. We gave him blood thinners to try to get past the clots, but that just didn't work. Once gangrene sets in, we have to amputate to keep the infection from spreading."

Nate plopped down in the seat in disbelief, and TJ looked over at Leroy.

"We needed to speak with the next of kin to get permission for amputation."

Nate didn't know what to do. He knew what type of person Leroy was, and amputation wasn't something Leroy would tolerate. But if he didn't do it, then the infection could spread and he could die.

TJ wanted to make sure he'd heard the doctor correctly. "You mean you want to cut off his legs?"

"Yes," Dr. Clinton responded.

TJ turned and walked over to the window. He looked out onto the streets below. He knew if Leroy came out of his coma and saw he didn't have any legs, he was gonna lose it. Leroy was a strong man, but he knew Leroy would never agree to something like that. TJ was glad he wasn't in Nate's position, to have to make an important decision like that. He sat on the windowsill and waited for Nate to give his answer to the doctor.

"OK, I'll sign whatever papers are needed," Nate finally blurted out. "Please do whatever you can for my father, and spare no expense. Money is not an issue. I'll pay for whatever."

"I will have the nurse bring you the documents to fill out, and we will schedule surgery for the amputation."

"Do you think this will help him come out of the coma?" Nate asked, his voice cracking a little.

"He's technically not in a coma. He's in a deep sleep, but we've had to keep him heavily medicated because of the severe pain he's enduring. The pain alone would kill him. When his condition gets better, we will be able to start treatment on the cancer, but to be honest with you, he is in the second stage of cancer, and I can't promise that the chemo will do any good. Frankly, I don't think he's strong enough to endure the treatment."

Nate's whole body felt numb. What he got out of the conversation was, there wouldn't be anything they could do for Leroy, and he was going to die.

TJ got up off the windowsill and walked back over between Dr. Clinton and Nate. He couldn't believe what he just heard.

Dr. Clinton saw the devastated looks on both men's faces and tried to make the bad news easier for them. "Let's not get ahead of ourselves," he said. "This is information I have to tell you, but anything's possible, Nate. Let's just handle one thing at a time, and we will see how things go. Shall we, fellas?" He looked back and forth between the two.

Nate plopped back down in the chair and interlocked his fingers, placing them under his chin, and leaned forward and rested his elbows on his knees.

TJ continued to stare at Leroy. His face had no life left to it. The reality of Big Roy dying was starting to set in. TJ felt sorry for Nate, but most of all, he felt sorry for Nyeem, who didn't have a clue that he was about lose his only living relative.

Nate didn't respond to the doctor's question. He looked over at Leroy and wanted to cry.

"Do you understand?" Dr. Clinton asked, trying to get Nate's attention.

Nate simply nodded, letting Dr. Clinton know that he understood, but never made eye contact with the doctor.

Dr. Clinton left the room, giving Nate and TJ privacy.

TJ didn't know what to say, so he didn't say anything. Sometimes some things were just best kept to yourself. He walked back over to the window and reclaimed his seat on the windowsill, and watched the cars drive by.

A few minutes later, Nurse Justine walked into the room with the papers Nate needed to fill out for the amputation.

TJ looked at the door as she entered, but Nate never looked up.

She saw TJ sitting in the window and gave him a warm smile, and he returned the greeting with a slight smile of his own.

Nurse Justine could tell that Nate was upset. She didn't say anything to him. She simply walked over to the bed and straightened out the sheet and bedspread over Leroy. She set the papers on the tray that sat next to the bed, and then she walked around the bed and stood next to Nate.

He finally realized she was there and looked up at her with saddened eyes.

Nurse Justine knew that there would have to be some heavy praying for Leroy, which she had done every day. She'd taken a liking to Leroy when he first came to the unit.

Nurse Justine didn't open her mouth to say anything to Nate. She just knew what needed to be done, and she did it. She gently placed her hand around Nate's head and pulled him into her bosom. She held him there while he released a flood of tears.

A shocked TJ sat in the window observing the interaction. Nate was the last man he thought would shed any tears.

CHAPTER THIRTY-SIX

SETUP

Star gave Jasmine Click's number as they both sat on the floor in front of the sofa, with Star facing Jasmine.

The phone rang three times before Click answered.

"Yeah," he said, not knowing who was calling him. He never got Star's number that night because he knew he wasn't going to call her.

"Hey, Click."

"Who dis?"

"It's me, Jasmine."

"What up, Jazz? This your number?"

"No, it's Star's phone."

Click was silent.

"Where you at?" she asked.

"I'm in motion. Why? What's up?"

"Oh, I was wondering if we could hang out and get a drink or something, like old times."

Star could tell Jasmine was nervous because Jasmine was biting her nails. She reached over, took Jasmine's finger out of her mouth, and held her hand, trying to comfort her.

"That's what's up." Click thought it would be perfect for him to link up with Jasmine, because he still needed to talk to her about the mysterious Spanish chick. "A'ight, so what time you want me to scoop you up?"

"It's whatever. Just pick me up at Star's house."

"A'ight, so I'll be by around four, 'cause I got some other shit to handle first."

"OK, cool. I'll see you then." Jasmine hung up before Click could say good-bye.

"You did good, Jazz." Star smiled at her.

Jasmine shook her head. "Star, I don't know if I can do this shit."

"Sure, you can. I'm gonna be there with you. Much as I can't stand his ass, I'm gonna take one for the team and then watch his ass get got!"

Jasmine sat there and watched her friend acting joyful, but she knew from experience that there was nothing joyful about that particular crew. Valencia had asked them that day at the pizza parlor a bunch of questions that neither of them could answer.

"So do you know Leroy Jones?" Valencia had asked.

"Who don't know him?" Star asked.

"So you know where I can find him?"

"No, Widow, she don't know him personally," Jasmine said. "She just saying everybody knows his name."

Valencia looked at Jasmine. "Do you know him?"

Jasmine was feeling uncomfortable now. The way Valencia looked at her was almost as if her blue eyes were cutting through her like a knife. "No, I don't know him."

"But she know people that run with him."

Jasmine could have killed Star. Neither of them knew this woman, and she could be police, for all Jasmine knew. But money-hungry Star was willing to tell it all. When Valencia mentioned the two grand, she didn't have to ask Star twice.

"So you do know his associates?" Valencia raised an eyebrow at Jasmine, making her feel even more uncomfortable.

"I know two people that's down with him."

Valencia didn't believe her, and it showed on her face. "And you don't know Leroy Jones?"

"No, I don't know Leroy Jones. I never saw him."

"So do you at least know if Leroy Jones is still alive?"

Both women looked at each other, because everybody in Newark knew Big Roy was dead.

"I heard he got killed," Star said.

"But do you know that to be true?"

"Well, that's what the news said." Star's naïveté was seeping out.

Little did Star know, she was already marked, in Valencia's book. In her opinion, Star would be the first to talk, and that was a chance she wasn't going to take.

Chapter Thirty-Seven

JACKED

"I know, baby, I know." TJ sat in the passenger seat while Nate drove. They had left the hospital and were on their way to Nate's security company to check on things.

"Baby, listen, my godfather needs me to help him handle some things. My godbrother's friend got killed, and he needs me right now too." TJ had a frustrated look on his face.

After hearing about the murder of Nyeem's friend, Dasia got nervous. She was trying to convince TJ to come back home on time, so he could keep his job. But Dasia didn't know that TJ had made arrangements to be out of work for a week. He told his employer that his grandfather had passed, so they gave him the time, understanding that he needed to comfort his family as well as make arrangements for the burial.

TJ had had a gut feeling that he would have to stay longer than the three days Dasia tried to get him to take. He'd never lied to her or betrayed her before, and he didn't feel good about it. But Nate and the rest of the crew were like his real family. He could deal with Dasia when he got home, but he only had one chance to be there for Nate and Leroy.

"A'ight, baby, I'll call you later," he said once he got Dasia to calm down.

"I love you?" Nate looked over at him and smiled.

"What are you talking about?" TJ asked, perplexed.

"Why didn't you tell her that you love her, man?"

"Whatever, Nate." TJ waved his hand.

"I'm saying, it's funny to hear you talk all grown-up," Nate said, teasing.

"Fuck you mean?"

"I mean, I remember when you were Nyeem's age, all quiet and shit, and now here you is, talking like you the man."

"Yo, I am the man." TJ smiled.

"Yeah, OK. That's why she had you stuttering and shit, talking 'bout, 'No, baby. I promise you, baby.'" Nate laughed.

"Fuck you, man!"

As they sat at a stop sign waiting to proceed, a gun was placed in the windows on both sides of the car, leaving Nate and TJ looking straight down the barrel of the guns.

"Get the fuck out the car, nigga!" one gunman yelled at Nate.

"What the fuck? You jacking me for my car?"

"Nigga, don't nobody want your shit!" the man yelled. "We want you, nigga!"

"I can't believe this shit!"

TJ sat there with a funny feeling in his stomach. The man that held the gun on him didn't say a word. It seemed as if he was taking his orders from the other one.

"Yo, man, what the fuck you want from me?" Nate asked.

"I want your life, nigga! You took my man's life, so now you gotta pay with yours!" The man looked dead serious.

"I don't know what you're talking about," Nate said calmly. He was thinking how dumb the dude was. If he really wanted Nate's life, he would have pulled the trigger when he stuck the gun in the window.

"Nigga, you lying!" The man punched Nate square in the face, snapping his head back.

Nate instantly put his hand up to his face to see if he was bleeding, but he wasn't. He looked at the man like he was out of his fucking mind.

"Get the fuck outta the car!"

The man tried to pull the handle on the door, and the other gunman proceeded to do the same to TJ's door.

"Yo, man," Nate said as his anger built, "I don't know what you're talking about, so if you are smart, then you need to roll out, and I'll forget about this little incident."

The man looked at Nate like he had four heads. He opened the door and snatched Nate out of the car.

Nate was fuming. He felt violated on so many levels.

The man yelled in Nate's face, "Nigga, do you know who I am!?" while holding the hard steel against Nate's temple.

In the meantime the other gunman opened TJ's door and waved for him to get out of the car. TJ cooperated with no resistance.

Nate didn't respond to the man. The stale liquor on the man's breath almost turned his stomach. The man was clearly drunk.

They were on a side street at the intersection. Minimal cars drove past, but no one stopped to assist. People simply minded their business, not wanting to get involved.

Nate continued to ice-grill the man.

"I'm Lex, nigga!" he yelled. "You know me now?"

"That name don't mean shit to me," Nate growled, transforming more and more into the demon he'd always held at bay.

"You killed my boy Mike! You fucking with the best right now, nigga! I'm gonna make you eat a bullet!" Lex pressed the gun harder into Nate's temple.

Lex and Devon had decided to go out and take revenge on Leroy's crew for killing Mike. They got drunk and amped themselves up to go out and look for any member of the crew. It just so happened that Nate pulled up to the stop sign as they were leaving the bar, giving them the opportunity to put their plan into play. Lex already thought Nate might have put the hit out on Mike anyway. He had been trying to get in touch with Tone and got no response, so this made him believe that they'd probably gotten Tone too.

Devon wasn't much of a gunman, but he was down for whatever was gonna bring him some street status.

The whites of Nate's eyes began to turn red, and his jaw muscles began to pulsate. TJ noticed and knew from years of knowing Nate that Nate didn't fear taking a bullet. He knew Nate would never go out like a coward. He'd go out fighting.

Devon and TJ stood there side by side while Devon held the gun to TJ's side. TJ saw that Devon was engrossed in what Lex and Nate were doing, so he took the opportunity and made his move, slowly reaching under his shirt. He gripped the butt end of the gun and slowly removed it from the holster.

Devon was so tuned in to how Lex was losing it on Nate, he never felt or saw TJ moving.

TJ reached down with his other hand and cocked the gun lightly, keeping his head forward as if he was watching the altercation as well. Once the hammer was cocked, he quickly shifted his weight to the right, out of range of Devon's gun, and let off two shots at point-blank range into the right side of Devon's neck, and then he quickly dropped to the ground.

Lex heard the shots and immediately trained his gun toward where he thought TJ was standing, giving Nate the opportunity he needed.

Nate grabbed Lex by the head and twisted with all his might, snapping his neck. He then picked up Lex's gun, which had fallen to the ground, and emptied it into his body.

TJ yelled to get Nate's attention when he saw a van slowly driving by. "Get the fuck in the car, man!"

Nate broke out of his trance and jumped into the car, quickly pulling away from the two dead bodies. As they drove, TJ kept looking behind them to see if anybody was coming. His adrenaline was in overdrive, and the rush made him feel like he was high.

Back at the scene, where Lex and Devon lay dead, the slow-moving van had circled back around the block. Blaze and his right-hand man observed the work Nate and TJ had put in, and then they pulled off.

Of course, the Chevy Impala wasn't far behind.

Chapter Thirty-Eight

THE HEARSE COMES A-CALLING

"Yo, Blaze, so what the fuck, man? We just gonna follow these niggas every day, all day?" one of Blaze's men asked.

The two men were tired of riding in the van with Blaze every day following Click and Nate around. They weren't making any money, and Blaze wasn't giving them the go-ahead for them to execute. They were bloodthirsty hitmen who wanted to do the hit, but Blaze was in charge and wanted to wait for the right time and place to do the job.

"Patience, man, you gotta have patience," Blaze said in a low whisper as he continued to follow Nate and TJ.

"I say we just buck on these niggas and then go after the rest. Fuck all this tailing muthafuckas like we security for them."

Blaze didn't say a word. He simply continued to follow behind Nate as he sped through the streets.

Nate pulled over in front of the Laundromat that Leroy also owned and hopped out of the car, leaving it running.

Blaze pulled over just a half a block behind him, put the van in park, and let it idle.

"OK, so why we just can't do the kid that's in the car and wait for the other nigga to come out and bust his skull when he walk out?"

"Yo, nigga, shut the fuck up!" Blaze screwed his face up. "You breaking my concentration."

The man turned around and looked at the other man, who shrugged his shoulders and checked the gun he held in his hand.

"Just let me ask you one thing," the passenger said.

"What?"

"Breaking your concentration from what? What the fuck? This is some ol' bitch move what we doing right now. I ain't never known you not to act on impulse." The man grilled Blaze.

Tired of the man's bitching, Blaze snatched the gun he had resting on his lap into his hand, cocked it, and put it to his friend's head.

The man simply looked straight ahead, not saying a word.

"Is this impulse enough for you, nigga?" Blaze yelled.

"Come on, man. Y'all niggas stop all that bitching. Y'all boys! What the fuck is you doing, Blaze?" the man in the back seat asked, trying to get Blaze to lower the gun.

In the meantime, Nate had come out of the Laundromat and hopped into the car while Blaze was threatening his friend with his gun.

Several minutes later, Blaze realized Nate had left. "Look what the fuck you did. You let that nigga get away!" Blaze yelled.

"I let him get away? You the muthafucka pulling your shit out like you gonna shoot me and shit. I told you a long time ago we shoulda just offed them niggas one at a time."

The man from the back seat yelled, "Come on, y'all! Damn!"

Before either of the men could react, they heard a shot, and Blaze's brain splattered all over the dashboard and his friend on the passenger side.

"Oh shit!"

Both men reached for their weapons.

"What the fuck?" the man in the back seat said. "Where they at?" He tried to look in the driver's side, side-view mirror while holding his gun ready to shoot.

The hearse had been equipped to conceal any possibilities of seeing inside. The van only had two windows, the driver's side and the passenger side, and the rear windows had been closed off for privacy. But, at that moment, it not only disabled the men from seeing their stalker, it was also a death trap for them.

"We gonna have to get the fuck outta here! Open the door!" the passenger said.

"Fuck no! As soon as we open that door, we could get twisted," the man in the back seat said. "Ay, just move Blaze and drive this muthafucka outta here."

"I ain't 'bout to touch that nigga," the passenger said. "Man, fuck this shit! I'm outta here!" He opened the door.

Just as the man in the back seat said, as soon as the passenger door was opened, bullets invaded the van, pierced the passenger's skin three times, leaving him slumped and leaking in the front seat.

Fear began to invade the man in the back seat. He knew he was already dead and couldn't even get a look at his killer before he died. Strangely enough, no one had come out of the Laundromat or walked down the street to witness the slaughter.

"Fuck it!" He'd rather take his own life. He placed his gun in his mouth and pulled the trigger.

Hearing the shot echo inside the van, the mystery man came walking out of the doorway of an apartment building in which he hid. He walked a block and a half back down to his Chevy Impala and pulled away from the curb.

Chapter Thirty-Nine

TRUST ISSUES

"What's up, Click?" Jasmine asked as she got into the front seat of Click's car while Star got in the back seat.

Click looked over at Jasmine and then rolled his eyes with a head nod back at Star.

Jasmine shrugged.

Click turned around to face Star. "Yo, Star, if you don't mind, I need to talk to Jazz alone," he said stone-faced, not feeling comfortable with her in the car. Just by the look in Star's eyes, he didn't trust her sitting behind him, not to mention the fact that during their last encounter he sodomized her.

Star sucked her teeth. "*¿Qué pasa, Jasmine?*"

"*Está bien, Star. Yo te llamaré cuando yo vuelvo.*" Jasmine told Star that she was fine and she'd call her when she got back.

"English! Why the fuck y'all speaking that shit? Get the fuck out of my car!"

"Calm down, Click. Ain't nobody saying nothing 'bout you," Jasmine told him.

"Then why you gotta say the shit in Spanish if y'all ain't talking about me?"

While Jasmine and Click were arguing, Star got out of the car. She wanted to spit in Click's face, but lucky for her she didn't. She slammed his door and pranced back into the apartment building.

"Bitch!" Click yelled.

"What is wrong with you?" Jasmine asked.

"I got a lot of shit on my mind and this bitch wanna play games. She gonna fuck around and catch a bullet," Click said as he pulled off from the curb.

"You must got a hell of a lot going on for you to just start blacking out, *papi*?"

"Man, you have no idea. We gotta find these niggas that tried to do Roy. I got niggas testing me and shit, fucking with my paper."

Click was racing through the streets, venting to Jasmine, no destination in mind.

From what Click had just said, Jasmine figured out that maybe Big Roy wasn't dead. She was sure she heard him say that they *tried* to do Roy.

"Click, you wanna slow down this car? You're scaring me."

"Oh, my bad, Jazz. I just got a lot on my mind. What did you want to talk to me about?" Click looked over at her and then back at the road.

"Well, after the way you blacked out, I don't even know if I want to even ask you."

"Naw, go 'head. You cool. What's up?"

"I was just gonna . . . um . . . ask you about what happened with Star?" Jasmine didn't want to ask him about Leroy after the way he'd behaved just moments ago. In fact, Jasmine didn't like the whole idea of it all, but she needed the money.

"Man, fuck that bitch! She sold herself short."

"Oh," was all Jasmine said. She could care less about what happened between them. "So do y'all at least know who tried to kill Leroy?"

"No, we don't, but I wanted to ask you if you'd heard anything on the streets?"

"Nah, I haven't heard anything like that."

"Listen, Jazz, I need you to do me a favor. Can you keep your ear to the streets for me? If you hear anything, let me know. I'ma throw you a bone for that."

Jasmine looked at him. She now realized that she could make money with Click too if she found out anything about who tried to kill Leroy. This would be the one deal she'd keep to herself.

"Sure, Click, I can do that for you. So how is Leroy?" she asked, reaching for some confirmation that he was still alive.

Click whipped his head around and looked at her sternly. He was looking at her so hard, she wanted him to pull over so she could get out and run.

"Who told you that Leroy ain't dead?" he asked, venom spilling from his lips.

"Nobody told me anything, Click. You said that some niggas *tried* to do Big Roy. I figured he wasn't dead from what you said."

Click continued his stare as much as he could, looking back and forth between her and the road. "Oh naw, Jazz, Big Roy is dead."

His answer didn't sit well with Jasmine. "Oh, OK. So when are y'all gonna have the funeral?"

"I don't know. I gotta see what Nate's gonna do," Click said, his thoughts wandering. Jasmine spoke as if she knew for a fact that Leroy wasn't dead, and then she tried to downplay it by saying Click implied that he wasn't dead.

"Jazz, you heard anything about a Spanish bitch out here doing muthafuckas?" he asked her, trying to get his mind right.

"Um . . . a Spanish *chica*? What do you mean?"

"I don't know. It was said that some crazy Spanish bitch might have had something to do with Big Roy getting murked. I was just asking."

A bell went off in Jasmine's head. Her gut instinct was telling her that Widow was the Spanish chick Click was referring to. Widow showed up all of a sudden, and then Click asked about a Spanish woman. Widow offered money for Leroy's whereabouts, like he was still alive. Jasmine knew at that moment that Leroy was still alive, and that they were probably hiding him out somewhere. She also figured that Widow and Leroy probably had some kinda beef, and were both out looking for each other. If she played her cards right, she could request enough money for the information she held for both parties, and then blow town.

Jasmine seemed to take offense. "Why she gotta be a crazy Spanish bitch?"

"I'm sayin' . . . you know y'all Spanish chicks are crazy. Just look at that bitch Star," he said, a slight smile on his face, trying to make light of the tense situation.

Jasmine sucked her teeth and rolled her eyes.

For a while, they both rode in silence, listening to the music playing over the speakers.

"There was this lady that came into the pizza parlor the other day," Jasmine said finally, looking out of the window while she spoke. She was afraid to give Click full eye contact, knowing he would see right through her lies.

"What about her? Was she Spanish? What did she say?"

"Calm down, Click. I don't know if this is the woman you are looking for. She approached me and Star, asking us all kinds of questions about Big Roy."

"Word? What kinda questions?"

"She wanted to know if we knew him. Then she asked, was he really dead and shit."

"So what y'all say?"

"Well, we couldn't say nothing, because we didn't know anything. I mean, everybody knows Big Roy got killed, and I thought it was strange that she would even ask that."

"What this bitch look like?"

"She was kinda tall, about my complexion, and she had really pretty, thick, curly hair. I mean, she's pretty and rolls with a big-ass Rottweiler in her car. She got a nice body, Click."

"Jazz, I ain't tryin'-a fuck the bitch. I want to know why she going around asking questions about Big Roy."

"I don't know, but like I said, we couldn't tell her anything. Oh, but she did give me her number in case we heard anything."

"Was she police?"

"I don't think so. She didn't show us any badge or nothing. She said her and Leroy had business and that's why she was tryin'-a find him."

"A'ight, Jazz, stay around, because I'ma get back to you, and I'ma need you to contact that bitch for me, a'ight?" Click looked over at her.

"Sure. Click, if you don't mind me asking, how much you gonna throw me if I can get you some information? I mean, a chick got bills to pay." Jasmine chuckled, trying to lighten the mood.

"I'll hit you off with five gees for the info, but if you set me up with this bitch where I can get close to her, I'ma throw you ten." Click looked at her to see how she would react.

Jasmine played it cool and just nodded. She knew she had to go home and plan it out right, so she could collect with both parties.

"A'ight, I'ma take you home. I got some moves I need to make."

"OK." Jasmine was already counting the money she would make.

Click suddenly pulled over to the curb and jumped out of the car. Jasmine didn't know what was going on. She watched him as he walked up on a crowded corner where several men stood.

When Click got to the corner, a few of the men turned to greet him, but he walked right by them and approached a dude who was leaning against the side of the building. The man saw Click coming and stood as if he was about to say something to him, but before the man could react, Click removed his weapon, placed it to the man's head, and pulled the trigger. The man's body dropped to the ground, and the inside of his head was now exposed for everyone to see.

The loud pop caused everyone to take cover.

Click simply turned on his heels and walked away from the corner like he hadn't just shot a man's brains out of his head.

Jasmine had seen worse, but watching that did something to her. She was shaking, and the events at the warehouse replayed in her mind. She had managed to push that day to the back of her mind and drown it with drinking, but now her fears surfaced again.

Jasmine's stomach began to turn, and she felt like hurling.

The menacing look on Click's face was enough to make a gay man go straight. He hopped back into the car and sped off down the street.

Jasmine covered her face, not wanting anyone from the corner to see her in the car and connect her with the murder.

After traveling for several minutes, Click looked over at Jasmine and noticed her uneasiness. "My bad, Jazz, but I been looking for that nigga. He and his boys robbed two of my spots, and they thought everything was everything. But niggas need to remember who the fuck I am."

Jasmine didn't respond. She continued to sit there praying he would hurry up and take her home.

"You know Mike and them, right?"

She nodded.

"Well, that was that nigga Tone that be with them. He was talking real slick about the shit, so you know me—I do what I do."

Jasmine was contemplating whether she should get involved with what they had going on with Black Widow and Big Roy, but it was already too late. She'd already told Click that she could contact the woman, and he wouldn't let things go now.

Chapter Forty

The Next Day

Nate was on fire. He had taken a trip up to the hospital and almost lost his mind after he saw Leroy lying there missing both his legs from the knee down. It hurt his heart to see that. It took Justine almost a half hour to calm him down and convince him he'd made the right decision. That, on top of the attempted murder on him and TJ, was enough to send him on a killing spree.

Nate and TJ walked into Nate's house after making rounds, and TJ sat down on the sofa. Nate walked around the living room in circles, trying to calm down. He had been trying to get in touch with Click, who seemed to be missing in action.

TJ picked up the remote for the television and began to flip channels. The news stated that two bodies were found lying in the middle of the street. Then the report went on to say that another body of a Tone Lewis was found in front of a liquor store with a gunshot wound to the head. Witnesses said a man walked up to him and shot him in the head, but no one had yet come forward to identify the gunman.

Nate stood there and watched the news, his hand resting on top of his head. After hearing Tone's name, it clicked with him about who the guy was that had held the gun to his head. He remembered the trio from back in the day—Lex, Mike, and Tone. But he knew he didn't kill Mike. If Lex was so adamant about him killing Mike, then there had to have been something going on that would suggest that Leroy's camp had something to do with Mike's death.

Nate placed a call on his cell phone and got no response. He was calling Click again, because the murder had Click written all over it. He waited for a few moments and called him back again.

"What up?" Click asked, finally answering.

"Yo, man, please tell me you ain't have shit to do with them niggas Mike, Lex, and Tone?"

"Why? What's up?"

"Yo, them niggas rolled up on us with burners out. They pulled me and TJ out of the car and put the steel to my head!"

"So what's up? You a'ight?"

Click was a little too calm for Nate's state of mind.

"Yeah, I'm good. Where you at?"

"I'm local."

"Yeah? Well, come through," Nate said, concealing his anger at Click.

"A'ight, I'll be there as soon as I handle some business." Click hung up. He didn't need to hear any more from Nate. He already knew what Nate wanted, but he didn't have the time. He had to go put some other cats in the ground for fucking with his paper.

"Yo, Nate, why don't you just sit down?" TJ finally asked after watching Nate walk around the townhouse several times. It was making him dizzy.

"I'm good," was all Nate said.

Before Nate could clear the screen on his phone, it began to vibrate again. He wanted to take the phone and slam it against the wall. It was irritating him that he was left in charge of everything, and Click was out there bringing heat to the organization.

He answered the call. It was the hospital.

A scared look passed over Nate's face, and TJ noticed it. He walked over to Nate and stood in front of him. Nate wasn't saying a word. Whoever was on the other end of the phone did all the talking.

"Let's go!" Nate yelled as soon as he hung up the phone, and they both bolted for the door.

Nate, TJ, Click, and Nyeem all ran out of the elevator and into the hospital hallway. The call that came on Nate's cell was from Nurse Justine. She told Nate that Leroy's condition was worsening and that hospice had been called in.

Nate and TJ had rushed to go scoop up Nyeem, and had called Click to inform him to meet them at the hospital. They'd all pulled up at the same time and were now speed-walking down the hallway.

Leroy's guards greeted them as they approached, but Nate brushed past them and headed into the hospital room, totally ignoring them. The rest followed in behind him.

Nurse Justine was standing by Leroy's bed with the hospice nurse.

Nate dismissed the other guard without opening his mouth, using hand gestures.

For the first time since Leroy had been in the hospital, Nurse Justine wasn't smiling. In fact, she'd been crying. She turned and greeted them. "I'll leave you to spend time with your father," she told Nate, squeezing his hand.

Nate's heart dropped when he saw the look in Nurse Justine's eyes.

Dr. Clinton walked in holding a chart in his hand. "How you

doing, son?" He extended his hand to Nate for a shake and nodded at the other people in the room. "I know the last time we spoke, I told you your father was stable, but sometimes things can change quickly. He has a weak heart, which also causes problems. His body functions are starting to fail, and there really is nothing else we can do for him. I'm sorry." Dr. Clinton placed his hand on Nate's shoulder. "Take as much time as you need. There is no limit to your visit." Dr. Clinton walked out of the room, followed by the hospice nurse.

They all gathered around Leroy's bed. It seemed he had deteriorated in just a matter of hours since TJ had last seen him. He couldn't look at Leroy anymore.

Click had walked away. This was the first time he had seen Leroy after he got shot. He walked over to a corner and punched the wall.

Nyeem stood there staring down at his natural grandfather, who had been hooked back up to the tubes to help him breathe again. He reached for Leroy's shriveled hand. It felt like a claw between Nyeem's fingers. He looked up at his grandfather and could see he had aged considerably. His hair had fallen out in spots.

"You not gonna miss my birthday, are you, Grandpop?" Nyeem asked softly.

Nate, who was sitting in the chair by the bed, lifted his head from his hands when he heard Nyeem talking.

Everyone else looked at Nyeem.

Click stood in the corner leaning against the wall, one foot resting against the wall, still stewing in his anger.

"You gonna at least stay for my birthday?" Nyeem asked.

Leroy lay there with his eyes shut while the machine pushed air into his body, making his chest and stomach rise each time.

"Grandpop, guess what? I saw my mother and father." Nyeem spoke softly and gently.

Nate sat back in the chair and looked at Nyeem. He was amazed at how calm Nyeem was. Listening to him talk to Leroy brought tears to his eyes. He felt bad for Nyeem. This was a kid who'd lost his parents when he was an infant. He'd only just found out about his biological grandfather, and now he was going to lose him too.

"They was a good-looking couple. My mom was so pretty. I do look like my dad. You did a good job, Grandpop." Nyeem smiled slightly as he spoke. "I know you gotta go see my mother and father. Please tell them that I love them so much and they will always be with me. I will always keep their picture with me." His voice began to crack.

TJ looked away. He felt Nyeem's pain, and it reminded him of his mother, Beverly. He wanted to break down and cry right there while sitting on the windowsill, but he couldn't. What he wanted more than anything was to kill the sons of bitches who'd done this to Leroy.

By now tears were already streaming down Nate's face. Although he didn't make a sound, the evidence was clear that he was saddened by the turn of events.

"I get it now, Grandpop," Nyeem said. "I understand what you been trying to tell me all these years. I remember when you told me about my parents and how much in love they were with each other. You told me they loved each other more than any couple in a lifetime, although they only had a small amount of time with each other. You told me that they made me out of true love, and that's why I was so special to everyone. I think you was trying to tell me then that you were my grandfather. I listened to all the things you told me growing up. Grandpop, I'm OK with it. I know you loved me. I know you made mistakes, and it's OK, because I don't want you to have pain anymore. Tell my parents I love them when you see them."

Tears streamed down Nyeem's face as well as everyone else's in the room, except Click's. He was so mad, his face turned red.

The heart monitor's faithful beeping stopped suddenly, and a constant long beep sounded off. It was loud and irritating.

Nurse Justine and two more nurses came running into the room. The security guards also came into the room.

Nyeem began to cry harder, and Nate put his head in his hands and cried silently.

TJ still sat in the windowsill, tears streaming down his face.

"I can't take this shit!" Click yelled, one tear running down his face. He bolted from the room and left the hospital.

The nurse began to check the equipment, and Dr. Clinton walked in to try to revive Leroy.

"Let him go," Nate said, speaking barely above a whisper.

They kept working.

"Let him go, I said! It's time for him. He will suffer no more." Nate stood, a menacing expression on his face. "Let's go," he said, and walked out of the room.

Dr. Clinton said, "Nate, we need to discuss the handling of Mr. Jones's body."

But Nate kept walking. The security men followed him out of the room, and so did TJ.

Before TJ walked out, he turned to Nyeem. "Come on, man," he said, his voice quiet.

Nurse Justine grabbed Nyeem and was holding him while he cried. She too cried a few tears for the patient she had come to care about. "I want you to call me." She shoved a piece of paper with her number scribbled on it. "You make sure you call me, you hear me?"

"Yes, ma'am," Nyeem said, continuing to cry.

"Go with your family. I will take care of your grandfather." She shooed him.

Nyeem walked out of the hospital room with his head held low and TJ's arm draped over his shoulder.

Jasmine, Star, and Black Widow sat in the same pizza parlor where they'd first met.

"So what did he say?" Valencia asked.

"I don't think he's dead, but he wouldn't tell me much." Jasmine looked out the window at the big dog sitting in the front seat of Valencia's car. He had his eyes trained on them as they sat by the window.

"I need to get in touch with this Click. And do you know Nate?" Valencia asked.

"Yes," Jasmine answered.

Star sat there stuffing her face with pizza, but Jasmine didn't have an appetite.

"Do you know where I can find him?"

"No, but I'm sure if you get a hold of Click, Nate will come for him," Jasmine said.

"Good. I need you to have him meet me here." She handed Jasmine a piece of paper with an address on it.

"I'll do my best." Jasmine felt uncomfortable around Valencia. Although she wanted the money, she didn't like dealing with her. She seemed evil, and the more she talked to her, the less she trusted her.

"When will we get the rest of the loot?" Star asked, her mouth full of food, making her sound funny.

"When I talk to this Click guy."

"OK, so let's make it happen. Jazz, call him now." Star handed her the prepaid cell phone she had.

Valencia looked at Jasmine while Star held the phone out to her.

Jasmine could have punched the shit out of Star for throwing her under the bus in front of Valencia. She took the phone and dialed his number, which was programmed into the phone. Click didn't answer, so she hung up. "He didn't answer." She handed the phone back to Star.

"Keep calling him, and call me when you give him the instructions." Valencia stood.

"Oh, Black Widow, I found out the house where he keeps his drugs. Maybe you can find him there too," Star said.

Jasmine kicked her under the table.

"Oww! Why you do that?"

Valencia looked at Jasmine with unsure eyes, but Jasmine never looked at her.

Valencia asked Star, "What's the address?" looking at Jasmine, burning a hole in the side of her face from her intense stare.

Star couldn't give her an accurate address, but she did give her good directions.

Once Jasmine went on her way, and Star went on hers, Jasmine stopped by a pay phone to call Click. She knew Click wouldn't answer the call when she'd called him from the pizza parlor, because he would recognize the number as Star's number, but when she called him from the pay phone, he picked right up.

"What's up?" he asked, not sounding like himself.

"Click?" Jasmine asked, not sure she'd dialed the right number.

"Yeah."

"Are you OK, *papi*?"

Click couldn't tell Jasmine that Leroy had died an hour ago. "Yeah, I'll be a'ight. I just got a lot of shit going on. What's up?"

"I got some information for you on the Spanish chick."

"Word? Do you have something real to tell me?"

"Yeah, Click, I do, but I'm gonna need the money before you do what I'm about to tell you to do."

"Why?"

"Because this bitch ain't no joke. I can tell. She travels with a mean-ass Rottweiler and she looks like she's holding. She's always wearing some type of jacket, as hot as it is out here, so that makes me think she hiding something."

"Oh, yeah? Ain't no bitch got nothing on me. Tell me what I need to know to put this bitch in the ground."

Hearing him speak the way he did sent a chill up Jasmine's spine. "She wants you to meet her at this spot tomorrow night." Jasmine read the address off to him.

"What time is she gonna be there?"

"I don't know what time she gonna be there, but she told me to tell you to be there at eleven. Oh yeah, she asked about Nate."

"Who is this bitch? How she know about us?"

"Her name is Black Widow."

"Black Widow, Black Widow." Click repeated the name, trying to see if he'd heard it before, but he didn't know anyone in the game that went by that name.

"I don't know where she came from, Click, but just be careful. She might not be alone."

"This my hood. I ain't worried about a bitch that don't even live here. You done good, Jazz, you done real good. I'ma give you a twenty spot for this. You just don't know how good this is for us. Good looking out."

"Twenty? Like in twenty thousand?"

At that point Jasmine no longer cared about the money Valencia was offering her and Star. She wanted the money Click was gonna give her, so she could leave town. She trusted Click more than she trusted Valencia.

"Yup."

"Oh, Click, *gracías*, *papi*! When can I come get it?"

"I'll let you know when I'ma be through."

"OK, I'm gonna go home."

"A'ight."

Jasmine hung up the pay phone and walked up the street. She didn't notice the man sitting on a milk crate drinking a beer. He had since walked up to her and took a seat without her having a clue that he was there.

The man walked over to the pay phone as soon as she walked away. He dialed the number and waited for the person to answer. "Yeah, I got some information for you," he said, watching Jasmine walk up the street.

Meanwhile, the mystery man sat in his car and listened to the informant spill all the juicy details he'd just heard Jasmine tell Click.

Chapter Forty-One

HELP

"Black Widow!" a short but handsome Spanish man called out, teasing Valencia as she walked into the unopened nightclub.

It was the afternoon hours and the club's opening was at nine at night. This was one of the businesses her father owned. Her older cousin John had been running it since his father died.

Valencia smiled at her cousin, and they gave each other a kiss on the cheeks before she sat down at the bar.

John was standing behind the bar, going over some paperwork. "*¿Qué le trae aquí?*" he asked.

"I come to you because I may need your help." She looked at him seriously.

"Oh." He stopped looking through the papers and looked up at her. "What is it?"

Valencia knew she had to find the right words and the best way to tell John, because he was a lunatic. John had once been the enforcer for their family. He was heartless and had no remorse. He was like the machine from the movie *Terminator*. He wouldn't stop until his victim ceased to exist. Most people underestimated his ability and strength because of his small size, but John delivered each and every time. Although those days of enforcement were now few and far between, John was still a beast, and would love the thrill of killing to run through his veins again.

Truth be told, Valencia realized she was gonna need some help. There were too many people involved that would get in the way of her getting to Leroy, not to mention, she had to manage Star and Jasmine as well.

Seeing the serious expression on his cousin's face, and knowing how vicious she could be, John got serious. "Anything. What do you need?" He leaned forward, eager to hear what she had to say.

"I thought I could handle things myself." Valencia stopped as one of the men who worked there walked over to her and handed her the keys to her car, which he had parked while she came inside. "But this organization is well established." She placed her keys on the bar. "They have a large army, and I can't do it alone. It's my poppa's dying wish, and I have to complete it before he dies."

John had never seen Black Widow look this stressed. Now even more concerned, he was eager to know what she needed. He yelled for her to stop procrastinating and get to the point.

Valencia looked into her cousin's eyes. "I need Leroy Jones dead!"

John felt heat move from his feet up through his body as the name Leroy Jones echoed in his head. "No need to ask, I would be happy to cut the heart out of that piece of shit!" John exclaimed.

He and Valencia talked for more than an hour on getting an army together to go over to New Jersey and wipe the whole crew out.

John did express that Valencia had gone about it all wrong from the beginning. "You no can be seen," he said, pointing at her. "You must always be invisible. You go to the ghetto driving your Mercedes?"

She nodded yes.

"*Tst! Tst!* Widow, you will stick out like a sore thumb riding around in such an expensive car. Those *negras* will notice you and finish you," he growled at her. "Leave it up to me and they will be a memory to their *madres*!"

TJ and Nyeem walked into Nate's house and took a seat. Nate was outside talking with the security men, who had all met and gathered out in the parking lot. He was going over specific instructions with them.

TJ looked at Nyeem, who seemed to have calmed down since leaving the hospital. "You a'ight, man?" he asked.

"Yeah, I'm OK. I'm just glad I was there when he took his last breath. I'm glad I wasn't at camp when all this happened."

"You still going to camp?"

"Yeah, I'm gonna go. I feel like my father, mother, and my grandfather never gave up, so why should I? It's in our blood to be fighters and never to give up. They told me how my mother was a crackhead, and she overcame that."

"Yeah, I know. Your mother was so cool. She stayed with us for a little while. Your mother and my mother died together, man. They was best friends. That's why I'm so close to you. I feel like you are my real brother, because my mother and your mother was close. That's why I know how you feel, Ny."

Nyeem chuckled.

"What you laughing at?" TJ asked.

"My peoples were real gangstas. They are legends, *T*. I get it now." He continued to smile. "My moms went to prison for orchestrating one of the biggest robberies in Jersey, man." His eyes lit up. "And my pops and my grandpops had the city of Newark on lock," he said, a wide grin on his face.

"Yeah, that's what they say." TJ half-smiled. "But that was then, and this is now. Shit ain't like that no more, so keep your head in them books and play ball. Fuck all that other shit."

"I know, big brother. They did enough for me not to want to do it. Living that lifestyle gives you a short lifespan."

"That's what's up. So you got a birthday coming up," TJ said, changing the subject.

Nyeem smiled, but then his smile quickly disappeared.

"It's a'ight, Ny," TJ said, immediately understanding Nyeem's thoughts. "Big Roy is in a better place, man. Just think, he can say what's up to both our parents."

The two gave each other an understanding look and continued to sit there, each sorting out their own thoughts.

Nate walked into the house to see the two of them sitting there quietly. TJ noticed that Nate had aged a good five years since Leroy's death.

Nate plopped down on one of the single chairs and sighed loudly. "Nyeem, are you up for going to Doc's funeral tomorrow?" he asked.

Nyeem had forgotten all about the funeral, with all that was going on. "Yeah," he said, sounding unconvincing.

"You don't have to go, Nyeem, if you can't handle it."

"No, he was my boy and my brother. I gotta go pay my respects."

"I feel you. I'ma be there with you, and we gonna be deep in security. I know you said he didn't bang, but he knew them muthafuckas, and they will show up to his funeral. I just want to make sure we're protected."

"I know," Nyeem said solemnly. "I'll be in my room," he said sadly before he walked off.

TJ's cell phone began to ring. It was Dasia. "Shit! I forgot to call her back."

"Handle your business," Nate said.

TJ answered the phone and then walked off into the spare room, closing the door behind him.

Nate continued to sit in the living room, massaging his temples. The doorbell rang. "Come in!" he yelled.

The door opened, and Click walked in.

"You a'ight?" Nate asked, genuinely concerned about the way Click had behaved at the hospital. He knew he was deeply hurt by Leroy's death.

"I'll be a'ight, but I got some shit for you," Click said, sitting down on the sofa.

"What's up?" Nate knew his friend must've found out who tried to kill Leroy, if he was coming to him now.

"It is a bitch that did Roy."

"Word?" Nate raised his brows. "So Roy was right."

"Yeah. And guess who told me?"

"Who?"

"Jasmine."

"Oh, the Spanish chick who used to run with Nettie? The one I told you to link up with?"

"Yeah. Peep this shit out—I think the bitch is working for her."

Nate frowned. "What? Working for who?"

"Some bitch that calls herself Black Widow."

"Black Widow, Black Widow." Nate repeated the name the same way Click did when he'd first heard it. He frowned, trying to remember if he knew anyone who went by that name, but he also came up with nothing.

"Man, I don't trust no bitch," Click said, "especially when both them bitches is Spanish. Plus, Jasmine run with this other shady

Spanish bitch named Star. Naw, man, all them bitches riding together." Click was convinced.

"How you figure?"

"Yo, man, I told this chick if she can find out anything about this Spanish bitch, I would hit her off. This bitch all of a sudden remembers talking to the Spanish chick now. So I don't say nothing. I let it ride. Then, all of a sudden she calls me quick as hell with all this new information."

"I'm hearing you. Continue," Nate said, deep in thought.

"So I said 'OK, so what's up,' and Jazz tells me this bitch wanna meet me at eleven o'clock tomorrow night. Then she says the bitch asked about you. I'm thinking, 'What the fuck did Roy have to do with this bitch?' So right after that she want to know when I'ma give her the loot."

"Yeah, dig it." Nate chuckled, shaking his head, seeing exactly where Click was coming from. His face turned serious. "They shut the security company down."

"What?"

"The cops shut my shit down because Andy and Dave got murked on the job, and I think it was the Spanish bitch that did it."

"Nigga, is you serious?" Click jumped up out of the chair and shouted.

"Yeah man, dead ass, and I never told anybody, but I'm almost positive it was the same bitch that did old Clarence down at the store. I think it's that Black Widow bitch."

"Why you ain't tell me that shit? See, that's the type of shit I'm talking about, you keep all that shit to yourself and we supposed to be a team!" Click beat his chest.

"Yo, man chill. I know how you get down and I ain't want you to fuck nothing up by doing something stupid to bring the heat on us."

"So that's what you think? Nigga, I bring the fucking heat so muthafuckas know! Nigga, that's what I do! I gets shit done!"

"I know, Click. Calm the fuck down. We gonna put that bitch in the ground," Nate stated.

"It's on, nigga. We 'bout to blow up that Black Widow bitch and her crew!" Click was amped. "And you know what? Jazz gonna say be careful because Black Widow look like she rolling heavy. Man, fuck that bitch! All of them!" Click swung at the air with his fist.

By then TJ had walked into the living room and was listening to the conversation.

Nate looked up and saw him standing there.

"Tell me it ain't a bitch who killed Roy." TJ was unsure of what he'd heard.

"Yup, a bitch." Click, too fired up to sit down, was walking in circles.

"Damn! Déjà vu all over again. Reminds me of Nettie," TJ said, sitting down.

"Word! See that's why I don't trust a bitch who fucked around with that crazy bitch Nettie!" Click shouted.

"Well, nigga, we gotta saddle up and handle business," Nate said calmly.

"That's my man!" Click slapped Nate's hand hard, giving him dap.

"Yo, fellas, I gotta bounce," TJ said.

"Why, man? You need to be down to buck off on these bitches!" Click said.

"I just started my new job, and really need to get to work. My girl is tripping out. She thinking I'm up here fucking an old girl or something." TJ shook his head, not quite believing Dasia was acting the way she was.

"Man, fuck that! These bitches think they rule the fucking world!"

"Naw, Click, let him go handle his business. He got a good career ahead of him. You go 'head, man. We got this," Nate said.

"A'ight, man, but you know I would have your back if I didn't have this new job," TJ told him sincerely.

"Oh, no doubt, baby boy, but you do what you gotta do. That's more important." Nate stood and leaned over to shake TJ's hand.

"A'ight, I'ma leave out tomorrow after Doc's funeral."

Chapter Forty-Two

THE FUNERAL

The church was filled to capacity, mostly with teens. Nate had spared no expense on Doc's funeral. Doc's real name was Walter Bolden, but everyone knew him as "the Doctor," or Doc. He fancied himself the doctor of basketball, like the legendary Dr. J. He was buried with a donated team jersey from his school team and his basketball, which was autographed by his team.

As everyone filed out of the church preparing to follow the limo to the cemetery, Nyeem and the other pallbearers brought the casket out to the hearse. Once the coffin was placed inside the hearse, Nyeem walked over to where Alicia was standing with her friends. She embraced him tightly.

Alicia wasn't only saddened by Doc's death, but she was also sad because Nyeem was leaving to go to camp. Although they talked on the phone frequently, they hadn't had the chance to spend much time with each other because of what had been going on. They spoke openly with each other about their feelings, and Alicia wanted to have sex with Nyeem in the worst way before he left for camp.

"You still coming by my house tonight, right?" she asked.

"I don't know." He kissed her on the forehead. "I'll see if I can get away. I'll call you later."

Nyeem had to leave because Nate had waved for him to come on. Security surrounded them like they were the family of the president.

Once in the security-driven trucks with tinted windows, Nate told Nyeem, "After we leave the graveyard, I gotta go take care of some business, and TJ gonna go with me because he gotta bounce in the morning, so I want you to stay in the house."

"A'ight," Nyeem said, still thinking about how his friend looked lying in the coffin.

"You gonna be a'ight?" TJ asked.

Nyeem nodded.

"I can stay until Nate gets back, if you want," TJ offered.

"Naw, I'm good."

"I'ma leave some people outside to look out for you," Nate said.

"You gonna go do the bitch that killed my grandfather?" Nyeem asked without raising his head.

Nate looked at him, shocked. "How you know?"

"I heard y'all talking. You gonna go do it or what?" Nyeem looked up at Nate.

TJ saw the same look in Nyeem's eyes that he had in his when he found out Nettie had killed his mother and they were going to let him kill Nettie for revenge. "Naw, Ny, don't even think about it," TJ said, shaking his head from side to side.

Nate looked at the two of them, not understanding what was taking place. "What?"

"Nyeem? You hear me?"

Nyeem looked at TJ. "Yeah, I hear you."

TJ held Nyeem's stare, trying to ensure the boy understood him.

"What?" Nate asked more loudly this time.

"Nothing," TJ said simply and looked out the window.

Nate was too exhausted to even bother pushing the issue. He had other things on his mind, like getting with the Black Widow chick.

Chapter Forty-Three

DESPERATE

The next day Nate left the house and once again Nyeem had to stay in. He felt trapped in his own home, and it was starting to get the best of him.

Nyeem placed a call to Nate because he wanted to go see Alicia like he'd promised her the day before but wasn't able to get out of the tight grasp Nate had on him. Nate was adamant about him not leaving the house. Nyeem was frustrated and didn't want to sit alone at home anymore. He had talked on the phone with Alicia for two hours. He wanted to see her.

TJ had left hours ago, and Nyeem had to admit, he missed his godbrother already. He wished he could have him around all the time.

Nyeem dialed TJ from his cell phone and spoke to him for a few minutes, expressing his frustration with Nate not letting him leave the house.

"Ny, they got a lot of shit going on. They about to get into a war with some other cats. Nate just wants to ensure your safety. You can't knock him for that."

"TJ, it ain't like I'm gonna be walking the streets. I'ma be at my girl's house. We gonna be in the house. Why can't one of the guards take me over there, wait for me, and bring me right back?"

"Because it ain't that simple. What if somebody following y'all and some shit pop off? If anything happened to you, Nyeem, there won't be no stopping Nate until he's dead, because he ain't gonna go to jail for nobody. And you already know that nigga will kill every muthafucka in Newark. I think you should stay put."

Nyeem sat there in silence. He was pissed. "How 'bout this then?"

"What?"

"How 'bout I have one of the guards pick up Alicia and bring her here? That way we ain't in the hood and we got them protecting us, right?"

"Well, I don't see a problem with that," TJ said after thinking about the suggestion for a minute.

Nyeem suddenly sounded happy. "So I can do that, right?"

"Oh, naw, Nyeem, you ain't 'bout to put me in that shit. Call Nate and pitch it to him like you did me. Maybe he'll go for it."

"A'ight," Nyeem said, sounding defeated.

"A'ight, man, call me if you need anything else."

After Nyeem hung up the phone with TJ, he took a deep breath and dialed Nate's cell again. This time Nate didn't answer. He got up from his bed and went to the front door. He opened the door, and the guard sitting on the porch stood.

"What's up, baby boy?" His deep voice boomed.

"My uncle said that my girlfriend can come over," Nyeem lied, "but one of y'all gotta go get her."

The big man looked unsure. "Nate ain't call me and tell me that."

"Well, I just got off the phone with him. They busy running niggas down, so he told me he would call me later," Nyeem lied.

The big man looked at Nyeem to try to detect if he was telling a lie.

Finally, he agreed to go get Alicia.

Nyeem gave the man the address, and after the big man told the other guard he was leaving, he pulled off to go get her, and left the other guard in his car to watch the house. Nyeem quickly called Alicia and told her he was sending a car for her.

Click had just left the stash house, while the other crew members sat around bagging up what was left of his product. It wasn't much, and soon Click would be bone-dry. He hadn't had the time to get with the connect and start up his other blocks. But, truth be told, he didn't want to invest any more money in those blocks. He figured if he supplied the corners now, then they would just get robbed again.

The workers, including the crew members that weren't working, sat in the stash house smoking and drinking, enjoying their time off. Click jumped into his car and pulled off.

Valencia and John, along with three other men, drove up in front of Star's house in a white van disguised as a Cablevision van. The van was tricked out with a ladder and the whole nine. Valencia pulled out her cell phone and dialed Star's number.

"Hey, Widow," Star answered.

"Star," Valencia said. "*¿Estás a solas?*"

"*Sí*, I'm alone."

"Where's Jasmine?"

"I don't know. I haven't heard from her. You can just give me her money. I'll give it to her," Star said eagerly. But Star had no intention of giving Jasmine anything. She still felt like Jasmine was at fault for setting her up with Click when she knew he was gonna treat her like he did. If Jasmine was a real friend, she wouldn't have done that to her. "Do you have the money?"

"*¡Dios mio!* This *puta* just won't stop," Valencia said to John after placing her hand over the phone to block what she was saying. "OK, I'm sending my brother Jose over with the money. And thank you again, Star, for all your help."

"You're welcome, and thank you." Star hung up and waited. She had no idea Valencia was right downstairs in the van in front of her house.

Valencia and her men waited in the van for several moments before Jose got out of the van with one of Valencia's Rottweilers. Jose was a short, stocky man. He held the big dog by his thick spiked collar.

The dog, his mouth open and breathing hard, seemed to know what he was supposed to do. He led the way, pulling the stocky man along behind him.

There was a knock at Star's door, so she jumped up and ran to the door to see who it was. "Who is it?" she asked.

"It's Jose. Is Star there?" the man asked in a heavy accent.

Star flung open the door, and the Rottweiler immediately pounced on her at Jose's command. When the dog stood on his hind legs he stood over five feet easily. His weight knocked Star to the floor, and she began to scream.

Jose stepped inside the apartment and closed the door. The dog never barked. Instead, he proceeded to mangle Star's body, shredding her legs and arms, as she tried desperately to fight it off.

Jose commanded the dog to finish the job. "*¡Finito!*"

The dog became a robot after hearing that command. He let go of Star's leg and wrapped his huge mouth over her neck and bit down.

Star began to hit the dog in the head and kick her feet as she tried to take in air, but her windpipes were blocked. Her efforts to fight became less and less persistent, the longer the dog held her throat.

Finally she stopped moving, but the dog didn't let go. He was waiting for the command.

"Back, Monster!"

Monster instantly let go and backed away from Star's body.

"¡Siéntate!"

Monster sat down, and a faint growl escaped his lips. Blood lined his snout and mouth. He had tasted blood and wanted more.

Jose bent down and moved Star's head to the side. He could see the deep gashes of Monster's teeth marks in her neck as he tried to find a spot to check for a pulse. Wearing a surgical glove, he checked for a pulse. Star was definitely dead.

"Good boy!" Jose whistled faintly, and the dog instantly fell in on the side of him. He then opened the door with the gloved hand and peeked out into the hallway to make sure it was clear before leaving Star's apartment.

Chapter Forty-Four

GOING SOMEWHERE?

Click pulled up in front of the apartment building Jasmine lived in. He killed the engine and hopped out of the car. Before he walked up onto the sidewalk, he looked at his surroundings. Adjusting his gun in the holster, he stepped up onto the curb, walked up the front steps, and entered the hallway. After arriving at Jasmine's apartment, he knocked on her door. She looked through the peephole and opened the door.

"Hey, *papi*," Jasmine said, smiling when she saw him.

"What's good, Jazz?" he asked, stepping inside.

Click looked around the studio apartment and noticed it was half-empty. There were no pictures on the wall and very little decorations. This struck him as odd for a female's apartment. Then he looked to his left and saw a few boxes and two suitcases that looked to be packed with things.

Jasmine locked the door and walked up next to Click. "What happened? I thought you was coming by. I was waiting for you to come through the other day."

"I know. I had shit I had to do, but I'm here now."

"You want something to drink? I don't have any food or I would offer you something to eat."

"Naw, I'm good." Click looked at the small kitchen and also saw that it was bare.

"Sit down." She pointed to the loveseat in the middle of the room.

Click took a seat.

Jasmine sat in another chair adjacent to the sofa. She rested her elbows on her knees and leaned forward. "So what's up?"

"A lot of shit. So, Jazz, be straight-up with me. Where you know this chick from?" he asked, giving her a chance to come clean.

"Click, I don't know her. I told you she walked up on me and Star at the pizza parlor."

"Why y'all?" He leaned back into the loveseat.

"I don't know." She shrugged. "I thought that was strange too. I mean, at first I thought she was the police, but the way she was talking, I knew she wasn't."

Click continued to stare at Jasmine. "So tell me again why she looking for us."

"She said she had some unfinished business with Big Roy. I don't know why she looking for y'all. But, trust, I don't think it's to talk."

"Do you know where she from?"

"Nope." Jasmine shook her head. She was becoming uncomfortable with the way Click was questioning her about the same stuff she'd already told him the answers to the first time they'd talked about it. She had to stay patient and cooperate with him after witnessing how he'd shot Tone at point-blank range. She tried to look relaxed, but she was on pins and needles. Her stomach was churning something awful, bubbling and making noises as she sat there trying to keep her game face on.

"And you said she rolls by herself with a Rott?"

"That's all I've ever seen her with, but I don't trust her. I'm telling you, she got something up her sleeve," Jasmine said, ready to get out of there. Her plan was to go to the airport and book a flight to Puerto Rico. She didn't care how long she had to sit at the airport, just as long as she was away from the hood and all the drama she knew was gonna build up to something ugly. After waiting so long for him to bring her money, she didn't want to waste another minute.

"Going somewhere?"

"Um . . . no. Why?" Jasmine tried to play it off. She hoped it didn't look too suspicious that she had cleaned her apartment and packed the things she wanted to take with her. She didn't have much there in the first place, and what she didn't want to take with her, she had given to her neighbors.

"I see you got your shit packed over there." He pointed to the boxes and suitcases.

"Well, the boxes are, er, going to the Salvation Army, and . . . um . . . I-I'm thinking about going to visit with my family in New York. I haven't seen my sister and my mother in a while."

Click reached in his pocket and pulled out a stack of bills wrapped with a rubber band. He tossed it over to Jasmine, who caught it in mid-air. She thumbed through the money and then got up to go put it in her purse that was sitting on top of one of the suitcases.

When she turned back around, Click was standing right behind her holding a gun in her face. She never even heard him get off the sofa and follow her over to the suitcases.

"*¡Dios mio!* Click, what are you doing?"

"You know what time it is," he said, an evil expression on his face.

Jasmine began to cry. "Why are you doing this?"

"Come on, Jazz, you should know me by now. You of all people should know not to fuck with me."

"But I didn't do anything."

"Bullshit, Jazz. You knew too much after I told you I was gonna hit you off. Before I said I was gonna give you something, you told me you didn't know shit. What the fuck you take me for?" he asked through gritted teeth. "Do I look like a punk to you?"

"No! I didn't take you for anything, Click. Please don't do this. I swear on my mother!" Jasmine made a cross over her chest and kissed her fingers and held her hand up to the sky. "I swear to you, I'm not lying to you! I don't know her!" Now the tears flowed like a river.

Without remorse Click pulled the trigger, popping her straight in the forehead, and Jasmine fell back hard to the floor from the force of the bullet. Click didn't bother to pump any more bullets in her. He liked Jasmine, but was disappointed in her. In his own sick way, he believed he was displaying sympathy for her by not emptying his clip in her already dead body. He reached over into her purse and removed the stack of bills he had given her then calmly walked out of the door.

Less than five minutes after Click pulled away from Jasmine's, Valencia and her boys pulled up in front of her house. Valencia couldn't call Jasmine like she did with Star, because Jasmine didn't have a phone, so she just took her chances that Jasmine was home. She didn't know where Jasmine lived at first, so she had her men do a little research to find out. So she opted to go home to see her father and come back another day to pay Jasmine a visit.

Valencia looked into the back seat of the van at Jose. He knew from her look alone what he had to do. They looked around to make sure the coast was clear, and then Jose jumped out of the van with Monster's brother, Beast. Beast was equally as large and just as vicious as Monster. Beast led the way into Jasmine's apartment building.

Jose knocked on the door, but he got no answer. He knocked again and waited.

Beast began to growl as he sniffed around the bottom of the door.

"What's wrong, boy?" Jose whispered.

Jose tried to turn the knob on the door, and it opened. Beast was ready to bust through the door, but Jose held him back. *"Suave."* He told Beast to be easy.

The dog sat down but still kept his focus on the door.

Jose eased open the door and then let go of Beast.

"¡Matanza!" He told Beast to kill.

Beast bolted into the apartment, and Jose closed the door behind him. He could hear Beast growling, but strangely, he didn't hear any screams coming from Jasmine.

Jose removed his gun and crept into the apartment. When he looked to his right, he could see that Beast had Jasmine on the floor with his mouth wrapped around her neck, choking her. But Jasmine wasn't fighting back.

Jose walked over to Beast, looked down at Jasmine, and saw the bullet hole in the middle of her forehead. "Down!" he told Beast, who let go of Jasmine's neck, backed up, and sat down, still growling.

"¡Ven acá!" He told the dog it was time to leave.

Once back in the van, Valencia saw the blood around Beast's mouth and snout, and a smile spread across her lips.

"The *puta* was already dead," Jose told her after he shut the door to the van.

"¿Qué?" Valencia was confused.

"Yeah, someone beat us to her."

Valencia looked over at John, and he simply started the van and pulled away from the curb.

About ten minutes later, they pulled up on the street in front of Click's stash house, which was located in a run-down neighborhood where very few people lived.

Chapter Forty-Five

SQUATTING

Later

Nate and Click met up with the rest of the crew, Leroy's security men, and the security men who worked for Nate's company. They were at Leroy's house preparing for war. Submachine guns, semi–automatics, and handguns were all being checked for readiness. Once everyone was locked and loaded, Nate stood to speak.

"Yo, listen up. Everybody already knows what they gotta do. We gonna roll over to the spot now and set up. That bitch said she wanna meet at eleven tonight. Well, when she calls herself coming through there early, we gonna light up that ass!"

Everybody mumbled and began to talk amongst themselves, getting hyped.

"A'ight, let's roll out!" Nate yelled.

Everyone rode in a hooptie to avoid being noticed. Three men rode in each car, with two in the front seat, and the third man crouched down in the back seat. Each driver knew to drive the speed limit and sit upright. No music was to be played in the car, because everyone needed to stay focused.

Nate, Click, and Ameen rode together.

Once everyone was in their cars, the caravan took off in different directions.

Valencia wanted Click to meet her in Port Newark because she figured it would be easy for her to spot anyone coming in, but Nate and his crew were smarter than that, and they'd be squatting in the port long before Valencia was scheduled to arrive. Each and every nook and cranny was covered. They were set. All they had to do now was wait, but the wait was gonna be a long one. It was only seven thirty.

Back on the stash house block, both vans sat and waited. One of the young boys inside the stash house stepped out onto the porch. He talked on his cell phone, and once he was done, he walked back into the building.

"Do you think that was him, Widow?" John asked.

"No." Valencia was going by the description she got from Jasmine and Star on how Nate and Click looked.

Two heavily tinted, navy blue Yukon Denalis drove down the street slowly, full of men John had summoned to come help with killing Leroy and his crew.

Meanwhile, at the hospital, Nurse Justine was standing in the empty room Leroy had died in. They hadn't put another patient in the room yet.

She couldn't understand why his death was weighing heavy on her heart. There was something about Leroy that took over her soul. Not to mention the fact, that she just seemed so close to Nate although they had spent minimal time together. She sat in the chair that she and Nate had always used when in the room with Leroy. She looked over at the bare bed and envisioned him lying there resting. Tears began to roll down her face. She felt like she'd lost a family member.

Nurse Justine lost her husband of forty years to cancer and had never remarried. She felt a certain type of closeness with Leroy, and now she felt empty again.

The door to the hospital room opened, and in walked the stranger who had come to the hospital the day Leroy was shot. Nurse Justine recognized him, since he'd been coming to the hospital every night since Leroy had come there.

He would get Nurse Justine to send the guards on different type of errands for her, so he could sneak in and visit with Leroy for a few minutes, before quietly slipping out of the hospital room unnoticed.

"How are you today?" Nurse Justine stood to her feet. She turned her back to the man and wiped the tears from her face. She began to continue doing her chores as if nothing was bothering her.

"I wanted to stop by and thank you for the way you took extra special care of Roy," he told her solemnly.

"It was no trouble. I was just doing my job."

"I know, but I also know you went the extra mile." He walked over to the window and looked out of it.

"Well, he was special in a way." Nurse Justine, in deep thought, stopped and stared at the wall.

"Yeah, I can definitely say he was special. He did something for me that I never thought he would. We hated each other, but he was the bigger man and did what he did for me willingly," the man said.

"Somehow, I knew he was that type of a person," she said.

"Yeah." He walked over to her and rubbed her shoulder. "Thank you again."

"Was he family to you?" she asked looking up at him from where she sat.

"No not at all. It's a long story," the stranger said looking over at the bed where Leroy once laid.

"I really would like to know something about him. All I've heard is what they put on the news. They say he was some type of king pin criminal. Say he killed a lot of people and sold drugs. But for some reason I just don't believe he was this mid-evil person they making him out to be," she looked at the stranger for answers.

The stranger pulled up a chair and sat in front of her.

"Well." He sat down and took a deep breath. "He was that kind of a man and more."

Nurse Justine was taken aback by the strangers response.

"Hold on," he held his hand up to stop her from over reacting. "Leroy was a criminal at best. He destroyed a lot of people lives. I had been trying to get close to him for years along with a list of other people. I hated Leroy Jones with a passion. I hated what he's done to our community. I hated the way he destroy lives. I hated how he flaunted in public like he was a hero."

Nurse Justine's face showed grave disappointment in listening to what the stranger had to say.

"But…here me out," he said. "I saw a side of Leroy that I never knew existed. I came down hard on Leroy as much as I could and he knew I didn't have any love for him at all. But when my life depended on it, he was right there to save my life despite all that we've been through." The stranger said sincerely.

"Who are you?" she asked.

"My name is Rick Daniels. I am a former detective of the Newark law enforcement."

"Oh, I see," Nurse Justine now understood. "Leroy musta' done something special for you to have a change of heart like you did."

"You have no idea. I was in a jam that not only forced me to leave to force here, but could have put me behind bars for the rest of my life along with the many criminals that I've put there."

"So you went to him for help when you was down and out huh?"

"No," Detective Daniels shook his head. "He came to me."

'Really?" Nurse Justine was surprised.

"Yeah I know right?" Detective Daniels chuckled. "This was a man who had me by the balls, excuse my expression. But, he could have spit in my face or worst. Fortunately for me Leroy Jones actually has a heart."

"I knew he was something special," she said with a slight smile on her face.

"I remember when he came to visit me at my home. I was on observation and could not leave my home pending the investigation. There was so much tension between me and my then fiancé." He stared off remembering that day.

"You got some pretty big balls to come to my house." Detective Daniels was not happy standing at his front door looking at Leroy on his porch.

"Hey brother, I come in peace." Leroy held his hands up in surrender with a smile on his face.

"I don't have time for this bullshit, Roy! I got enough shit going on now, and I don't need you coming over here to rub your nuts in my face!"

"Easy, easy, Rick. I think I can help you out with your little situation."

"What are you talking about?" Detective Daniels was trying to figure out where Leroy was going with all this.

"I know some people that know some people in the world of judges. I

may be able to pull a few strings for you."

Detective Daniels stared at Leroy, trying to see if there was some truth to his madness.

"You gonna let me in so we can discuss this?" Leroy asked.

"I don't know if I should. I don't trust you."

"Listen, at the end of the day, we are brothers whether you like it or not, and them cracker muthafuckas you work for and love so much? They about to stick it to your black ass good. So right now, at this point, you don't have another choice but to trust me." Leroy was serious.

"Yeah, I let him in that day, and that was the day Leroy and I bonded."

"Do you mind me asking what did he do for you to keep from going to prison?" Nurse Justine asked.

"I was set up by a fellow officer. I was being charged with rape on a minor and kidnapping. There was so much evidence that led right to me, and God as my witness I didn't touch that girl. Hell, I didn't even know her. I never saw her a day in my life." He stood up and walked the floor slowly back and forth.

"But whoever Leroy talked to helped to get the case thrown out. I retired and Leroy helped me to relocate and continue to do law enforcement. Needless to say, my fiancé left me because she believed I would rape a thirteen-year-old."

Nurse Justine could see the hurt that still lingered on his face.

"You really loved her, didn't you?" she asked.

"You have no idea the luck I have had with women that I've fallen in love with." He chuckled.

"Just give it to God, honey. He will come through. You just have to believe." She stood. "Well, I better get back to work before somebody come looking for me. It was really nice to meet you and I'm sure Mr. Jones knew you were coming to visit with him. So I guess your work here is done."

Detective Daniels didn't respond.

Just as Detective Daniels got to the elevators, he received a call on his cell phone from his informant. "I'm on my way!" he yelled into the phone, continuously pressing the elevator button before deciding to bolt for the staircase.

While watching the stash house, Valencia got a call telling her that her father was taking a turn for the worse. This news rested heavily on her mind. She needed to finish this job so she could get to him before he died. So much death had come to their family. She couldn't let her father die without him knowing she had gotten his so-called revenge.

As she thought about her father, she remembered from the story she'd overheard how his hatred for Leroy began. Leroy and Vinny used to be good friends in the business, until Leroy got too cocky and greedy. Although Vinny moved to New York and became successful in the drug business there, he still held animosity against Leroy for forcing him out of Newark. Vinny trained Carlos, Valencia's brother, to get revenge on Leroy, but Carlos had other plans. He wanted to kill Ishmael Jenkins first.

Ishmael and Carlos had been the best of friends, until Carlos saw that his father treated Ishmael more like a son than he did him. Carlos became jealous of Ishmael's and Vinny's relationship. He felt like Ishmael was trying to move him out of the way to take his spot as second-in-command. Carlos began to distrust Ishmael and told Vinny that Ishmael couldn't be trusted, but Vinny just dismissed Carlos's suspicions and told him to focus on killing Leroy.

Then Sasha, Valencia's and Carlos's sister, started sneaking around with Ishmael, which was all the ammunition Carlos needed to get Vinny to turn on Ishmael. Carlos got Vinny to believe that Leroy had sent Ishmael to infiltrate the family business and destroy him for good. But Ishmael fell in love with Sasha, and Leroy had nothing to do with him seeing her.

Vinny and Carlos banned Sasha from seeing Ishmael and kept a close watch on her. They tried to convince Sasha that Ishmael was trying to destroy the family and was using her to do it, but she wouldn't believe them. Her love for Ishmael was too deep for her to believe their warnings.

Then one day Sasha snuck off to meet Ishmael at a hotel, and she never came back. Carlos told Valencia that Ishmael Jenkins had Sasha killed by Leroy Jones. There was a huge gunfight that day, and Carlos was shot many times, but he survived. He ended up with a metal plate in his head and several bullets still lodged next to his spine.

A year or so later when Carlos went to hunt down and kill Ishmael Jenkins and Leroy Jones, he never returned. He was missing for two weeks before her father got the call from New Jersey authorities stating they'd found his body.

As Valencia thought about the senseless deaths of her sister, brother, and mother, and the impending death of her father, her anger boiled over, because she also thought about the conversation she'd had with her father the other day. It was the day that she and her men went back to New York to take a break while she left a couple of men to do research on where Jasmine lived.

She walked into her Long Island home when she was met by her two small dogs as usual. She gave them attention like she normally did when the housekeeper Shelly walked into the foyer.

"Hello, Madam."

"How are you, Shelly?" Valencia asked.

"I'm well, but you father, he no doing good today," Shelly told her.

Valencia turned on her heels and headed for the staircase leading to the second level and her father's bedroom.

When she walked into the room she could smell the sickness seeping from her father's pores. She sat down in the chair next to the bed and stared at him. Vinny was in a deep sleep and didn't know she was there. Valencia sat there for about twenty minutes when Vinny started to cough uncontrollably. She stood up to comfort her father and when his coughing fit was over she poured a glass of water from a pitcher on the night table. She put the cup to his lips so that he could take a sip.

Valencia set the cup down and sat on the bed next to Vinny and held his hand. She rubbed the back of his hand and could see all the age spots that blotched all over his hand and arm.

"How are you today, Papa?"

"Is the *maricón* dead?" Vinny asked of Leroy.

"Papa, I've been thinking, maybe he is dead. No one seems to have any information on him. I have killed for you and still I have no answers to his death. I'm starting to think that I am chasing a ghost. I'm running around in circles, and I am still coming up with nothing. This is like a story in a book with no ending; the pages seem to go on and on, and it's getting tiresome."

"So you give up?" Vinny croaked barely above a whisper.

"No, Papa, I've just been thinking that soon the police will be on to me and I don't want that kind of trouble."

"So you rather give up then to honor your *familia*? I've fought for decades to make a good living for my *familia*. I've killed hundreds to protect my *familia* and you sit here and disgrace us for a *negro*!"

Valencia didn't respond as she saw her father getting upset. He was a very sick and weak man and didn't need to be angered.

"You promised me, *hija*," he said sternly, cutting through her with his aqua eyes.

"Papa, why would that man kill my brother and sister? Was there something that you did to cause him to do such a thing?" Valencia asked.

Not once was she ever told why Leroy and his crew would murder her siblings. She just knew from childhood those type of things happened when you're in the business. She just knew she had so much anger built up inside her and she had wanted revenge for her siblings' deaths since she was a young teen. But she knew her father didn't have much time to live, and before he died, she at least wanted to know the real story behind this war between Vinny and Leroy.

After an hour of talking with her father, she left the house pissed. What she got out of her stubborn father was that Leroy had run Vinny out of town, but the story was different from what she knew it to be. Come to find out Vinny and Leroy had both been sleeping with Ishmael's mother. Ishmael's mother was in love with Vinny and Leroy knew this, but his ego and pride would not allow Vinny to be the victorious one. When it all boiled down to it, neither man could claim her because Willie Jenkins, the man thought to be Ishmael's father, had the claim.

But no matter how Valencia felt behind the ice walls around her heart, she knew her obligations were to her family. Revenge was her father's dying wish for the death of his two children, and revenge was what she was seeking.

"Send the dogs in!" she yelled, unwilling to wait any longer. She was hoping that this act would lure the crew to this location. She no longer wanted to wait to catch them at the previously scheduled location.

Jose grabbed the chain-linked leashes and began to hook them onto the dogs' spiked collars. The dogs got excited, growling and breathing heavily because they knew they were about to taste more blood.

Before Jose opened the van door, John made a call on his cell phone, and seconds later, two men emerged from one of the SUVs and walked over to the van.

The three men walked up the front steps and disappeared into the house. What came next was like something right out of a horror movie.

Screams, shouts, barking, and growling could be heard coming from the house. The occupants of both vans and the SUVs all watched from their positions, waiting to see what was gonna happen.

Suddenly gunfire could be heard coming from the house.

Meanwhile in Port Newark, Nate, Click, and Ameen sat in the car listening to a DMX CD for the second time. Although no one was supposed to be listening to music, Click needed the music to get into his killing mode. Nate was trying to tune out the music so he could focus, but he was finding that hard to do since Click rapped along with DMX loud enough to make Nate want to backhand him.

Click's cell phone rang, finally making him stop rapping.

"Thank you," Nate said quietly.

"What the fuck!" Click yelled into the phone. "Yo! What's going on? . . . We on our way!" Click started the car.

"What's up?" Nate asked.

"Some Spanish muthafuckas just ran up in my shit with some dogs, trying to murk everybody in the house!"

"That's our bitch!" Nate said.

Nate got on his phone and started to call the rest of the crew to tell them where to go. But as Click raced through the port, passing some of the setup spots where their men were squatting, he realized he didn't need to make any more phone calls, because all the men started their cars and pulled in behind Click.

Chapter Forty-Six

GROWN MAN'S DECISION

Nyeem paced the floor, walking from his bedroom to the living room window. He peered out the window, wondering what was taking the guard so long to come back with Alicia. He'd called her five minutes ago, and she'd told him no one had come for her yet. The guard left twenty-five minutes ago, and it didn't take but a good fifteen minutes to get to her house.

Nyeem could still see the other guard sitting in the car and talking on his cell phone, so he decided to get dressed and sneak out of the house to see Alicia. He had already taken a shower and was walking around shirtless, wearing just a pair of basketball shorts. He had the evening planned out because he knew Nate wouldn't be home until late. But the longer it took Alicia to get there, the less time he would have with her.

After putting on a colored T-shirt and his sneakers, he grabbed his keys and some money, and put them in his pocket. He was just about to drop his cell phone in his pocket when the doorbell rang. He walked over to the door with a smile, expecting to see Alicia standing there. When he opened the door, he was surprised to see the guard from the car standing on the porch.

"Let's go, kid," the guard said. "I gotta drop you off someplace safe because Nate needs me."

"Well, where is the other dude? He went to go get my girl."

"I don't know. Let's go, kid."

Nyeem was mad because nothing was going as planned, and he was tired of being pushed around by the guards. "Man, why don't you call that cat and see where he's at?" he asked. "I don't want him to bring her here and I ain't here."

"Yeah, a'ight," the guard said as they descended the steps. "I'll call him when we get in the car."

As the guard raced through the streets, Nyeem knew something was wrong, but he didn't know to what extent. He hoped nothing had happened to Nate. Just as the thought entered his mind, the guard's cell phone chirped. He had a Nextel phone and pressed the button for the direct connect.

Nyeem could hear Nate spitting instructions to the guard. From what he got out of it, Nate and the crew were all heading over to Click's stash house to battle with some Spanish gang. Nate sounded like he was about to blow his top.

After Nate finished speaking to the guard, the guard connected with the other guard, who was supposed to get Alicia. He'd never made it to Alicia's house because he was stopped and rerouted by Nate.

"Where you taking me, man?" Nyeem asked.

"I'm taking you to Big Roy's house, where you will be far away from this shit," the guard said, his eyes on the road.

"I don't want to go way out there. Why can't you drop me off over at my girl's house?"

"Because I have orders, and my orders are to take you to your grandfather's house."

The siren of a police car sounded behind the guard's car. He looked in the rearview mirror. "Shit!" he shouted.

Nyeem looked behind them and saw they were being pulled over.

"These muthafuckas!" the guard yelled.

Once the officer came up on the driver's side of the car, the guard rolled down the window, letting out all the cool air.

"License, registration, and insurance card," the officer said.

The guard presented everything to the officer and then rolled the window back up. He picked up the phone and chirped Nate.

"What?" Nate said, sounding irritated.

The guard explained to Nate that his paperwork wasn't right on the car.

"What?" Nate shouted. "You gotta be fucking kidding me! I told you to take care of that shit before!"

Nyeem listened to Nate blacking out on the guard, telling him he was supposed to have gotten the paperwork straight on the car a long time ago.

The police officer came back to the car with another officer, who then walked up on Nyeem's side of the car. The guard hung up the phone and rolled down his window.

"Step out of the car, sir," the officer said.

"What's the problem, officer?" the guard asked, playing dumb.

"You're under arrest for driving with an expired license and no insurance on the vehicle."

"Officer, I have the correct insurance card at home. I forgot to put it in the car," the guard tried to explain.

"I understand, but you're driving with an expired license, sir, not to mention, you have a loaded gun on your person." The police officer handcuffed the guard.

"I got papers for that too. I'm a licensed guard," the guard explained to deaf ears.

The other officer asked Nyeem to step out of the car. "Hold your arms up, young man," he said to Nyeem.

Nyeem did as he was told. The officer half-searched Nyeem because he was too busy watching the officer with the guard.

"What did I do?" Nyeem asked, his heart racing a hundred times its normal speed.

"Nothing. I just want to search you." The officer kept his gaze on his partner and the guard. The officer didn't find anything illegal on Nyeem. "Do you have any ID on you, son?" the officer asked.

"No."

"How old are you, kid?"

"I'm fifteen."

"Stay right here." The officer walked a little closer to his partner but kept his eyes on Nyeem as well.

After a few minutes, the officer walked back over to Nyeem. "You need to make a call, so someone can pick you up. This car is gonna be towed, and your friend is going to jail."

After placing the guard in the back seat of the squad car, the other officer came over to the car and began to search it. He looked up and saw Nyeem still standing there on the sidewalk. "Do you have anything in the car?" he asked.

Nyeem shook his head no, but then he saw the guard's cell phone still sitting on the console and decided to take it. Nyeem started to walk down the street. He called TJ but didn't get an answer, so he tried calling Nate. Of course, Nate didn't answer either.

Nyeem didn't know what to do, so he decided to walk to Alicia's house, which was more than a half-hour walk.

As he walked, the Nextel phone came alive. He could hear different conversations. Nyeem didn't know much about the phone, but it seemed like the phone was grouped with the other phones to be on the same channel. He could hear the chaos going on. Then his BlackBerry rang. It was TJ.

"What's up, baby bruh?" TJ asked.

"TJ, I'm out here walking on the streets right now."

"What? What are you doing, Nyeem? Didn't Nate tell you to stay in?"

"I did! It's not me. Unc called the guard and told him to take to me to Grandpop's house. Well, we got pulled over, and he ain't have no license, so now I'm out here on the streets walking."

"Where you going?"

"I was gonna go to Alicia's."

"Shit!" TJ was pissed. This day wasn't going well. He'd traveled four hours and was at a rest stop getting something to eat. He hadn't had much sleep before he left, and every time he tried to drive, he would get sleepy. This was the longest trip back to Virginia he'd ever made. "A'ight, hold up. Let me think."

Nyeem kept walking while he listened to the Nextel phone spit slander and yells from different voices. He also heard gunfire. He was now starting to get worried because he didn't hear his uncle's voice over the phone.

"Nyeem, go ahead to Alicia's. Stay there and don't leave!"

"A'ight, TJ."

"You got loot on you?"

"Yeah," Nyeem said.

"Call a cab. You don't need to be walking."

"A'ight."

"I'ma hit Nate up to let him know. Call me as soon as you get there."

"I will," Nyeem told him.

Nyeem flagged down a cab. While in the cab, he turned the volume down on the Nextel so the cab driver couldn't hear what was going on.

Once he got to Alicia's house, he went inside. She immediately embraced him, and they hugged each other for what seemed like an eternity.

As they stood there embracing, Nyeem heard what he thought was Nate's voice over the Nextel.

"What's that?" Alicia asked.

"Shh!"

Sure enough, it was Nate giving orders to the others. Then there was more gunfire, and Nate's voice screaming that they were losing men like crazy.

"Look out!" Nate shouted over the phone.

Nyeem's heart dropped to his knees, and sweat began to form on his forehead. He didn't know what to do.

"What's wrong, Nyeem?" Alicia asked, as if she didn't just hear the same thing he heard.

"I gotta go. I think my uncle's in trouble."

"Trouble? What's going on?"

"I can't explain it to you right now, Alicia. Do you know where your father keeps his gun?"

Alicia gave him a confused look. She'd told him about her father's gun that he thought no one in the house knew about. But she didn't tell him about the gun to actually give it to him.

Nyeem noticed how hesitant she was. "I need you right now, Alicia, more than anything in this world. I need you to trust me. I have to go see if my uncle is all right. I would never put you in harm's way, but I need you . . . please." His eyes showed sorrow, fear, and concern all at the same time.

"Yes, I know where he keeps it. I'll get it for you." She dashed off and disappeared into her parents' bedroom and returned just as quickly with the gun. She placed the hard steel in the palm of his hand. She stood back and looked at him, waiting for him to say something.

Nyeem looked at it for a minute before he gripped it tightly. Then he leaned over and kissed her on the lips softly.

This sent chills up Alicia's spine. She wanted to grab him and hold him. She felt like that was the last kiss she would ever get from him.

Nyeem turned and walked out of the front door.

"Nyeem!" Alicia called out to him.

Nyeem turned around.

"I love you," she said.

"I love you too."

Nyeem ran up the street at top speed. He knew where Nate and the rest were, but he didn't know what he was gonna do when he got there. All he knew for sure was that he had to get to his uncle and save him. He hailed a cab and jumped into the car. He blurted the street to the cab driver.

"Oh no. Me no go there," the Spanish cab driver protested.

"Please mister, just drop me off close by there."

The driver looked back at Nyeem, seeing the desperate look in his eyes and reluctantly drove off. Nyeem sat back in and looked out the window.

CHAPTER FORTY-SEVEN

BATTLE ZONE

When Nate and the rest of the crew arrived on the block, they saw that there had indeed been a battle going on. They spotted a few of Valencia's heavily armed men coming out of the stash house. The rest of Valencia's men, who were sitting in the Denalis, also got out of their vehicles when they spotted Nate's crew pulling up. Valencia and John remained inside the cable van, while Nate and his crew began to battle with Valencia's crew.

Valencia was getting antsy just sitting in the van doing nothing while she listened to the gun battle that went on outside. So she decided to join her men in battle. She climbed into the back of the van and removed the windowpane on the back of the door. Picking up her assault rifle with the telescope connected to the top, she placed the nose of the gun on the ledge.

Valencia put her sharpshooting skills to work, picking off Nate's crew one by one.

More of Nate's and Leroy's crew arrived onto the scene.

Valencia scanned the area with her gun, and when she locked on Click, he was now aiming his gun at the back of the van. She dove to the floor just seconds before a barrage of bullets slammed into the van. She crawled up to the front of the van and noticed that John had been hit in the back of the head by one of the bullets. Rage filled her body as she crawled out of the van and onto the ground.

Nate spat orders over the Nextel, while Click sat beside him behind the row of parked cars.

Suddenly a switchblade flew past Nate and lodged itself into a tire of the car, and air rushed out of the tire.

"What the fuck?" Nate looked at the knife sticking out of the tire.

Click looked over, saw the knife, shrugged his shoulders, and kept firing. "Damn! Where all these muthafuckas coming from?" Click asked, as more Spanish crew members arrived on the scene.

Another switchblade flew past Nate and lodged itself into the same tire. As Nate looked around, a third blade whizzed by and landed in the same tire. He stared at the three blades sticking out of the car's tire right next to him and realized someone was fucking with him.

Valencia stood behind the building, a smirk on her face. She was clearly toying with the men and could have easily killed either one of them if she wanted to. This was something she liked to do at times, just like a cat loved to play with a mouse before getting bored with it and killing it.

"Yo!" Nate called out to Click just before he sent a slew of bullets into the alley, causing some of his men to do the same.

Click looked at Nate, and Nate pointed to the knives. Click was confused. "What's up?" he asked.

Just then another switchblade came spiraling from the alley, and it landed on its intended target—right in Nate's left bicep. Nate grabbed his arm in pain. Click witnessed the event and his eyes widened.

Nate grimaced when he snatched the knife out of his arm. Luckily, it didn't go in deep. "Go get that muthafucker!" He pointed toward the alley, where he thought the knives came from.

Click stayed in his crouched position, while Nate covered him, and he took off running through the space between the two buildings.

As the gun battle raged, two patrol cars drove onto the scene only to be over powered by both crews. The crews didn't hesitate to pop off on the cops, and in no time the police cars looked like Swiss cheese. The scream of the patrol cars' screeching tires and smoke from burning rubber filled the air as the cops sped backwards down the street, trying to escape the barrage of bullets.

Nate lost several of his men, and so did Valencia.

When Nyeem arrived on the street, he saw everyone shooting at each other. He could hear the popping of guns, but he didn't know which way to go or where to find his uncle. He decided to walk up the next block and work his way through the backyards of the other houses on the other block, hoping he would end up back in the war zone, on the right side of the fence.

Click heard somebody step on a piece of glass. He whirled around with his gun extended to find Valencia standing there, her hands behind her back, and a sinister grin on her face. He marveled in the glory of having his gun trained on her. "So you the Black Widow, bitch?"

Valencia stood very still, and watched her stalker closely.

"If the circumstances were different, I would fuck the shit outta you Click-style before I made you eat a bullet. But they aren't, so I'ma make you eat this bullet right now." He smiled.

Valencia also held the smirk on her face. "You must be Click," she said, stopping him from pulling the trigger.

"Oh, most definitely. Did we fuck or something?" He laughed.

Valencia snickered. “No, we did not. I know you because you were in the crew that Ishmael ran.”

Now this got Click’s attention. Just the mention of Ishmael’s name did something to him. “A’ight, bitch, start talking!” Click steadied his automatic weapon, ready to blow her brains out if she didn’t give him some answers.

“I know Ishmael because his father Leroy was best friends with my father, and Ishmael was best friends with my brother Carlos. Leroy killed my brother and sister, so now I am here to kill Leroy.”

Click was confused because he never knew anything about Leroy being Ishmael’s father. Only Nate and Dak knew about that.

Click figured Valencia was just talking shit to try and throw him off. “Listen, bitch, I don’t know what the fuck you talking about or who those other muthafuckas you talking about, ’cause that ain’t got shit to do with me and Nate. But, in case you haven’t heard, Leroy is dead.”

“Well, then if he’s dead, his crew must die.”

Before Click could even think about pulling the trigger on his gun, Valencia threw the retracted switchblade she was hiding behind her back.

The blade hit him in the hand just before he pulled the trigger, causing him to miss his mark and drop the gun to the ground, and they both dove to the ground trying to get the gun.

Click’s adrenaline was pumping so fast, he couldn’t feel the pain from the blade that was embedded halfway into the back of his hand. He managed to overpower Valencia and get the gun from her. While he tried to gain his balance, she took off running down the alleyway of the next building, but Click fired the gun anyway.

Once he stopped firing his weapon, he steadied his hand and snatched the blade from his hand, frowning his face a little. He still felt minimal pain in his hand as blood leaked from the open wound.

Just as Click stood to his feet and prepared himself for the chase, he heard the clicking of a gun being cocked. When he looked up he saw Officer Kimble.

Officer Kimble had come to the battle after being tipped off by his informant. "I knew I would get your ass sooner or later, nigga."

Click was pissed. He was tired of Officer Kimble's harassment. Of all the people to be in his face at that moment, the officer was the last person he wanted to see. "What the fuck you want, cop?"

"I see somebody done did you wrong." Officer Kimble looked at the knife Click held in his hand.

"Fuck you, cop!"

"No, nigga, it looks like you're the one that's fucked. I'm gonna do what I have been wanting to do for years. I'ma put you to sleep." Officer Kimble smiled.

Click squeezed the trigger on his gun, and several bullets slammed into the officer's chest and abdomen. Officer Kimble fell to the ground, kicking up dust when he hit the dirt. "Stupid muthafucka!"

Click heard another sound coming from the adjacent backyard of a house behind him. He held his gun steady, waiting for whoever was going to show up. When Nyeem appeared holding a gun, Click's eyes got as wide as saucers.

"Yo, Nyeem, what you doing here?" he yelled.

"Well, for one, I heard everything on the Nextel, and I thought y'all could use my help." Nyeem was thankful that he ended up on the right side of the fence, but he was still afraid of what might happen to them all.

"Man, you shouldn't have come here. Nate is gonna kill your ass! Come on!"

The two of them took off down the alley that led them back to where Nate and the rest were battling.

Valencia made her way behind one of the parked cars her men used as a shield, and one of the men passed her a gun.

"*¡Venid!*" she yelled, and took off running down the alleyway behind the buildings. She had two men with her—one in front, the other behind. She had no clue of Click's whereabouts. "You stay here in case someone tries to come back here," she told the man behind her.

The other man was in front of her to make sure the backyard was safe to enter.

Nyeem followed Click back over behind the cars to avoid getting shot.

Nate looked over and saw Nyeem with Click, and he could have busted a blood vessel. He stared at Nyeem with intensity.

Nyeem had never feared his uncle, but at that very moment he feared Nate something terrible. He had never seen that look in Nate's eyes before.

"What the fuck!" Nate shouted.

"I didn't bring him out here!" Click yelled back, firing more shots over the hood of the car.

"Get the fuck over here!" Nate yelled more out of fear and concern for the young boy than anything else.

Nyeem was afraid to move, but he figured if he didn't do as he was told, Nate might shoot him.

Nyeem practically crawled on his belly over to Nate, while bullets rained.

Nate snatched him and met him eye to eye. "What are you doing here?" he growled.

"I-I wanted to come and help you. I didn't know if anything

happened to you or not. Unc, are you OK?"

"I'm so pissed at you right now. Do you understand that this shit is not a fucking game? I don't know what I would do if something happened to you. Why would you come here?"

"I heard you on the jack, and I had to come help you."

"I told you to stay in the house!"

"The guard took me out, and we got stopped. The cops took him to jail, so I was left on the streets alone."

"I'ma fuck you up when this is over!" Nate began to shoot his gun and then sat back down behind the car to re-load. "I'm gonna deal with your ass when this shit is over, and trust, you ain't gonna like the shit I'm gonna do to you!"

Nate noticed Nyeem was holding a gun. "Where you get that shit from?" he yelled. "Never mind; don't tell me. Here, you gonna need another one!" He handed Nyeem another handgun he'd pulled from his holster and forced the boy to the next car over, hoping no one would shoot at that vehicle. "Get over there and stay the fuck down!"

"Leave the kid alone!" Click yelled. "That's little Ish right there. He got it in his blood!" Click stood to shoot his gun, yelling like a maniac.

Nate looked at Nyeem, and for a second he could have sworn he saw Ishmael squatting there in front of him. That was when he knew he had to end this war and get the boy to safety.

Behind them, coming from the side of the buildings, were five more of Leroy's men, but before they could make it over to the cars that Nate and the other crew members were hiding behind, they all got shot and fell to the ground like bowling pins.

Nyeem jumped up from his crouching position when he heard the gunshots.

Nate shouted, "Get down!"

"Are you OK, Unc?" Nyeem asked again, still concerned because

Nate seemed to be a different person altogether.

"Yeah, I'm good. Don't worry about me!" Nate stood and let off shots then ducked back down. Nyeem watched him from the sitting position he was in.

That's when it happened. Nate was shot and Nyeem witnessed it. No one seemed to notice that one of Valencia's men was creeping on the side of the building behind them and had killed all five of the men who had tried to come up the alley.

Nate fell to his knees and turned over in a sitting position with his back resting against the car. Nyeem could see the blood seeping from Nate's stomach. The bullet seemed to have gone through Nate.

Bullets began to fly over Nyeem's head when he saw Valencia's man shooting from the alley behind them. Nyeem pointed both his guns and squeezed down on the trigger with all his might. Bullets flew from his guns and hit his mark, sending the gunman falling to the ground. That's when he looked over and realized his uncle wasn't moving.

Meanwhile, Valencia took this as her opportunity to finish them off as she watched Nyeem kill one of her men. She crept along the wall, crouched low to the ground. She laid her body on the ground at the rear of the alleyway and set herself up to take aim and pick Nyeem and Click off. She thought Nate was already dead.

As she took aim lying on the dirty, glass-strewn ground, she placed her finger on the trigger and began to pull it back slowly. Just then she felt the hard, cold steel on the back of her head. She stopped moving and thought of a possible way to defeat the intruder who had her pinned to the ground.

She thought about her dying father back at home. She thought about how she knew the risks of the job, but always thought she was smart enough and skillful enough to never be caught in the position she was now in. But most importantly, she thought about how out of loyalty to her father she was now gonna lose her own life.

Before she had the chance to even put her expert skills to use to disarm her attacker, the bullet shattered her brain, and all her thoughts came spilling out onto the ground.

Detective Daniels made his way back to where he came from, all the while ducking stray bullets. As he walked past Officer Kimble's corpse, he fired two more bullets into Officer Kimble's face.

"Payback's a bitch, bitch!" he said and kept walking, never breaking a stride.

Nate began to cough up blood, and Nyeem noticed.

"Click! Cover me!" Nyeem yelled.

Click stood to his feet like Rambo and let the bullets rain. "Aaaahhhh!" he yelled.

Nyeem ran over to Nate, ducking bullets as they flew past and around him. He dove to the ground next to Nate.

When he removed Nate's limp hand to see how bad the wound was, a glob of blood spilled out from the hole. He pressed Nate's hand back over the hole. He could see the distant look in Nate's eyes. "Unc, stay with me! Hold on, man!" Nyeem said. "Click!"

"Yo!"

"I gotta get Unc outta here. He needs to get to the hospital!"

For the first time Click actually looked over at Nate and saw how bad he was. "Oh shit! Yo, I don't know how we gonna do that shit without getting dumped on!"

"Call in reinforcement then!"

"Nigga, look around you!" Click yelled.

Nyeem looked around. "Everybody's dead."

"You think?" Click asked sarcastically, referring to the men from their crew that lay dead all over the area.

Nyeem didn't know what he was going to do. He looked at Nate and saw that his eyes were closed. "Unc!" He panicked, shaking him.

Nate barely opened his eyes.

"Unc, I'm gonna get you to the hospital. Just hold on!"

Nyeem looked around frantically. He was trying to find an escape route to get Nate out of there.

Meanwhile, Click was reloading clips into his weapons. He stood just in time to meet one of the gunmen making his way into the street. Click unloaded into the man's face, making him unrecognizable as his face tore away piece by piece before he hit the ground. He ducked back behind the car just before bullets hit the car he hid behind.

Several seconds later, the gunfire ceased. Nyeem and Click looked at each other, wondering what had happened.

Click positioned himself to the rear of the parked car in an attempt to peek out from behind the car. Just as he did, he saw two Spanish men running in a crouched position toward them. He immediately began to let off shots at the two men, hitting one of them in the leg. The man fell to the ground, screaming in agony. Click then shot the other man in the chest several times. He carefully took aim and silenced the screaming man on the ground by hitting him in the face.

Just then another man made his way cross the street, but Click couldn't get him.

"Yo, Nyeem, I think he's coming up on your side." Click pointed his weapon in the direction he thought the gunman was going to come from.

Two more men started making their way over to them.

Nate had passed out, and Nyeem was ready to shoot the gunman as soon as he peeked out from around the car.

One of the men stepped around the car on Nyeem's side. The young boy panicked, and Click shot the man several times in the stomach, and he fell to the ground several feet away from Nyeem.

Suddenly, bullets sounded off, and Click yelled out. It seemed as if everything moved in slow motion. Nyeem turned to see Click on his knees, his body jerking as he was riddled with bullets. As the force of each bullet pierced his body, small particles of flesh and blood leaped from his body to the ground. He still held his gun and fired straight up into the air before he fell to his death.

One gunman trained his gun on Nyeem and walked toward him.

"*¡Lo conseguimos!*" the gunman yelled to the others, letting them know that they got them. He looked around for the others that he'd summoned, but no one came. He turned his attention back to Nyeem, looking at him with evil eyes.

Nyeem looked over at Nate and then closed his eyes, accepting his fate.

Chapter Forty-Eight

NYEEM'S FATE

Shots sounded, there was a loud grunt, and then there was silence. Nyeem didn't feel any pain, but he knew he'd heard gunshots. He opened his eyes slowly and saw his godbrother TJ and a tall, brown-skinned man wearing a fitted cap standing in front of him with a smoking gun. "Ny, you alright?" TJ asked.

TJ's friend looked down at Nyeem and then knelt down in front of him. "You all right, kid?"

Nyeem couldn't speak. He couldn't believe he was still alive. He nodded in response.

"Who are you?" Nyeem asked the man with the smoking gun.

"I'm former Detective Rick Daniels." That name meant nothing to Nyeem, but he was glad that the detective was there.

TJ helped him to his feet and gave him a bear hug. He looked back at Nate and closed his eyes tight, hoping his uncle wasn't dead.

"How is he?" TJ asked.

Thoughts of Nate dying made his heart pound hard in his chest. "Is he dead?" Nyeem asked as he looked down at Nate and saw that he wasn't moving.

Detective Daniels reached over and felt Nate's neck for a pulse. "He still has a pulse. Let's get him outta here and to a doctor."

Nyeem stood and looked down the street and saw bodies everywhere. It was like a scene straight out of an old World War II movie he'd seen. Bodies lined the street like they lined the battlefield in the movie. There was nowhere to walk without touching a body.

Two more men ran over and helped carry Nate to a waiting car that pulled up in the middle of the street.

Nyeem looked at Click as he walked by him. "Can you check him?" he asked Detective Daniels.

Detective Daniels glanced at Click and saw multiple gunshot wounds. "There's no hope for him, son. He's dead."

Nyeem and TJ got in the car with Detective Daniels, and they followed behind the car that held Nate. They drove through the streets very slowly, trying to avoid running over dead bodies.

Now that Nyeem knew Nate was alive and on the way to the hospital, he wanted to find out more about the detective who was helping to save his uncle.

"How did you know where to find us?" Nyeem asked TJ.

"I didn't. I was thinking about you and I couldn't keep driving knowing you were out here on the streets. So I turned around and came back. I was driving all around looking for you and the good ole detective here side swiped my car. He was hauling ass down the street looking for the same battle I was looking for," TJ responded.

"Really?" Nyeem asked.

"Yeah, and once I got out of the car ready to whoop his ass, we recognized each other. I knew who the detective was back when I was around your age. One thing led to another, and then we were both in his car heading over here."

"That shit is crazy," Nyeem said.

While they drove, Detective Daniels answered all of Nyeem's questions. He explained that he had owed Leroy a favor. He told Nyeem how Leroy had pulled some strings and got him set up in the South on a police force there. Daniels always kept in touch with some of his loyal officers on the Newark police force, and when he got word that Leroy was sick, he decided to pay a visit. But before he could get over to Leroy's house, he heard the news that Leroy had been shot that same night.

After speaking with an employee on the police force, he found out that Leroy was taken to the hospital, so he made his way there to check on Leroy's condition.

To get information about Leroy, Detective Daniels portrayed himself to Dr. Clinton as an investigating detective on the case of Leroy's attempted murder. When Dr. Clinton informed the detective that Leroy was alive, he figured he could pay back Leroy by telling everyone that Leroy was dead. He made Dr. Clinton aware that the case was sensitive and told him he needed full cooperation from him and the staff regarding the ploy.

Detective Daniels knew that someone had put a hit out on Leroy. By making Leroy's death public, he ensured Leroy would have some safe time to recover in the hospital.

Meanwhile, Detective Daniels monitored Nate and his crew, knowing Nate would be seeking revenge. The detective also used his own resources to try to discover the identity of Leroy's shooter, but he had no luck. He had an informant that he used on the streets sometimes, and paid him to give him information when needed.

Then he got a call from Officer Kimble's partner, one of his inside connections. The partner told Detective Daniels what was going on with the two crews shooting it out, and that Officer Kimble decided to investigate the shootout alone. Kimble's partner never trusted him, so he made the phone call to Detective Daniels. Detective Daniels' informant also made a call to him, confirming the war between the two crews was definitely gonna go down.

After hearing the whole story, Nyeem was in total shock. He had never imagined that loyalties went that deep. His family really had pull. They looked out for him, even when he didn't know they were looking out for him, so now he needed to look out for his uncle, who just had to get better.

Chapter Forty-Nine

Five Years Later

A crowd of thirty thousand filled the Amway Arena in Orlando, Florida. Music played over the speakers and strobe lights flashed, illuminating the gymnasium. Glow sticks and glow necklaces shined brightly in the darkness.

The announcer's voice boomed over the speakers, "Ladies and gentlemen, welcome to the Amway Arena, home of the Orlando Magic!"

The crowd roared, and then the music lowered. The crowd stood to their feet, waiting to hear the home team members introduced.

The Orlando Magic players all stood and made two lines in front of the bench.

"Introducing the point guard for the Magic, standing at six feet six inches tall, Nyeeeeeemmm Jenkinnns!"

The crowd clapped and yelled as Nyeem ran through the double lines his teammates had formed. He slapped hands with each player and headed toward the middle of the floor.

Once Nyeem made his way to the middle of the court, he looked up to the ceiling and pointed, giving a shout-out to his mother, father,

Leroy, and most of all, Doc. He then ran over to shake the hand of the head coach.

As the announcer continued to announce the names of the other players, Nyeem looked over at his family and pointed to them as they stood and waved at him.

Alicia, TJ, Dasia, Nurse Justine, and Nate all cheered him on from their front row floor seats.

Nyeem eventually got his life back together and was drafted right out of high school into the pros. He signed with the Orlando Magic and moved to Florida. Alicia registered for college in Orlando, so she could be close to him, and was now studying physiology and living the life of a baller's girlfriend to the fullest.

Eventually a small, quiet, private funeral was held for Leroy, and he was buried next to Ishmael and Desiree in New Jersey.

TJ moved to Florida with Nyeem to start his own accounting firm, which was doing very well. He and Dasia got married and were now expecting their first child.

Nurse Justine became like a grandmother to Nyeem after Nate's injuries. When Nyeem arrived at the hospital after the huge shootout in front of the stash house, he'd called her and they talked.

Soon after, she quit her job at the hospital to handle all of Nate's and Leroy's affairs. She sold off each of their businesses, making enough money to last Nyeem and Nate for a lifetime. Nurse Justine took Nyeem into her home and gave him plenty of love and spiritual guidance, keeping him grounded and focused.

Nate didn't fare as well as Nyeem. Black Widow's bullet had severed his spine, destroying it, and he was now paralyzed from the neck down. Surprisingly, Nate remained in good spirits throughout his ordeal, and seeing Nyeem's success helped him avoid any bitterness over his injuries.

Nyeem couldn't be happier. He was a professional basketball player, and all of his family constantly encouraged him, supported him, and loved him. He prayed each day and spoke to his mother, father, Leroy and Doc regularly. This was something Nurse Justine had taught him to do, and believe it or not, it really helped him with his pain and heartache.

Although he had grown into a spiritual adult, Nyeem would always have the hood in his heart. After all, that was where he was conceived and where he grew up. He would always be a boy from the hood.

Book Club Discussion Questions

1. Do you agree with the way Leroy and Nate were raising young Nyeem? Why or why not?

2. What are your thoughts on the character Nyeem?

3. Nate is running a legitimate business now and doesn't have his hand in the drug aspect of the business. How do you feel about people who've walked away from the drug business with a nest egg saved and now own several businesses, making more money than the average honest-working individual?

4. Violence still plays a major role in the organization Nate is running for Leroy in his absence. Does that make Nate any different from drug dealers although he doesn't deal drugs? Why or why not?

5. What are your thoughts on Leroy's death?

6. What are your thoughts on Valencia (Black Widow)?

7. Did Valencia have the right to seek revenge? Why or why not?

8. Was Valencia any different being raised in an upscale organized crime family, versus Nyeem being raised by Leroy and Nate living in Newark, NJ?

9. How did you feel about TJ coming back to Newark? Did you expect him to get re-involved with the business?

10. What are your thoughts on Nurse Justine?

11. How did you feel when Nyeem's friend Doc was killed? Did you feel Nyeem's pain?

12. What are your thoughts on the pressure that Nyeem had to deal with growing up without his parents?

13. Do you think children without parents living in the hood who have to face harsh realities are having a tough time? Why or why not?

14. Who was your favorite character? Explain why.

15. What are your thoughts on Click?

16. Nyeem was accused of being involved with gangs, which now make up most of the drug dealings and crime rates. What are your thoughts on the wide spread of gangs in the inner cities?

17. There are hoods all over the world that have these battle zones amongst the residences. Innocent people are caught in the middle because they have to live there. Do you think the police are allowing some of these battles to happen? What do you think could be done to stop this?

MELODRAMA PUBLISHING ORDER FORM

WWW.MELODRAMAPUBLISHING.COM

Title	ISBN	QTY	PRICE	TOTAL
In My Hood	0-971702-19-5		$15.00	$
In My Hood 2	1-934157-06-6		$15.00	$
In My Hood 3	1-934157-62-7		$14.99	
Myra	1-934157-20-1		$15.00	$
Menace	1-934157-16-3		$15.00	$
Cartier Cartel	1-934157-18-X		$15.00	$
10 Crack Commandments	1-934157-21-X		$15.00	$
Jealousy: The Complete Saga	1-934157-13-9		$15.00	$
Wifey	0-971702-18-7		$15.00	$
I'm Still Wifey	0-971702-15-2		$15.00	$
Life After Wifey	1-934157-04-X		$15.00	$
Still Wifey Material	1-934157-10-4		$15.00	$
Eva: First Lady of Sin	1-934157-01-5		$15.00	$
Eva 2: First Lady of Sin	1-934157-11-2		$15.00	$
Den of Sin	1-934157-08-2		$15.00	$
Shot Glass Diva	1-934157-14-7		$15.00	$
Dirty Little Angel	1-934157-19-8		$15.00	$
Histress	1-934157-03-1		$15.00	$
A Deal With Death	1-934157-12-0		$15.00	$
Tale of a Train Wreck Lifestyle	1-934157-15-5		$15.00	$
A Sticky Situation	1-934157-09-0		$15.00	$
Sex, Sin & Brooklyn	0-971702-16-0		$15.00	$
Life, Love & Loneliness	0-971702-10-1		$15.00	$
The Criss Cross	0-971702-12-8		$15.00	$

(GO TO THE NEXT PAGE)

MELODRAMA PUBLISHING ORDER FORM
(CONTINUED)

Title/Author	ISBN	QTY	PRICE	TOTAL
Stripped	1-934157-00-7		$15.00	$
The Candy Shop	1-934157-02-3		$15.00	$
				$
			Subtotal	
			Shipping**	
			Tax*	
	Total			

Instructions:

*NY residents please add $1.79 Tax per book.

**Shipping costs: $3.00 first book, any additional books please add $1.00 per book.

Incarcerated readers receive a 25% discount. Please pay $11.25 per book and apply the same shipping terms as stated above.

Mail to:

MELODRAMA PUBLISHING

P.O. BOX 522

BELLPORT, NY 11713